A PERFECT

"*A Perfect Machine* is like ste[...] blindfold on and finding your[...] in a boosted tube that slithers and loops you down into a sensory deprivation tank where you didn't think to take one last breath first, but it's pretty down here, isn't it? Either that or all the blood vessels in your eyes just burst."

Stephen Graham Jones, author of Mongrels

"Savory deserves to make a great impression on both our highly mutable genre and the reading public."

Peter Straub, multi award-winning author of
Ghost Story *and* The Talisman

"A wild and exuberant concoction of horror, science fiction and crime thriller, Brett Savory's *A Perfect Machine* hurtles along like a runaway train, picking up speed, belching smoke and shooting out sparks before erupting into an explosive, mind-shattering finale. Terrific stuff!"

Mark Morris, author of the Obsidian Heart series

"A wildly inventive, swiftly paced, brutally fun mindbender of a novel. *A Perfect Machine* envisions a future gone crazy with unsettling parallels to our own world."

Benjamin Percy, author of The Dead Lands

"Imagine that the godlike aliens from *2001* paid a visit to *Dark City* – except instead of uplifting us to sapience, they got their shits and giggles by pulling off our arms and legs and forcing us to kill each other. Welcome to *A Perfect Machine*."

Peter Watts, author of Blindsight *and* Echopraxia

BY THE SAME AUTHOR

In and Down
The Distance Travelled
No Further Messages

BRETT SAVORY

A PERFECT MACHINE

ANGRY
ROBOT

ANGRY ROBOT
An imprint of Watkins Media Ltd

20 Fletcher Gate,
Nottingham,
NG1 2FZ
UK

angryrobotbooks.com
twitter.com/angryrobotbooks
Running beneath the skin

An Angry Robot paperback original 2017

Cover by Erik Mohr at Emblem
Set in Meridien and Conduit by Epub Services

Distributed in the United States by
Penguin Random House, Inc., New York.

ISBN 978 0 85766 630 7
Ebook ISBN 978 0 85766 631 4

Printed in the United States of America

9 8 7 6 5 4 3 2 1

for Sandra Kasturi – best of all possible monkeys

ONE

The bullet tore a thin strip of flesh from his cheekbone, drove into the brick wall behind him.

He turned a corner, cut swaths through the steam rising from sewer grates – smoky ghosts wrapping around his skinny legs. Dissipating.

Gone.

More bullets flew past his ears as he ducked around another corner, legs pumping hard, breath coming in thick rasps. He didn't know this section of the city very well, so it was just a matter of time.

Always just a matter of time.

Voices. Loud, harsh. Guttural bursts exploding from thin lips, wide mouths: find him, fuck him up. The words didn't matter, but their speakers did. The people who spoke these words could run hard and for a very long time.

Gas lamps swam by on his left, shining, flickering, watching the man run. Chasing away the shadows in which he wanted to hide.

The man heard more shots behind him, wished for a dumpster, a garbage can, another brick wall, anything to hide behind. Then one of the bullets slammed into the back of his right knee. He gritted his teeth, continued running.

Another bullet caught him in the left shoulder. He plunged ahead, driven forward by the momentum, listing to one side, nearly losing his balance. But his left knee held him, and he kept running.

More shouting. Now coming from two directions.

He turned another corner, saw four men standing there, weapons raised, aimed in his direction. He stopped, stumbled backward, teeth clenched tight against the pain in his leg and shoulder. Two more men and one woman stood the way he had just come, grinning, their mouths black holes in their faces.

The shouting stopped.

Nowhere to go.

Seven distinct cocking sounds, as bullets entered chambers.

The man took a deep breath, held it. Closed his eyes.

The night burst open with muzzled fire. The man crumpled. Red seeped out from under him, glistening in dim gaslight.

Hospital green.

Walls rippled when he opened his eyes. Fluorescent ceiling lights rotated blurrily. He looked to his right. The woman in the bed beside him wavered, floated on crisp white sheets.

The man rubbed his eyes, heard a door open, whisper closed. Heard a voice, looked up, saw a young woman at the foot of the bed. A nurse. Her mouth moved, but the man heard no words. She held a clipboard, her eyes sweeping it, her mouth moving again. Her brow crinkled, maybe frustrated she was getting no answers to her questions.

The man thought the nurse was beautiful, and he would have answered her questions had he heard them, had he been capable of hearing anything but his own pumping blood.

Faraway sounds filtered into the man's ears. Mumblings in a tin can. He shook his head, cleared the cobwebs. The sounds swirled, formed words to match the nurse's red, red lips. She was asking how he was feeling.

The man put a hand to his head, glanced at the woman in the bed next to him. She had almost stopped floating on her sheets, was now staring at him hard, frowning. The man looked up at the nurse, smiled as best he could, and said, his voice a jumble of cracked rocks, "Not particularly great. Uh, how about you?" He tried to smile, but he wasn't sure if his mouth moved at all.

The nurse – very familiar to him for some reason, what was her name? – returned the smile, then mouthed more words to him, lost again to the pounding in his ears. He shook his head to let her know he couldn't hear her. She reached down and patted his hand. She was warm. He wanted to move his other hand on top of hers, to feel the smooth skin there. He tried, but nothing happened. He looked down and saw the sling in which they'd put his arm. His leg, too, was bandaged.

He wanted to tell the nurse – Farah? Frieda? – they'd made a mistake. He didn't need to be here.

The sling and bandages were unnecessary. Some kind pedestrian had probably brought him in, or at least called an ambulance to take him away. But they were wasting good hospital supplies on him when they could be used for people who really needed them – perhaps like the woman next to him.

He looked again at this woman, and saw her frown had softened. The lines in her forehead smoothed out to show that she approved of the nurse's job, approved of compassion shown to another human being.

But she didn't know him. Didn't know what he was. If she did, the frown lines would most certainly reappear.

In past hospital experiences, the doctors usually discharged him very quickly once they identified him. But the doctor who'd scribbled the man's name on his chart might have been in too big a rush to figure it out, or maybe too new to his job to notice the signs.

The way the hospital staff looked at him – and others like him – was always with a touch of faint disgust, but mostly indifference. Once they realized he was one of *them*, they'd ask two security guards to walk him down the hall, the automatic doors would slide open, and they'd stand there silent, waiting for him to leave. Just staring. Afraid to touch him. Pushing him out into the cold with their eyes, their fear. Sands in their minds shifting already to cover the experience. They would gradually forget they'd even met him. The memory erased entirely.

He did not know why this happened, but it had always been so, for as long as he could remember.

The nurse patted his hand again, released it, smiled

once more, and walked out the door.

The woman beside him looked away, focused on the mounted TV across the room, high up on the wall.

The man tried to move his injured leg but, as with his arm, no dice. Actually, both arms. He must've caught a few more bullets before he went down. His chest felt tight, too, so probably one or two more in there. He'd have to wait another hour, maybe two, before he could walk with any degree of comfort again.

He gingerly touched the bandage on his face where the first bullet had grazed his cheekbone. He knew by now it would be nearly healed. By the time the program currently on TV had ended, the wound in his shoulder would be closed up, scar tissue already evident. Then, another hour or so after that, his knee would operate as it always had – smoothly, and without a hint of pain.

Exhaustion overtook him, then, and he slept.

When he woke again nearly two hours later, the nurse – her name finally came to him: Faye – stood over him and was looking down. She held his hand.

"How you feeling now, Henry?"

"About how I probably look."

"Oh, OK, so you *do* feel like shit."

The man laughed a little. Faye glanced over at the woman in the next bed. She was scowling, probably at the language.

"It's OK," Faye said. "We know each other. We're friends."

The woman just huffed and looked away.

"Friends? Is that all?" the man said. Not only had

her name come back to him, but his relationship to her had returned, as well.

"Well, you know. Maybe a little more," Faye said, teasing. "Look, I gotta go. I can't walk you out, but call me later, OK? Let me know you got home safe."

When he was finally discharged from the hospital an hour later – amidst the requisite complement of security guards, and exactly the amount of indifference he had anticipated from the attending doctor – Henry walked straight home to his one-bedroom apartment, where the phone was ringing.

"Hello?"

"Henry. Milo."

Henry's friend Milo figured that, despite his best efforts, the flesh beneath his skin was now only about ninety-percent lead, give or take.

"Caught another few slugs tonight, brother," Milo said. "What about you? Examined yourself yet?"

"Not yet, just got home."

"How long's it been?"

"Since I examined myself?" Henry said. "Couple of weeks."

"What's the matter – afraid to check?"

Fucking Milo. Always on Henry's ass about the same goddamn thing.

"Listen, why don't you lay off me for a while, alright, Milo? Don't you have anything better to do? Christ."

"You know I don't. Neither do you."

Henry sighed, looked out his living room window. Snow was falling – big fat flakes that stuck to the window, melted, vanished. No lights on in his apartment yet, so the lone gas lamp outside his building shone in, illuminating his sparse furnishings with a sickly yellow glow.

As if somehow sensing Henry's thoughts, Milo said, "You know what you need? You need a woman's touch over there, my friend. Someone to bring some fucking *life* to that shitty little hole you call home."

"I'm hanging up now, Milo."

"Alright, alright, but check yourself out, chickenshit!" Milo blurted. "And let me know how things're going with Faye. You really do need–"

Henry hung up.

He crossed his living room, touched the base of a lamp. Slightly less sickly yellow light suffused the room. Henry touched the lamp's base twice more, until the light was closer to white than yellow.

More than just sparse: stark. Empty. Hollow. Gutted. A home to match his personality. But that was Milo talking. Henry knew better. Tried to convince himself of better, anyway.

Shower. Maybe some TV, then bed. Fuck the examination. It could wait.

Henry hung his leather on the coat rack near the front door, made his way to the bathroom. Past piles of mystery novels stacked halfway to the ceiling; past a computer that he never used on a desk at which he never sat; past pizza boxes empty but for the crusts of each slice, turned rock-hard, forgotten.

Henry flicked a switch on the inside of the bathroom doorway; a fluorescent light above the sink flickered, shot to life.

He pulled his shirt over his head as he walked in, dropped his pants around his ankles, stepped out of them. He took his underwear off, then stood up straight, turned to his left, saw himself in the mirror. Nearly every inch of his torso was composed of scar tissue; his legs more of the same. There were only small patches of skin left unmarked.

No way I'm even close, Henry thought. *Not a chance I'm anywhere near Milo's percentage… But fine, fuck it, I'll check.*

Fingers trembling, heart thudding, Henry brought his hands up from his sides, placed them gently on his chest… and moved them around in slow circles. He rubbed around his nipples, pushed in near his armpits, squeezed the flesh around what remained of his ribs, sank his fingers deep into his stomach. Both arms. Pressing, concentrating, trying to feel as deeply within his body as possible. It was a crude manner of examination for the information he was trying to obtain, but it was all he and others like him had. Someone had stolen an X-ray machine a few years back (Henry had no idea how), but it broke down – got shot up, actually – so they were back to these hands-only self-examinations.

Down to his legs, pushing, kneading, prodding around the knees. To his calves, the tops of his feet. Standing back up, checking his groin, buttocks, up to his neck, his hands roaming over his scalp as if washing his hair. But feeling gently, listening to the song of his skin.

Steel-jacketed lead. Not pulsing through his veins, but replacing them, replacing flesh, tissue, organs –

everything but bone. And even a good portion of that had been shattered, replaced by rows of bullets or clumps of shot.

Everything except skin – the skin remained, but forever changed.

Scarred.

The bullets in his body pushed flush to one another inside him. When he pressed on his abdomen, he felt them clink together. They rippled under the skin of his forearms, writhed in his thighs.

Henry *had* caught up to Milo – had likely surpassed him. He estimated about ninety-five percent, maybe more. His head was the least-affected part of him, as most of the bullets were naturally aimed at his body, but there was still a lot there.

And when he reached one hundred per cent...

But no one knew what happened then, because no one in living memory had reached one hundred percent. Maybe no one had *ever* done it. Or at least that's what the Runners had all been told. Maybe the Hunters knew different.

Henry showered, dressed quickly, flicked on the TV, and stared out the window again at the steadily falling snow. He gathered his thoughts, then dialed Milo's number.

Milo picked up almost immediately. "Well?"

"Dunno, exactly, of course, but... ninety-five, give or take," Henry said, sweat on his brow, hands slick. His voice was edged with a nervous tremor.

"Ninety-fucking-five," Milo whispered, then whistled low. "Holy shit, man."

"Yeah. I know."

"So – belief?" Milo asked. "Which crackpot theory do you subscribe to these days? Transformation into a steel kraken? Eternity in some kind of bullet-time hell? Just plain flat-out death? Or maybe you finally show up on God's radar and he strikes you down for the freak of nature you are. Any or all of the above?"

Henry thought for a moment, chewed his lip. "I don't know, Milo. I have no clue about any of it."

The snow blew hard against Henry's window, whipping up a white storm of flakes that mesmerized him as he stared outside, lost in thought.

"… still there, dipshit?"

"Yeah … yeah, still here, Milo. Gotta go. Have to call Faye, let her know I got home alright. See you at tomorrow's Run."

"Alright, see you there, chimp."

Henry hung up.

On TV, the news had just started. The weatherman called for four inches of snow tonight, another three tomorrow afternoon. Wind chill creating a deep freeze to smash all previous records.

Henry and Milo, frozen metal statues, running every night. Because they had to. Because they *all* had to.

TWO

This was the only rule that mattered: if you didn't run every night, someone you loved would disappear. Simple as that. No one knew who took them, or how. But if you didn't show up for the Run, the next morning they'd be gone without a trace.

It had never happened to Henry or Milo because they'd never missed a Run. But they'd known other people who had, for whatever reason, and they'd watched that person crumble little by little in the weeks and months that followed.

One guy in his mid twenties, Jonathan Witters, an old acquaintance of theirs from high school (the *Inferne Cutis* – the ridiculously pretentious name of their society – weren't required to run or hunt until they'd graduated high school) didn't go to a Run because his mother was sick, dying. He stayed by her side the night of her death. He went home, went to bed with his wife. The next morning, his wife was gone. The blankets were undisturbed, a depression still visible in the pillow where her head had been.

She'd simply vanished.

Jonathan, obviously severely distraught, tried

first appealing to the leader of the Runners, Edward Palermo.

"She's my fucking *wife*, Ed! Bring her back, for Chrissakes!"

"I don't know where she is," Edward said. "You knew the rules. You chose to disobey them. I cannot help you."

Jonathan had needed to be escorted out of the warehouse where the Runners met before their nightly Run. He then barged into the Hunters' warehouse where *they* met each night before the Run, strode into James Kendul's office (Kendul being the leader of the Hunters), grabbed him by the throat, slammed him against a wall.

"Give her back, you fuck!" Witters screamed in Kendul's face.

Two Hunters had followed Witters into the office, each grabbing an arm to restrain him. Word of the disappearance had traveled fast through the society, so Kendul knew what Witters was upset about. He maintained the same calm demeanour as his colleague, Palermo, but was perhaps a little colder.

"We do not know where they go when they disappear," Kendul said. "I'm sorry for your loss. Go home, Witters. She's not coming back. The sooner you wrap your head around that, the sooner you can get on with your life. Lashing out accomplishes nothing. This is the way it has always been. You knew that before she vanished, and you know it now."

Witters was then roughly thrown out of the Hunters' warehouse.

From that day forward, he did nothing but drink

– never showing up to another Run – until everyone who mattered to him disappeared.

Jonathan Witters died alone of liver failure in his shitty little apartment.

And there'd been more than a few others like him over the years Henry and Milo had been running. They had discussed this particular series of disappearances more than most because they'd known Jonathan so long. Not long enough to get close, to become someone they – whoever they were – would target, but long enough to do more than just register he was gone.

"Taken by God," Milo said the day after Witters' body had been found. They were at Henry's apartment, drinking, playing video games. "All of them."

Henry had remained silent at first; just took a sip from his can of stout, frowned, mumbled something Milo couldn't make out.

"What was that?" Milo asked.

"Doubtful," Henry said, clearer this time.

"Why doubtful? What else could it be?" Milo said.

"Look, we always go round and round on this, Milo, and I don't want to do it again. You know I don't believe in any of that shit. I don't know where they go when they disappear – just like I don't know what happens when we 'ascend,' or whatever the hell you wanna call it. If that's even true, and there's no proof that it is."

"Alright, alright, settle down," Milo said. "Just trying to give their lives a little more meaning than if they'd vanished into the fucking void, you know?" He took another swig of beer, glanced sideways at

Henry. "So sensitive, my word."

Milo grinned, nudged Henry with his elbow, trying to lighten the mood, but Henry wasn't having it.

"Nah, man, I'm just not interested in assigning magical explanations to real-world events. I don't know where they go, but who's to say that real *people* don't come and take them away? We don't know that for sure. All we know is what Kendul and Palermo tell us, and what our ancient –" and here Henry put down his controller to make air quotes with his fingers "– holy books –" picking his controller back up again "– have to say on the subject. And that's less than useful, since they're as vague as humanly possible in their descriptions, saying only that they're 'removed from the offender's life.' Shit, I'd be more inclined to believe aliens steal them than some god has anything to do with it. What kind of shitheel of a creator would do that? And if he did, then fuck him."

The two clattered their controllers for a while in silence, destroying aliens on Henry's TV screen, then Milo said, "God doesn't give a shit what you think, Henry. If he exists, he will fuckstart your face for that level of blasphemy. And then your mom's. And then your cat's. He will fuckstart all the faces, and there's not a goddamn thing you can do about it."

Milo grinned, glanced over at his friend.

After a moment, Henry grinned a bit, too, said, "Shut up, dickhead. I don't have a cat."

Tonight, shadows moved quickly against a backdrop of random white, like the snow on a TV screen. Same running crew as always. Same Hunters, too, save for a few new faces on both sides. Young faces – fathers teaching sons.

Each side of the city attracted different kinds of Runners and Hunters. But with one thing in common: both operated below the collective conscious. For most intents and purposes – invisible.

Everyone in this particular Run thought the gas lamps in this part of the city – east of the railway tracks that cut through the city's center – made for the best ambience; the electric streetlights to the west side of the tracks were too garish. Too modern.

Henry and Milo sprinted side by side, two strips of black cut out of the fabric of the storm. Henry had brought a gun this time – to present a danger, keep interest up. Prevent boredom: Hunters' flesh was not nearly as bullet-friendly as Runners'. Officially, Runners bringing weapons was intensely frowned upon, but certainly not unheard of. There were consequences, but you had to be caught to suffer them, so as long as you could manage to avoid that…

A shotgun blast cracked nearby. Three Hunters spread out, settled in behind dumpsters in the alleyway Milo and Henry had entered, coming in off a main street. The wind cut to a minimum here. Henry recognized the area – it was very near the same part of the city he'd fallen in last night. He and Milo hunkered down behind some trash bins, caught their breath, listened for movement from the dumpsters.

"Fuckers hemmed me in last night," Henry whispered, pointing behind them to the corner where he'd gone down in a quickspray flash of red.

"Tired of the chase?" Milo said.

"Must have been, yeah. Though I like to think I provide a reasonable challenge, you know?"

Another shotgun blast crisped the night, lit up the graffiti-strewn brick walls around them.

"That's why tonight," Henry said, cocking his Magnum, "we piss them off a little." He stood up fully, in plain sight, popped off a round in the direction of the closest dumpster, where one of the Hunters' feet was visible through the blowing snow. Henry's shot pulped it.

The Hunter fell to the side, propped against the wall. Screamed his lungs out. Henry ducked behind the trash can again, leaned to his right, just enough to see his target's head through the heavy snow.

Fired.

A clump of bone and gristle slapped against the brick wall, silencing the screams.

Words of anger filtered out from behind the other two dumpsters. It was rare that the Runners fought back.

"Oh, shit. That did it," Henry said.

A shotgun exploded from behind one of the dumpsters; machine gun fire opened up from behind the other. Wails of pain filled the thin spaces of silence between the metallic staccato.

Henry popped his head up quickly to see if he'd killed the Hunter or just badly wounded him. (He was only aiming to wound, but he might've fucked up, blown the guy's whole head off.)

Five bullets from the machine gun fire whistled into his cranium. The first two slammed out the back, but the last three stuck hard. Two more sliced through his neck, butted up against several others already lodged there. Henry fell backward, exposed to the gunfire, unconscious. Four more bullets found their home in his chest as he lay there, then the firing stopped.

Milo swore and moved to pick Henry up.

The two Hunters ignored Milo and shuffled to the dumpster where their friend had fallen. Low, muffled curses whipped by wind found Milo's ears.

The Hunters picked up their friend – each to an arm – and dragged him backward out of the alley, his booted feet leaving trails through the snow.

"Idiot," Milo said. "Idiot with shit timing." He hoisted Henry up and over his shoulder in a fireman's carry. A feeling of distinct unease swept through him, and he hoped like hell that Henry hadn't killed the Hunter – that maybe by some miracle he was still alive, just very badly wounded.

Milo trudged through the deep snow of the alley, past the three dumpsters where the Hunters had been, walking in the grooves left by their boots. He squinted against the wind, was nearly blinded by the street lamp's glaring reflection off the crisp, fresh snow. At the mouth of the alleyway, down and to his right, Milo spotted a dark shape, a man, lying on the ground, most of his head pulverized, a misshapen, bleeding lump in the darkness. Definitely dead.

Oh fuck, he thought. He looked up from the Hunter Henry had shot, saw the man's two friends coming toward him. Scowls under hoods.

The closest one stopped in front of Milo, blocking his way; the other stood behind the first, at his shoulder, glaring, stonefaced. The first one spoke: "This ain't how the game's played, motherfucker." He pointed to Henry, a deadweight sack slung over Milo's shoulder, still out cold and leaving a trail of blood in the snow behind them: "He killed my friend; now I'll kill his."

"Whoa now, hang on a minute, fellas," Milo said. "Henry was just trying to liven things up a little, you know? He didn't mean to–"

Something metal glinted in the gaslight, catching Milo's eye. He looked down. The Hunter had pulled a machete from a sheath.

Milo backed up a step, shook his head once.

The machete swung, sliced through air, through snowflakes, through Milo's windpipe, vertebrae.

Three crumpled heaps, lying still in the dark. Bleeding.

When the machete sliced through Milo's neck, he felt almost human.

With hardly any lead lodged in his neck, the blade sliced clean through, only knocking up against one, maybe two bullets. When his head fell from his shoulders, his eyes blinked one last time. And then he was suddenly floating about four inches off the ground, just hovering, swaying in the cold winter wind. Dead but dreaming.

He stared at his corpse, wished he could reach down, move his body, then grab Henry by the collar, lift him back into the fireman's carry and move up the street, closer to the warmth in Henry's apartment. But he knew now that was impossible.

He turned his gaze on Henry's body, watched his chest move up and down ever so slightly. *Still alive. Good. Someone will find you in the morning.*

For now, the comforting warmth of Henry's apartment called to Milo, just three or four blocks away to the north. *I'll see ya soon, Henry. Meet you at home.*

Milo drifted up the street, the sensation of not pumping his legs to walk, of not feeling the ground under his feet, was surreal. Whatever he'd become, it was *lighter* than what he was before. Everything else seemed the same. Eyesight, hearing, thought processes – all working as they had before. Only his sense of touch was gone.

Snow created tingling sensations wherever it filtered through him. One block, two blocks. He passed an old man crumpled in the corner of a storefront, mumbling to himself. The old man paid him no mind. He passed a cat. The cat did not hiss at him. The cat saw nothing, sensed nothing.

The wind died down a little. Milo picked up speed. Rounded a few more corners, then saw Henry's building ahead. When he got to the bottom of the building, he looked up through the snow, saw Henry's south-facing apartment window. A dim light glowed inside.

He tried to will himself straight up, felt he could drift right up through the night, coast inside Henry's apartment through the window like a ghost. But no dice. All he got for his mental effort was a silly look of intense concentration on his face and a sincere flush of embarrassment.

As though people could actually see him trying to fly.

He shook his head, frowned, and floated forward, through the same front door that the living used. Up the stairs, instinctively maintaining the four inches he'd had outside on the street. Up to Henry's apartment on the third floor. Through the locked door.

Inside, it was probably warm, Henry's living room radiator hissing out heat. But Milo couldn't know for sure. It felt the same temperature to him as it did outside. Cold.

The coldest he'd ever felt.

Milo floated into Henry's bedroom, saw the covers on his bed flung back. Clock on the nightstand flashing 12:00.

Outside, the sky was getting lighter. Someone would soon find Henry's body, even if the usual society cleanup crew was asleep at the wheel: a waitress on her way to work, a construction worker crossing the street for his morning coffee.

Milo considered leaving Henry's apartment to wait for Henry at the nearest hospital, but he couldn't summon the courage to go back out. The apartment was comfortable. Familiar.

The curtains were open and the light coming in was thin and wan. Milo moved over to the window, reached up a hand to close them, but couldn't get a grip. His hand didn't pass right through; it brushed the curtains a little, made them move, but it was as if he wasn't strong enough to grip the material.

Morning hands, he thought.

He concentrated harder, felt his grip tighten a bit. The curtain moved a little more, as though being brushed by a draft. Milo tried a few more times, but couldn't get a firmer grip. He left the curtains alone, stood by the foot of the bed. Stared at the flashing clock.

Waited for Henry to come home.

An hour later, when the sun tinged the sky dark red, a passerby noticed Milo's and Henry's bodies in the street (the Hunters had taken their friend home to be buried): one was headless, and the other might as well have been. But the latter was still breathing. The passerby called 911; an ambulance picked Henry up, took him to the hospital he'd been at the previous night. Upon examination, the paramedics on duty quickly figured out what he was, had seen plenty of his kind during the course of their jobs, but since there had never been any clear directive about how to handle them – and since the memory of treating them would fade from their minds like a photograph in the sun, anyway – they just treated them like they were normal people in need of assistance. Let someone else deal with them once they got to the hospital.

Henry woke up a little during the bumpy ride. He wondered briefly what his percentage was now. He guessed it wasn't a hundred percent because if it had been, shouldn't… *something* have already happened? He wondered, too, if maybe Milo had been taken in another ambulance. Maybe Henry would see him at the hospital.

Henry closed his eyes, wished he were outside again, feeling the night's fat snowflakes falling gently on his lips.

Again – hospital green.

And again, the same nurse. His girlfriend, Faye.

"You here again?" she said, smiled a little, leaned over Henry, fluffed his pillow. Faye was used to seeing Henry brought in to the hospital, had come to relax about it much more than when they'd first started dating. Back then, about a year ago, she regularly panicked, didn't know how to react, what to do, what to say. But you get used to anything, as the saying goes. She knew what Henry was – to a certain extent, anyway. Her repeated exposure to him – day in, day out – helped shore up his personality in her mind, like sandbags against a flood. In this case, the flood was a mysterious memory wipe that came, presumably, from the same place the bodies of loved ones went when they vanished.

Henry's mouth felt stuffed with cotton, his head packed with burnt chestnuts. "Sure looks that way. Not for long, though, I suspect, once the doctors get wind of it."

Faye said nothing, just kept smiling.

Looking up at her pretty face, Henry suddenly remembered something Milo had said on the phone last night: *You need a woman's touch over there, my friend. Someone to bring some fucking life to that shitty little hole you call home.*

And he decided to give it a shot... before his head fully cleared and he was capable of talking himself out of it.

"Hey, uh, so, when I'm feeling better and stuff, you wanna maybe, I don't know…" Shit, this was going well. "Like, kinda… fucking, um, move in with me?"

A few seconds passed. Faye smiled wide, said, "Yes."

Henry was blushing, and was prepared to backpedal the moment her refusal was out of her mouth. When she didn't refuse, he didn't know what to say. He hadn't banked on an acceptance.

"Uhh, OK," he said. Then trying to act cool, added, "Good deal."

Henry, wanting desperately to change the subject now, asked where Milo was.

"Henry, listen…" Faye said, her smile quickly vanishing, brow furrowing. She took his hand, squeezed it. "Milo's dead."

Faye waited a beat, swallowed, locked eyes with Henry. "I'm so sorry."

Inside Henry, metal shifted. Bullets and shot moved slowly, piecing themselves together. Like a puzzle.

"I, uh… I have to go now," he said, some base instinct taking over. A need to be home. To be warm, somewhere familiar.

Henry swung the sheets back from his legs, got to his feet. Staggered, nearly fell. Faye caught him, steadied him.

"Henry, your head. Jesus. You can't just walk out of here with–"

"Jesus Christ, I'll be fine!" he shouted in Faye's face.

Henry took a breath, put a hand to his head – the walls swam and rippled. "Look, I'm sorry, Faye,

I just… I can't be here right now. I need to…" He
moved forward, hugged Faye hard, kissed her head.
"I'll call you later, OK? We'll sort out moving in and
all that, and we'll figure out Milo's… arrangements,
or whatever."

Henry'd never had anyone die on him, and he'd
only ever been to one other funeral in his life – his
grandfather's. Three quarters full of lead, but dead
simply of old age. He hoped he'd be as lucky.

Henry turned and walked out the door.

Faye followed, trying to convince him to go back
to bed, stay and talk for a while. Just until he calmed
down. But he kept walking, would no longer look at
her.

She gave up at the front door, where it was clear
she wasn't going to stop him, no matter what she
said. She watched Henry from the hospital's front-
entrance window. Watched him stumble slowly out
into the blowing snow. Trip. Fall. Collapse on his
side.

She cursed under her breath, threw her coat on,
ran through the double doors, across the parking lot.
She knelt down, tried pulling him to his feet, but he
was too heavy.

Faye stood up, left him lying in the snow, ran to
the curb, flagged down a cab. The cabby pulled over;
she approached the driver's side and explained the
situation. The cabby put on his hazard lights, jumped
out of the car, moved to help Faye.

Together, they lifted Henry to his feet, shuffled him
through the snow and ice to the back door of the cab.
Faye ran quickly inside the hospital, fished around for

some bills in her purse, came back out, paid the cabby, told him Henry's address.

The car pulled away from the curb, soon lost in a white sheet of snow.

THREE

It snowed for another three days straight, then cleared up suddenly to usher in sunny, blue skies. But colder now. Much colder.

Henry shivered in his apartment. Not only had the temperature dropped, but his bedroom radiator had shut down. So much for getting warm.

He was too tired to move out into the marginally warmer living room, so he wound the blankets around him as tightly as he could to keep in the heat. But no matter how many blankets he curled around himself, or how snugly he wrapped them around his frame, the cold still got in.

The cold of ice on steel.

His teeth chattered. He swam in and out of consciousness. Several times he hallucinated Faye coming to see him, stroking his brow, telling him it would be alright, that he just needed to rest to get through this, just needed to sleep a while longer.

Sometimes during the three nights of the storm, he dreamed of Milo: Milo standing at the foot of his bed, floating a few inches off the ground, smiling. Just smiling. Snow in his hair. Then he'd drift out of the room, disappear, and Henry would wake up. Cold and alone. With pieces of the metal puzzle inside him still shifting around. Faster than at the hospital, steadily picking up speed.

In the chill of dawn, when the apartment seemed at its coldest, Henry felt he knew what the pieces of the puzzle were doing. They were moving within him to touch each other, form something. But what – and for what purpose – he had no idea. He believed in nothing. Expected nothing. The only thing Henry wanted now was to close his curtains. Since the storm had subsided, the sun streamed through his bedroom window too bright for Henry's eyes, which now glinted in the light. He didn't know it, couldn't see it, but they'd turned from deep brown to metallic silver.

The day after the storm passed, Henry felt the puzzle inside him slowing, calming.

Milo came to visit him in his dreams one last time, late that fourth night: he hovered at the foot of the bed, as he'd been doing the last few days. Only this time, before he left – a look of intense concentration on his face – he floated over to Henry's bedroom window. Tried, and failed, to close the curtains for his friend.

The night before Henry would wake up changed forever – five days after coming home from the hospital – he dreamed a memory of him and Milo as kids of about twelve years old:

"What do you think happens?" Milo asked Henry, a more innocent precursor to their discussion the week before Milo's death.

They were in Henry's backyard. Just sitting in the dirt, playing with plastic action figures from their favorite movies.

"Happens when?" Henry replied. He held one action figure in each hand.

"When ya get all filled up with bullets. Or whatever."

"Dunno. Don't care," Henry said, and pummeled one of the action figures into the other.

Milo shifted his position in the dirt. Something about Henry not caring what happened when full lead content was reached bugged him. "How can you not *care*, dummy?"

Henry shrugged. "Just don't. Maybe one day I'll find out, but till then it's stupid to waste time thinking about that crap."

Milo dropped his own action figures in the dirt, glanced up at the sky. Blue, clear, the sun shining so fiercely, he couldn't look anywhere near it. He dropped his eyes again, looked at Henry. He hesitated a moment, as if considering something, then spoke, hesitantly: "Well, I think … I think you become, like, this awesome monster robot machine! I think you become really big, and you go around saving people trapped under cars and in burning buildings and stuff. I think you become a lot happier, too. Like, way happier than in regular life. You know?"

When Henry didn't immediately answer, Milo picked up one of his action figures – an army guy missing an arm – and tossed it across the yard.

Sensing his friend's frustration, Henry said, "OK, here's what I honestly think: I think whatever you become, it's not good. It's bad. I think you become something else. Not even yourself anymore. And maybe you do bad things to people, but you can't control yourself. And yeah, maybe you're all cool and robotic and metal and gigantic and everything, sure. But I think –" and here, Henry droppped his action figures on the ground, and stood up "– I think you hurt people. People you hate. People you love. Everybody."

The dream ends as Henry walks back into his house, leaving Milo outside in the blistering sun.

Faye knocked on the door.

No answer.

She knocked harder. Still nothing.

She fretted about whether or not to keep trying this late at night. Decided to forget about knocking again and just open the door with her key.

She'd tried calling the past couple of days, but there'd been no answer, and she'd been run off her feet at the hospital so there'd been no chance to check on Henry in person till now. It wasn't abnormal for them not to see each other for days at a time, given their abnormal schedules, but after her second or third call attempt, Faye began to worry just a little bit – and that feeling had only grown worse with each passing hour.

She turned the key, pushed gently. The door swung open.

The apartment air was frigid. Faye shivered and pulled the gray scarf tighter around her neck.

She walked in slowly, called out, "Henry, are you home?"

Silence.

She poked her head around a corner, looked in the kitchen which branched off from the living room. Nothing.

The bathroom light shone bright in the relative gloom of the apartment.

"Henry?"

No one in the bathroom. Only one more room in the place.

The bedroom door stood slightly ajar. Faye pushed on it softly, peeking inside. It was hard to make out anything. Shadows layered on shadows. Faye whispered Henry's name once more as she walked through the door, but her stomach was already sinking. It was so quiet. No hiss from the radiator, and the sound of the refrigerator running didn't make it to this side of the apartment.

No breathing sounds came from the bed.

"Oh, God," Faye said, putting a hand to her mouth. "Henry…"

He lay still on the bed. Bundled in blankets. Only his head uncovered. His shoulder-length dark hair, threaded with gray, hung in strings to the sides of his face. Unwashed for days.

For a brief moment, Faye thought maybe he wasn't dead. His cheeks seemed rosy in the dirty light filtering in through the window from a streetlamp. She moved forward, tentatively put a hand on his forehead. He was warm. Not only warm – burning up. But somehow there was no life in him. No breath. Just a wall of heat, emanating from his body.

She stood like that for a long while, looking down

at him, feeling the warmth still coming from his body in waves, as if something inside were generating it. Gears spinning. Clockwork, winding itself up.

Impossible.

"Where have you gone, Henry?" she said, though she didn't understand why she'd chosen those particular words.

No breath, she thought. *He is dead. He* must *be dead.*

Faye quietly left Henry's apartment, tears just beginning to form in her eyes.

Later that night, a dark, heavy shape rose from Henry's bed, moved around the room as if waking from a deep sleep.

Outside Henry's bedroom window, a single snowflake drifted down, stuck against the pane, melted.

Vanished.

The first of a new storm.

FOUR

"I know this sounds terribly corny, but haven't I seen you somewhere before? Like, legitimately?"

Henry turned toward the voice. *Wow, a girl is talking to me*, he thought, cleared his throat, and said, "Uh, hopefully?"

She frowned.

"I just mean that, well, if it keeps us talking, then yes, you've seen me somewhere before."

She grinned a little, maybe blushed just the tiniest bit. "Well, OK. Where was it?"

They were in a shitty little bar downtown. Henry frequented it often to unwind after Runs, and Faye occasionally came in when the loneliness of her apartment became too much to bear.

"Maybe..." Henry began, turning fully toward Faye where she sat on a stool next to his at the bar. "I dunno." He took a shot in the dark: "Milo's?"

"Don't know anyone named Milo," Faye said.

"Oh."

"Maybe if we tell each other our *names*, that might jog something," Faye said, and smiled.

Henry laughed. "Yeah, that might help. I'm Henry."

"Faye."

They shook hands, awkwardly.

"Lovely to meet you, Faye."

"Likewise. Now, let's see," she said, taking a sip from her rum and Coke. "Where do you work? Maybe I saw you there."

Ha. Where do I work.

"Um, you haven't seen me at work," he replied. "Pretty certain."

Warning bells sounded in Faye's head at this evasion, but she decided to press on. "OK, well, I'm a nurse. Maybe you were recently hospitalized?" She'd intended it as a joke, but Henry didn't laugh.

"Actually, that coulda been it. I go there more often than... normal people." He smiled, and did manage a little chuckle that calmed Faye's nerves a little.

"Street fights?" she said. "You a big badass?" More joking.

"People shoot me a lot."

He'd talked like this before to interested women. He found that telling the truth disarmed them, since they always thought he was just joking. The relationships never got much further than this because he kept strange hours and didn't have much of an interest in pursuing a relationship anyway.

"Well, I like people who get shot a lot. Gives me job security."

Henry laughed loudly at that. They continued chatting for hours, till the barkeep called for last orders.

They walked out together, awkwardly shook hands, then, taken by an impulse neither of them understood, they hugged. They knew it was strange, but they held each other for much longer than two people who've just met normally would.

And then it didn't feel so strange anymore.

Half a year later, Henry was reading over Faye's shoulder where she sat at her computer in her apartment. Henry had brought her some tea, and as he leaned over her shoulder to set the cup down on a coaster, he glanced at the document, said, "Hey, what's this? Are you cataloguing my hilariousness?"

"Yep," she said, kept typing.

Henry looked closer, read a little, then stood up straight again. "Oh, come on. No one else is going to find this shit funny."

"They did when I posted them on social media."

"People on social media don't count. For anything. Ever."

"Says you."

"It's true. I did just say that."

"Thanks for the tea. Now go away."

"I'm never going away. You're stuck with me until that murder-suicide pact I mentioned the other day. I don't want to live without you, and I'm just going to assume you feel the same way."

"Look, just let me finish this, OK?"

Henry leaned in closer again, read the following under the heading "Boyfriend Funny du Jour":

> *Henry:* Check out this video with a deer kicking the shit out of a hunter.

Faye: [watches video] That's awesome! Too funny.
Henry: I'm going to post it on the Facebooks. Ummm…
Faye: Yeah?
Henry: Uh… do deer have hooves?
Faye: [laughing] Yes. Yes they do.
Henry: What? I just wanted to make sure.
Faye: I am seriously booking a zoo visit.

"Animals are hard," Henry said. "I'm taking that tea back, meanface."

"Are girls hard, too?"

"Oh, the one after we ate at Roy Rogers? Classic Kyllo right there."

Henry: Who was Roy Rogers, anyway?
Faye: An American movie cowboy.
Henry: Oh.
Faye: With his sidekick Dale Evans. Who was a girl.
Henry: Who was a what?
Faye: A girl.
Henry: Oh! I thought you said a robot.
Faye: Yes, that sounds a lot like "girl."

"You know what's fun," Henry said. "Not this, that's what. How many of these do you have written down, anyway?"

"Pages and pages," Faye said. "And I'm going to show them to our kids one day, show them that Daddy can't tell the difference between a lemur and a meerkat. Or a tiger and a lion." Faye turned in her chair, looked up at Henry pointedly. "*A hippopotamus and a pig!*"

"The hippos were pink. No fair."

Faye laughed, turned back to her screen, read the next one out loud:

Henry: Monkeys are better than gorillas.
Faye: That's because monkeys have tails. Apes don't have tails. Like gorillas and... orangutangs... and... are baboons apes?
Henry: Ha ha ha ha ha!
Faye: Why is that funny?
Henry: I thought you said "legumes" instead of "baboons."
Faye: Yes, legumes are apes.
Henry: Legumes are the apes of the bean world.

"This right here. This is why I love you, Henry." Faye pushed her chair back, stood up, hugged Henry where he stood pretending to be hurt, his face turned away from her.

"You don't even have my favorite one in there," he said, smirking.

"Which one's that?" she said playfully, slapping his butt.

"The one where I called a ski mask a face cozy."

"Ha! Forgot about that one. I also loved when you couldn't remember who Batman's partner was. You said it was 'Batman and Robert.' I thought I was gonna die laughing."

"Speaking of dying, I think it might be murder-suicide o'clock if you keep this up."

Faye kissed Henry's face gently, said, "You are the

best of all possible boyfriends."

"I can think of better," Henry said. "I can certainly think of better *girl*friends."

"Haha. Hardly. Wait, okay, one more. Honest!"

Henry: Look at the T-Rex on that poster over there.
Faye: It's a frog.
Henry: Oh man. I just keep walking into these things. Well, at least it's a lizard.
Faye: No.
Henry: Oh, right. A reptile.
Faye: No.
Henry: What?
Faye: An amphibian.
Henry: Oh. It's amazing I passed science.
Faye: It's amazing you haven't been eaten by an animal.
Henry: Yeah! I'd go "Oh, look at the nice kitty" and it would be, like, a werewolf.
Faye: A werewolf!
Henry: No! I meant, like, a really big wolf. A wolf-wolf.

Faye pulled away, smacked his butt again, said, "We're adorable. Let's go eat."

They went downstairs together, decided they were both too tired to cook, ordered pizza, drank wine, watched some TV, and generally had a night like any other.

Neither of them with the slightest inkling of what was to come.

FIVE

Henry stumbled out of his apartment and into the hallway, a dark blot well over six feet tall, still shifting, changing shape. In flux. Milo stayed well back from Henry, but kept him in sight. The ghost of a man following the ghost of something perhaps more than a man. Perhaps nothing like a man at all.

Henry crashed down the stairs, bumping into a woman, knocking her flat. The man the woman was with narrowly sidestepped Henry's blundering descent, turning and opening his mouth, thinking about saying something. But the man had no way of rationalizing what he'd just witnessed, so he closed his mouth, bent to help his girlfriend off the ground.

Milo floated past the couple, unseen.

When Henry reached the bottom of the staircase, he flung his massive arms at a door with an "Exit Only" sign hanging over it. The door crashed open, knocked against the cement wall behind it. He emerged into the parking garage of his apartment building, immediately fell to his knees, then rolled over onto his back. He let out a strangled cry from between steel, blackened lips. One of his legs kicked out convulsively, knocking out a low section of a nearby concrete pillar. Pieces sprinkled the front-left tire of a car parked in the closest stall. His other leg shot out, denting the same car's driver-side door. He'd grown about half a foot overnight and, in places on his body where muscle and bone used to be, now metal existed, or at least something *becoming* metal.

Milo told Henry to calm down. Told him to take it easy. *Relax. It'll be alright. Just settle, man. It'll pass. No worries.*

But Henry couldn't hear Milo – not that Milo knew if this convulsion *would* pass, anyway; they were just words of comfort for comfort's sake – so Henry thrashed some more, took another small chunk out of the pillar, this time a little higher up.

Milo watched, fascinated as Henry took shape. His new shape.

When he rose again, his knees shook, clattered together. He reached one part-metal/part-flesh palm out to steady himself against the pillar he'd kicked.

Henry breathed in, breathed out. Slowly. Like great bellows. Chunks of shot poked from his ribs; tips of bullets littered one side of his face, both arms, most of his left leg; strips of smooth steel ran down both sides of his torso, glinting in the dim underground light.

Another breath, slow. The expansion of Henry's chest caused a few bullets to dislodge from his body, clatter to the ground.

He turned his head a little. Eyes gray, nearly solid metal. Ball bearings set deep in his skull. Somehow seeing, collecting information.

Milo shivered as his friend's eyes settled on him.

But they did not see him – rather saw *through* him, behind him. Milo turned around.

A small boy and his mother stood at one of the exits. The mother's keys rattled in one hand. Neither she nor the boy had yet looked up to see Henry. They held each other's hands as they walked, the mother looking down at her son, the boy prattling on about some video game he'd been playing. The mother's boots shattered the previous quiet; the boy filled the spaces between each heel's connection with excited patter.

They passed very near to Milo; he smelled – or perhaps imagined he could smell – the woman's perfume. Henry's head tracked them as they strolled by, still not noticing him. Milo wondered what this new Henry would do if the mother and the boy looked up and saw him.

The mother's car was opposite Henry and Milo, two rows over. She opened the passenger side for her son, sweeping her arm in front of her. "After you, m'dear," she said, and laughed a little.

The boy giggled, got in the car. The mother closed the door. Crossed to the driver's side, head still down, digging for something in her purse, smiling. Opened her own door, slipped inside. Slammed it shut.

Started the engine. Backed out.

And drove away.

Henry watched the car turn up a ramp, the engine sounds drifting farther and farther away. His neck relaxed, head drooping. A dandelion too heavy for its stalk.

"Henry," Milo said. "Henry."

But Henry just stared at his heavy, gray-black hand, still plastered against the pillar. And breathed.

Waiting for whatever came next.

Milo hovered nearby, of two minds about watching his friend go through another change. On the one hand, he wanted to be here for Henry – as physically ineffectual as he was; on the other, he didn't want to witness again what he'd just seen: the mad thrashing, the roaring, the pained look on his face of a kind Milo could scarcely imagine – his face that was now beginning to look like something else's face. What made it Henry was the way the body moved. Milo had run enough with his friend that they knew each other's physical movements inside out. Henry had always been fluid, sleek. Even changing into whatever he was becoming, Milo saw that he had not lost that.

Henry gained control of himself, leaned against the car he'd bashed up, near the front-right wheel well. He examined his hybrid hands, moved them around in front of his face, rubbing them, clinking together fingers nearly the size of screwdriver handles. He held them up to his ear as he clinked, as if trying to figure out what they were made of.

What *he* was made of.

He knocked his deformed knuckles on the car's panelling. Metal clanged loudly, reverberated off the wall. He tilted his head to one side, positioned one knuckle to stick out farther from his hand than the others. He raked it across the panel he'd just rapped against. A thin strip of paint curled under the pressure, flaked off, fell to the ground beside him.

Milo watched as Henry's face contorted. Metal grating against metal. A Frankenstein's monster of steel, patched together, forgotten before it was complete.

Move on, Henry, Milo thought. *You can't stay here forever. Someone's gonna come down here and see you. Come on, brother, let's go.*

But Henry was fascinated with himself. Intrigued by his transformation.

He opened his mouth. A thin gray sliver about the width of a watchband slipped out from between his serrated lips: pink tongue mixed with gray metal. Henry bit down gently with iron-tombstone teeth, grimaced. Snaked his tongue back into his mouth.

A few minutes passed with Henry just staring ahead, breathing, perhaps feeling the power, the efficiency, of his new lungs. Milo heard doors slamming shut in the stairwell nearby.

Henry, please…

Henry stood up slowly, back bent. He opened his mouth again, this time looking as though he were trying to speak. He fish-gaped for a few seconds, then clamped his lips shut, closing his eyes, defeated, when nothing came out. Then he put one foot in front of the other – just like in his old life – and shuffled toward the exit ramp clumsily, nearly falling over several times.

Milo followed his friend out into the cold white of the storm. Followed him as his balance improved, his step became surer, his footing more solid. Followed him when others would run in the opposite direction. But Milo believed that a friend is a friend is a friend.

And he soon saw that Henry had a purpose, a direction.

Henry stuck close to the sides of buildings, hunkered behind cars, dumpsters, anything big enough to hide him when people came into view. Though it would be hard for them to see him through the blowing snow, Milo knew Henry realized what he was – or if not *what* he was, he knew what he certainly did not appear to be: human. And yes, people somehow forgot their encounters with his kind, but how much of that was tied to the fact that they looked human? Would this mysterious force continue to work when people were confronted with a giant metal/human hybrid bumbling around their streets? Probably best not to find out.

The storm picked up, dumped layer after layer of crisp, crunchy snow under Henry's feet. The sun dipped below the horizon. Gas lamps flickered on. Henry moved carefully down back alleys, crossed nearly deserted streets with special care not to get caught in the pools of thin yellow light from the lamps above.

As deeper darkness fell, Milo caught sight of a large blue "H" limned against the swirling white.

Where are you going, Henry? Milo thought, drifting above the snowy ground. *What's drawing you here?* But then it hit him: *Of course. The hospital. Faye.*

Henry trudged across a muddy field, ducked under several trees with low-hanging branches as cars in the hospital parking lot drove by, their lights cutting conical swaths through the curtain of snow. Light shone out of one of the rooms on the first floor of the hospital. It bathed a patch of sidewalk a well-defined white, as if cut with scissors.

Without understanding where the thought came from, Milo found himself repeating, *Henry, I'm here, I'm here*, over and again in his head.

Henry moved away from the last tree he'd stuck himself against, headed toward the light from the room on the hospital's first floor.

Milo followed Henry across the remaining patch of field, the snowflakes feeling colder than ever where they passed through him.

SIX

The day after Faye left Henry's apartment, she walked to work through the new storm that had started the previous night. A squat man in an ill-fitting suit and overcoat approached her, stopped her before she crossed the street to the front entrance of the hospital.

"Excuse me," he said.

"Yes?" Faye replied, glancing across the street, reflexively checking that she was in plain view of other people.

"Do you know Henry Kyllo? I believe you do," the short man said, speaking quickly; his words meshed into one another to the point that Faye wasn't quite sure she'd heard him correctly.

"Pardon me?"

"Kyllo," the man said, took a step back, perhaps to ease Faye's obvious discomfort at being stopped in the street by a stranger. "Do you know him?"

The little man had squinted eyes, which were not helped by his horizontally thin glasses. His close-cropped helmet haircut only added to the severity of his other features – hawk nose, thin lips, pointy chin – and Faye found it increasingly difficult to concentrate on his words rather than his off-putting appearance.

"Um, sorry, who are you?" Faye glanced nervously across the street again. Gerald Haines, a co-worker, was out front having a smoke. She unwound a little, knowing someone she knew was within view.

"You helped him yesterday, didn't you?" The man sniffed sharply. "Don't lie to me. I saw you with him, right out front here –" he swept one of his stubby arms around and pointed to the front of the hospital where Faye had helped Henry into the cab the previous day "– so just nod *yes* like a good little girl, and we can continue."

Faye raised her eyebrows at the man's rudeness, but nodded. "Yes. Yes, I helped Henry Kyllo." Memories of Henry swam up from the back of her brain, edited, distorted, changed slightly to minimize things that may have struck her as odd about him. This always happened, but due to her repeated exposure to him on a near-daily basis, enough of what made Henry *Henry* stayed with her. "He was in no shape to help himself, which, if you were watching us yesterday, as you say you were – which is creepy, obviously – you should know. Who are you, anyway, to stop me in the street and–"

The man held up a pudgy hand. "Ah-ah," he said. "No need to get your knickers in a twist, my dear." He smiled. Most of his teeth were black, as though stained by soot. "I just want to know what happened to our Mr Kyllo, that's all." He spread his arms wide, palms open, facing her. Crudely drawn tattoos covered his hands, snaked up into his coat sleeves. Faye tried to make out some of the shapes before he brought his arms back down, but could only see that they were symbols of some kind.

"Why do you–"

"I want to know because I am an interested party, young miss. That is all. I am a friend of Mr Kyllo's and his wellbeing is of great importance to me."

Faye's friend, Gerald, butted out his half-finished smoke and headed back inside the hospital. Faye felt suddenly desperate. The man continued to block her way, and there were no other people around now. There might have been someone farther down the street, but the heavily falling snow obscured her view, and she couldn't be sure if the thin black lumps she saw were people or short lampposts, bicycle stands, post office boxes.

"Well, he's dead," Faye said, a wave of sadness falling over her. "At least I think he is." She didn't know why she added that last. Surely he was dead. She must have simply imagined the heat coming from his body. Wishful thinking. The clear light of day had convinced her of this. There was no breath. No breath equals no life.

"He's not dead, miss. The dead do not walk around. The dead do not vanish from their tiny apartments in the night. At least not the dead I know." He winked, and it sent a small shiver creeping down Faye's back.

She ignored the content of the man's words, and just reacted to his haughty tone. "If you're his friend–"

"Oh, I am probably his *best* friend right now, I assure you," the man interrupted.

"–then you'll know far more about where he might be than I do. Now, if you'll excuse me, I have to get to work."

She made to move around him, but he stepped quickly in her way again.

"You *will* let me know if you hear from him, won't you? It really is in his best interest."

"Yes, yes, I'll let you know." She made to move around him again, and again he stepped in front of her, head tilted to one side.

"Now how will you let me know, if you don't have my contact information?"

"Look, I don't know who you are or what exactly you want, but–"

"Here's my card," the man said, his voice dropping several octaves. Deep, dark wood. He slipped a business card into Faye's hand, wrapped his stubby fingers around her long, elegant ones. "I'll never be too far away."

The man turned around quickly and walked into the storm, hands in his coat pockets.

When he disappeared into the swirling snow, Faye looked down at the card. There was a telephone number and a name: Edward Palermo.

All throughout that day, Faye felt odd. Somehow just *off*. As if she'd done something out of habit, and it had put her out of sync. It wasn't just the visit from Edward Palermo on her way to work. It was the combination of the ceaseless storm, the visit from

Palermo, Milo's death, and now Henry's death – and surely he must be dead, despite Palermo's insistence to the contrary. All of these things, plus something else she couldn't quite put her finger on. Something that made her feel cold inside. Empty. Something that replaced her general feeling of loneliness with a hollow ache.

Then a thought struck her: *If I truly believe Henry's dead, why haven't I called anyone? Why haven't I at least reported the body to the police?* She had no answer, and the niggling feeling that perhaps this Palermo was telling the truth would not go away. *And why aren't I more upset? If I knew in my heart he was gone, I'd be a wreck. Or at least I* imagine *I'd be a wreck.*

As the sun went down – the storm picking up even more, wind battering against metal doors, shaking them on their hinges, snow pelting windows in furious sheets – Faye neared the end of her shift. She was on the first floor, changing an old man's bedpan in the bathroom, talking with her friend Marjorie, who was changing the patient's sheets. Marjorie had a strong lisp, but loved the sound of her own voice nonetheless. Short, broad-shouldered, and a tiny bit cross-eyed. You couldn't really tell unless she got mad at someone.

Marjorie stripped the sheets from the old man's bed, snapped them tight as she folded. One room away, another nurse bathed him; Marjorie and Faye did not envy this other nurse whatsoever.

"That old man is one dirty motherfucker," Marjorie said, snapped another sheet briskly.

"I know," said Faye. "The other day he tried to kiss me. Full on the lips. I couldn't believe it."

"*I* can believe it. Old bastard grabbed one of my tits when I leaned over to change his pillow. Little shit. Tries it again, I'm gonna sock him one."

Faye smiled, came back into the room with a clean bedpan. Marjorie folded, continued detailing ways in which she would beat the crap out of the old man if he so much as looked at her for too long. She soon got bored of this topic, though, and switched to bitching about one of the other nurses.

A shadow crossed the window. Marjorie kept talking.

Faye didn't notice the brief darkness. She continued listening.

"… so then she asks me to take her shift! I ain't taking that bitch's shift, not after what she said about Herman. Herman wouldn't do nothin' to nobody and there she is badmouthing him right in front of me! 'Course she didn't know I was listening, but that sure as shit…"

Marjorie blathered on and on. But her lisp soothed Faye and she found herself drifting off. She helped Marjorie put new sheets on the old man's bed. Tucked in the corners good and tight, smoothed it out flat. Not a wrinkle in sight.

She drifted further into her own thoughts, Marjorie's voice becoming a dull brown tone at the base of her neck, its pitch wavering ever so slightly, creeping up into her brain, massaging her consciousness.

Snap. Fold. Tuck. The soft murmur of linen hugging bed corners.

On to the pillows.

Suddenly, Palermo popped into Faye's head. *Henry,* she thought. He seemed to float in and out of her thoughts – sometimes right at the forefront, other times just the flicker of a memory that she had to concentrate on very hard to pull near the surface.

If he is dead, it'll get harder and harder for me to remember him, until he's completely gone from my memory. How long will it take? A week, a month, a year? The thought caused a lump to form in her throat – the closest thing she'd had to tears since leaving Henry's apartment last night.

Another shadow whipped by outside the window. Again, Faye did not see it.

Marjorie prattled. Pillows swished into pillowcases.

More darkness. Only this time, it lingered at the window, a hazy figure, unclear had anyone been looking from the inside. But no one was.

Breath fogged up the window. Close now. Closer still. Almost a discernible shape.

Then it backed off, moved away. This time the movement *did* catch Faye's attention. The condensation from the breath dissipated slowly. Nearly gone. Faye caught sight of a tiny wet circle on the window just before it disappeared.

The nurse who'd been washing the old man returned with him in tow. He leered at Marjorie's breasts as he passed. Marjorie warned him to watch his step. Then Faye and Marjorie changed sheets on the next patient's bed.

A whisper of dread threaded through Faye's body

as she stepped near the window.

Snap. Fold. Tuck.

Outside the window, Milo hovered near Henry's back, trying to make his voice heard. *I'm here, I'm here* were the only words that made any sense to say, stuck in his head like sticks in mud.

When Faye turned her attention to the window, Henry ducked back out of sight, leaving a small circle of breath dissipating in the cold. He whipped around, his back to the concrete wall beside the window. His face creased up. Etched pain. He slumped down against the wall, folded his legs under him as best he could, panted quick breaths into the night.

Finally, the logjam in Milo's head cleared enough to let in another thought. *All night? You're just going to sit out here all night and wait for her? For what, Henry? If anything, you're just gonna terrify her, and she'll run screaming into the night.*

Milo sighed. Drifted over to his friend, sat cross-legged, floating several inches off the ground, like a genie out of his bottle. But he had no magic carpet. And no matter how much he wanted to, he could not grant Henry three wishes. Could not even grant him one.

Concentrating as hard as he could – as he'd done back in Henry's room when he'd tried to close the curtains for his friend – he reached his hand up to a part of Henry's head that was more or less completely turned to metal. His fingers brushed through the solid steel there, no friction whatsoever. He tried again, this time slower, eyes closed, visualizing his fingers gaining purchase on the smooth, blackened metal of Henry's skull – this close to it, it looked scorched, as if burned by fire. But again, it just passed right through.

Around them, the snow piled up thicker, blown into drifts by the wind. Above the nearby street, a gas lamp flickered, blew out, deepening the shadows cast by the other lamps around it.

One more try.

His eyes as tight as they'd go, Milo imagined harm coming to his friend, imagined this transformation leading to nothing of any worth, of Faye running screaming from Henry, of Hunters killing him out of fear, or simply reprisal for what he'd done to one of their number. Milo imagined these things and felt the near-tangible dread of being left alone in this new world – this world that, to him, was a world in which only he existed, in which he could communicate with no one else.

His fingertips touched Henry's head, then, just the tiniest bit. An emotional and physical connection formed, however briefly. Milo brushed his fingers near Henry's left ear, which now looked more like a blistered spike jutting from his skull, and Henry turned his face slowly in Milo's direction, squinted hard gray eyes against the wind and snow, as if someone had called his name.

I'm here, Milo said, taking up his mantra again, *I'm here, Henry. I won't leave you tonight. I won't.*

Henry, unsure what he was feeling, moved his head away from Milo's hand. Furrowed his brow.

Metal crunched as he lowered his head and waited for the night to end.

SEVEN

At the far north end of the train track that ran through the city's center, an abandoned caboose sat huddled against the winter storm. Inside, a lantern burned. By the lantern's light, Edward Palermo, leader of the Runners, wrote on a yellow notepad. He gazed out one of the little windows in the caboose that he'd turned into his home, and documented the storm.

If one recorded the weather, Palermo believed, documented each snowstorm, each calm day, each rainfall, how *much* rain or snow fell on any given day, the temperature, and other variable factors, one might glean just a little of what events lay ahead. He'd learned this practice from his father. Not everyone could do it, but Edward and his father seemed to just have a natural knack for it.

There were no calculations, no formulae, no mathematical equations to apply to it. Palermo just recorded the weather in a journal in his own words, described it with whatever emotions it stirred within him. As he wrote, images came into his mind. Sometimes he recognized the events playing out in his head; other times, they were foreign to him, like scenes from someone else's dreams. He then recorded those scenes in a separate journal. Palermo – as well as those under him – believed this attempt at reading the passage of time through shifts in the weather had successfully guided him in his decision making.

But this snowstorm was like nothing he'd ever seen before, had lasted longer already than any in recent memory, and showed no signs of abating. It had caused his dreams to darken, his visions of events to blur, become indistinct, shadowed. A white curtain dropping on everything.

The wind whipped the caboose, rocking it on its tracks. Nearly two feet of snow lay on the ground, which would make tonight's Run more challenging… if Palermo decided to continue with it. Given what had happened with Henry Kyllo and his friend, Milo, Palermo thought maybe a cooling-down period of at least a day or two might be advisable. Although what might happen if the Run was cancelled was something Palermo didn't want to deal with. Under his guidance, a Run had never been missed – one had happened once a night for as long as he'd been in control. Nearly thirty years now. Individuals occasionally missed a Run, and that came with a heavy price, but to cancel the entire thing? Palermo shuddered at the thought.

If no one showed up, would we all just disappear? Or would people defy the order, too scared to think of the consequences? Happier to face my wrath than… whatever or whomever truly runs the show?

What Palermo didn't know was that upcoming events would render the question moot, anyway.

He finished writing his entries for the day – including as a side note the fact that he'd located Henry Kyllo through various intelligence sources earlier that day – sat back in the antique oak chair at his little desk, and closed both journals. The lantern light flickered briefly, a particularly strong gust of wind sneaking in through a small crack in the wall.

The wind died down for a few seconds, and Palermo heard boots crunching snow beside the caboose. Closer. Now the ring of metal steps. Palermo turned in his chair, waited for the knock on the door. When it came, it sounded thin, the latest gust whipping it from the knocker's knuckles.

"Enter," Palermo said.

The door opened just a crack, closed a little, opened again as the opener struggled to keep it from being ripped out of his hands. Snow blew in, dusting Palermo's dark red Persian rugs and Sri Lankan wall hangings. To Palermo, the elephant was the most exquisite of animals and everywhere in the caboose sat statues, photographs, miniatures, and paintings of the creature.

"You'll do well to close that door in a hurry, Marcton. Either in or out, make up your mind," Palermo said calmly.

Another few seconds of struggling with the door and finally Marcton squeezed inside, the door battering him on the shoulder as he did so. The door slammed shut behind him. A final puff of fine white powder settled on the floor at his feet.

"Kendul's here, sir."

"I told you not to call me 'sir,' Marcton. You know my name; I expect you to use it."

"Right," Marcton said, uneasy in his own skin. "Well, he's here, like I said. Shall I bring him in to see you, or will you go out to see him? Derek and Cleve patted him down already; I gave him some coffee. Warm him up."

Then Marcton just stood there, head bent, chewing his lips. His thin frame shivered from the cold. He'd gone out into the storm – as always – wearing only a thin black T-shirt and loose fitting blue jeans.

"Send him in here," Palermo said. "You get him, and only *you* come back with him. I don't want Derek and Cleve in his company for too long, understood?"

Marcton nodded, swallowed, shivered harder. He turned toward the door in his heavy boots, the laces flapping behind him. He burst outside this time, rather than play push-and-pull with the wind. The door cracked on its hinges, nearly flew off, then slammed shut again, Marcton's boots now thundering down the metal steps. Boots crunched on snow again, the top layer a thin sheet of ice driven through with every step.

Palermo knew that when Marcton came back with Kendul, he would not step in the holes already made by his boots, but would go out of his way to avoid them. Palermo never asked why. Just as he'd never asked why Marcton refused to wear a coat, a hat, or anything else that might help keep him warm in winter months. He respected his people's privacy above all else, and never wanted to pry into their personal lives – unlike Kendul, who made it his business to know everything he could about his Hunters. But then Hunters and Runners had always been fundamentally different – always would be.

Palermo swiveled in his chair, picked up his journals, pulled open a drawer in his desk, and placed them gently inside. He shut the drawer and stood up, breathing deeply of the crisp night air. He glanced back at the door; the snow Marcton had ushered inside had already melted into his rugs, sunk into his wall hangings. Only a sprinkling remained near the foot of the door where a thin strip of the caboose's original hardwood lay exposed.

He walked to the dresser next to his small bed, examined the framed photographs there, searching for one in particular, but not finding it. He frowned, tried to remember where the photo might be. It'd been so long...

Then he remembered. He reached across his bed to the tiny nightstand. Pulled out the top drawer, dug under some papers, his gun, and a bottle of whiskey. The picture he pulled out was not framed like the others. It was in terrible shape: burnt-edged, sun-faded, bubbled, and warped. A decade of neglect, both emotional and physical. Until last night, he had barely thought of the girl in the photograph. It was just too heartbreaking.

Palermo stood up straight again, back popping,

fingers brushing the girl's photo. Over the years, pain had settled into the creases of Palermo's face, but when he touched the photograph, he felt a thin smile playing about on his lips, easing – if only momentarily – some of the heartache imprinted there. He still loved her, of course he did, no matter what had happened. He always would.

When the door suddenly flew open again, Palermo nearly dropped the picture, but caught it at the last second, thrust it deep into his coat pocket. Turned to greet his visitor.

Snow blasted in again, swirling around the caboose, creating little blizzards for the elephant statues peppered throughout the furniture surfaces.

Marcton escorted James Kendul, leader of the Hunters, inside, pulled a fold-out chair from inside the redwood armoire, snapped it open, motioned to Kendul to sit.

Kendul thanked Marcton, sat down, and sniffed. Once.

"Thank you, Marcton," Palermo said.

Marcton nodded, shivered, and bounded out the door, slamming it behind him.

Palermo bent to look out the window, watched Marcton plod up the path toward the warehouse – careful, of course, not to step in any of the footprints already made. He watched Marcton knock at the warehouse door, shift from side to side as he waited for it to open. Cleve's bulky frame filled the doorway, then Marcton was in.

Palermo looked back at his guest, sighed, pulled out his own chair at the desk, and plopped himself in it. The two faced each other. Old friends, occasional enemies.

"What are you doing here?" Palermo said. "Why now? Why not just send one of your boys?"

"Want something done right, do it yourself," Kendul said. James Kendul was fairly short like Palermo, but built thinner, sleeker. Kendul's crisp blue eyes rarely left the person to whom he was talking. "You know that as well as I do, Edward."

Palermo nodded. "So why now?"

"You know why."

"Because one of your boys got killed in a Run? Goddamnit, it happens; not very often, but you know it happens, so–"

"One of mine saw him, Edward. Near the hospital this side of the tracks. Luckily, one loyal to me, one I can trust not to say anything about it to the others."

Palermo thought of carrying on with the ignorance act, but knew it would be pointless. Kendul knew. Kyllo'd been seen.

"How long were you going to wait before telling me, Edward?" Kendul asked, anger rising. "How fucking long?"

"We knew it would happen again one day," Palermo said, resigned, unable to look his old friend directly in the eyes. Palermo put his hand inside the coat pocket where he'd stuffed the picture of the girl. His fingers stroked the burnt edges of the photograph. "I just always wished it wouldn't be on my watch."

Kendul nodded, shifted his weight in his chair, glanced out the caboose window at the warehouse.

The light from the top windows made the snow glow a dirty yellow. "We have to find him," he said, brushing his hands once down the creases in his pants. "See exactly what he's become. We on the same page here?"

Palermo pulled his hand from his pocket, gestured vaguely at nothing. "Of course." Kendul usually made him a bit nervous – the same way Palermo made *other* people nervous – but he was determined not to show it. At least determined to *try* not to show it.

"You OK, Palermo?" Kendul asked, shifting the full weight of his gaze onto Edward. "You seem… distracted. More distracted than usual, I mean."

Always with the little digs, Palermo thought.

"No, I'm fine, Kendul. We dealt with this situation before, and we'll do it again. Let's not make it worse than it already is by getting at each other's throats. It's wholly unnecessary and, frankly, beneath us."

Kendul sniffed again. Twice this time. Looked away.

"I'll be in touch," Kendul said, then stood up, extended his hand. Palermo stood and shook it. Kendul moved toward the door. "And Edward," he added, opening the door, letting the screaming night inside, "see what your weather visions have to say about this. I'm open to taking advice from any source willing to offer it up."

Kendul stepped outside, his floor-length weathered brown trench brushing the lip of the doorframe. He turned around. Squinted against the snow and wind.

"What's his name, anyway, Edward? Not that it matters. But what's his name?"

"Henry Kyllo," Palermo said, unsure whether his voice had been loud enough to carry over the storm. "Been with us some time now. I had no idea how close he was, though."

"Kyllo," Kendul repeated, rolling the name around on his tongue.

Palermo nodded. More snow to sprinkle his elephants, more cold to freeze his photographs into place.

Kendul slammed the door hard, stomped down the caboose steps, crunched across the lot toward the warehouse's back door.

Palermo rolled up his coat sleeves, caressed the tattoos there, brushed his fingers lightly over the symbols. They felt hot, burning beneath his skin. He made sure the photograph of the girl was still in his pocket, then put on his boots, wrapped a dark blue wool scarf around his neck, put his collar up, and stepped out into the storm.

"Good?" Cleve grunted as he opened the warehouse door to let Marcton back inside. But Marcton's gaze was locked elsewhere, toward the street.

"Yo, dingus, wake up," Cleve said. "I'm talkin' to ya."

"Yeah," Marcton said, slowing down, squinting, still looking toward the street. "Fine."

Cleve followed his gaze. "What are you so enthralled by, dummy? I swear to Christ you get more spaced out with every passing day.

Marcton's expression changed, then. He went stonefaced. As he pushed past Cleve, stepping inside the warehouse, he said simply, "Company. Follow me."

Hidden in the long shadow of a building across the street from the Runners' warehouse, a man in a ratty, logoless baseball cap sat in a VW Beetle doing a crossword puzzle by the low light of a nearby lamppost. The tip of his cheap pen was chewed like a dog's toy. The cigarette dangling from his lips was unlit.

On the passenger seat beside him sat a small spiral-bound notepad filled with the night's scribbling.

When James Kendul walked out the front entrance of the darkened warehouse toward his beat-up old jeep parked on the street, the man in the car put his puzzle aside, reached inside his fake leather jacket, pulled out a crappy ninety-nine-cent lighter, and lit his cigarette. The ember glowed bright in the dark interior of the car when he inhaled, illuminating the steering wheel, the man's lap, and part of the passenger seat.

He started the engine, put the car into gear, and rolled out of the shadows, snow crunching under the tires. The heater in the man's car was broken, so every once in a while he lifted his hands from the wheel and breathed on them.

As Kendul pulled away, the chrome on the back bumper of his jeep flashed, momentarily blinding the man. Every time this happened, he had to refocus his mind, remind himself what he was looking at, or else, he knew from experience, the memory would fade and he would simply drive home, forget about the warehouse, forget about Kendul, Palermo. The whole evening would become a blank, with only his scrawled notes an account of what he'd been doing. But even those would soon cease to make any real sense to him.

The decaying warehouse seemed to lean in at the man as he drove by it, tilting down toward him, its roof slanted at a curious angle. The rumble of his car's engine lulled him, made his eyelids heavy. Fifty feet. A hundred. Flash of chrome. *Refocus*. Flash of chrome. *Refocus*. Concentrate. *Remember…*

A dream within a dream within the darkness – then suddenly jolted awake when two loud pops split the stillness. The man lost control of his car, tires spinning, careening to one side. He barreled into a parked station wagon. Metal crumpled, glass shattered. His car tilted onto two wheels – the other two useless, flapping strips of rubber on warped rims – then flipped over onto its roof not two hundred feet from where he'd started. Crashed against the side of a red-brick bank building. The tires spun. Snow fell, dusting the little car's undercarriage. A beetle on its back, legs in the air, trying but unable to right itself.

Glass tinkled, then silence crept in as the wheels slowed down, stopped.

Kendul's jeep disappeared around a corner up ahead.

The man in the car hung upside down, suspended from his seat belt, unconscious – and unaware that two of the men he'd been spying on earlier that night were approaching his car. One smiled; the other did not. One wore heavy winter clothing; the other did not.

Both were visibly upset about something. And each carried a smoking Magnum at his side.

EIGHT

Pitch dark. Absolute. Save for the tiniest sliver of light wriggling in under the back door of the warehouse.

The man's baseball cap still sat on his head, though skewed – like the chair he was tied to, tilted at an uncomfortable angle. The man felt sweat drip from the band of his hat, trickle into the corner of his open eyes, stinging. He clamped them shut.

All around him, breathing; some of it short and quick, some deep and slow. Sounded so close, he thought maybe it was just in his mind. Until someone coughed lightly. Someone else wheezed.

The man moved his head around, looking for any sign of where he was, any shape in the darkness. To his left, he caught a glimpse of light, someone moving behind stacks of... stacks of what? He watched the light move closer, intermittent. Brighter, dimmer, brighter, dimmer. Crates of something. *Warehouse*, he thought. *I'm inside*.

Footsteps now, echoing around his head, mixing with the chorus of uneven breathing, and the light flitting closer, nearly upon him. A face swam out of the darkness. Round, pitted. Acne-scarred. Breath like sulfur, puffing on him. The candle in this man's hand was tall and thick, like its carrier. Built for war.

A voice from one of the crates: "Cleve, step back. Give him some fucking breathing room."

Cleve grimaced, bared crooked, tombstone teeth. "Breathin' room, yeah," he said, and leaned back out of the candle's light. Stood up straight.

His eyes adjusting a little more to the gloom, the man in the chair saw that the chorus of breathing he heard was made up of twenty-five, maybe thirty men sitting on large wooden crates of various heights – some stacked two, three high – in a rough circle.

He recognized a few faces in the crowd, men whose pictures he'd taken earlier that night – and other nights.

As the cobwebs in his head cleared, the man pieced together what had happened, how he'd got here: driving after Kendul's jeep, trying to focus, concentrating as hard as he could on the task at hand. Flashes of chrome blinding him under each gas lamp. *Two pops. Shot out my tires, flipped the car.* Then, nothing.

"Shot out my tires," the man said, enunciating as clearly as possible. He felt something sticky near the corner of one of his eyes, felt burning across his forehead, figured his face was cut up pretty badly.

Cleve just grunted.

The voice again from one of the crates. "Yes, we did. Cleve and Marcton did, anyway. You were… watching us."

The man said nothing, just breathed.

"Why were you watching us?"

Again, nothing but a subtle shift of weight from the

man in the chair, the click of tiny bones in his neck as he tilted his head to the side.

Edward Palermo jumped down from the crate on which he'd been sitting. Boots echoed, sharper than Cleve's workboots. Cleve glanced behind him, handed the candle to Palermo, took a seat on a nearby crate.

Palermo leaned in very close, said, "What did you want with the man you were following in the jeep?"

"James Kendul."

"Yes, James Kendul."

Silence.

"Look, you're going to talk. You know it as well as I do. Cleve loves to hurt people. And he would love to hurt you. So you're either going to tell us–"

"Save the Hollywood bullshit, pal. This ain't some fucking action movie. You won't touch me. People know where I am. You kill me, they come looking, you're fucked. End of story."

Palermo leaned back out of the candlelight, breathed deeply. Then his free hand moved forward, reached inside the man's fake leather, found something in the inside pocket, pulled it out.

"Yeah, my wallet, imagine that," the man said, a big, cocky grin slapped across his bleeding face. "Inside you'll find out that I'm some guy none of you know named Carl Duncan. Then you'll get all pissy and have one of your dim-bulb bruisers threaten me, maybe even go so far as to break some of my fingers until I tell you everything. You'll tell me I'll never see my baby girl again unless I spill the beans." Duncan snorted. "But I ain't got no baby girl. And I've been alive long enough to know when someone means to kill me and when they don't. You fuckers won't do it. You'da done it by now if you'd meant to. 'Cause you know I ain't bluffing when I tell you that people are watching the watcher, and if you kill me you'll be exposed. This whole fucking freakshow will—"

Palermo's hand suddenly shot forward, cramming Duncan's wallet into his mouth. Then he drove his clenched fist five times into Duncan's face, knocking out three teeth, and splitting his lip in two places on the last punch.

Unconscious, Duncan's head lolled to one side, resting on his left shoulder. Blood dribbled onto his striped shirt. One of his dislodged teeth fell from his mouth into his lap.

"Cleve, Derek, Marcton: take some of the boys, go outside and make sure our friend was alone. If he wasn't, bring in whomever you find."

Boots slapped concrete. Motion. Gruff voices, plans of action.

The last thing Palermo wanted his Runners doing tonight – or, really, any other night – was hunting humans. But they'd only ever had one person snooping around before, a reporter. At least in as long as Palermo had been running things. And he'd been a bluffer. Trying to save his life, he went down the same fictional road as this new guy – lying about people watching him, people who'd break things wide open. Expose their society.

Palermo knew then as he knew now that even if this pompous sack of shit wasn't lying, and there actually were others with him, exposing their society wasn't as easy as he made it out to be. Because no one really wants to know the *details* of the disease they're carrying, no one wants to understand it, admit it even exists within them.

They just want rid of it.

The snow had still not stopped, and it was now so high that Marcton's boots were barely enough to protect him from it. Not that he appeared overly concerned.

"Why don't you ever wear a fucking coat?" Cleve said, as they marched out into the warehouse yard. Figuring on a bluff, they weren't being particularly stealthy. "Stand around shivering like an idiot when you could just throw on a fucking coat."

Marcton shrugged. "Don't want to wear one."

"Yeah, but why not?"

Marcton shrugged again. "Don't like how close they make me feel. Always feel too tight. Don't like the rubbing on my arms."

Cleve shook his head. "You're such a dick, Marcton. You know that?"

Marcton broke away from Derek and Cleve, swept his arms around, motioning for the five other Runners they'd brought with them to separate and search different areas: two to go across the street where the man's car still lay upside down; two to go up on the warehouse roof to get a bird's-eye view; and one to stand guard at the back entrance. All connected by walkie-talkies.

"Hey," Cleve shouted over the wind, "why aren't you avoiding my footsteps like you do Palermo's and your own?"

"Quit needling the poor bastard, Cleve," Derek

said, scanning the tracks that disappeared into the blowing white haze.

"Shut up, Derek," Cleve said. "Answer me, Marcton."

"Don't always do it," Marcton said. "Just sometimes. You know, like you and thinking before you open your fool mouth. Now let's be quiet and keep our eyes peeled, yeah?"

Cleve frowned, unsure whether or not he understood the insult. He stomped in the snow, mumbling under his breath.

The Runners grew quiet as they approached their designated search areas. The two on the roof slipped up via a rusty fire escape pinned to the back of the warehouse; the two out front drew their guns, more exposed to street-fire than the others; the guy at the back door just stood smoking, swiveling his head back and forth like an oscillating fan; and Cleve, Derek, and Marcton drifted slowly apart from each other along the tracks, a lantern Cleve had stolen from a neighboring factory trying like mad to illuminate their way through the storm.

Marcton's walkie crackled. A thin voice squawked out from one of the guys on the roof: "Nothin' up here. And nothin' movin' down below. Not that we can really see shit through the storm, mind, but still. You guys? Over."

Marcton tapped the side of his walkie. "Nothing so far here, either. Just a pile of snow getting blasted into our faces. What about over at the car? Over."

Marcton released the walkie's button. Waited.

Nothing. Cleve and Derek started pulling away

from him on the tracks. He wanted to shout at them to wait up, but thought better of it. They pulled farther away still, and Marcton decided to risk raising his voice. "Hey! Slow down!"

Cleve spun around and gave Marcton the finger, kept walking. Derek slowed a bit, though, now about halfway between Cleve and Marcton.

Pressing the walkie's button down again, Marcton said, "Hey, everything cool by the car? Anyone copy? Over."

More silence.

Then finally, something: "Yeah, rooftop here. Trying to see what's happening down by the car, but tough to tell, so much snow. Looks like movement other than our two guys, but can't be certain. Just waiting to see whether–"

Then shouting filtered through the walkie system. Marcton brought the walkie to his mouth. "Report! Over."

Rooftop answered: "Fuck! Christ. Both men down. Repeat, two men down, front of warehouse, near the overturned car. No one other than the bodies, though. Not sure when it happened. Killer could be…"

"Shit," Marcton whispered, turned, yelled for Cleve and Derek: "Two men down out front! Get your asses back here now!"

Cleve turned, started walking back; Derek turned, too, but then a dark shape, one arm raised, sword in hand, seemed to materialize from the swirling snow about three feet from where Derek stood. Derek, completely unaware, opened his mouth to shout something to Marcton farther up the tracks. But instead of words, only silence came out. Then Derek's head toppled from his shoulders, his body following it to the ground a moment later.

But just as Derek had been taken unawares, so was the killer, as Cleve fired two shots into him as soon as Derek dropped. The first pulped the killer's right eye, the second burst his heart. He crumpled and lay still in the snow.

Cleve, now squatting low, looked all around him, gun tucked in close to his body. Without another word, Cleve and Marcton searched the area carefully while shouts on the walkie confirmed that the two Runners out front had been beheaded. Satisfied that there were no other immediate threats in the area, Marcton and Cleve headed back to the warehouse.

The guard at the back door stepped aside to let them in, said he'd seen nothing, just heard the shouting on the walkies. The interior of the warehouse was bustling as Cleve and Marcton came in. Palermo barked orders in all directions. "Total lockdown!" he said, pointing at the exits and first-floor windows. "No one in or out unless it's on *my* say so, is that fucking clear!?"

Concern about whether or not a Run would happen tonight – and the consequences of such – hung in the air, but no one spoke, just went about securing the building.

Marcton approached Palermo, leaned in close, spoke in low tones near his ear. "Derek's dead, too, sir. Beheaded like the other two. Cleve got the fucker who did him, though. Dead, as well, not more than a few feet from Derek."

Palermo closed his eyes, took a deep breath. Exhaled slowly.

"We're locking down till further notice, Marcton. Get word to Kendul. He'll want to keep his eyes peeled for a similar attack on his Hunters. Maybe the Run happens later than usual, maybe not at all. But we need to regroup, figure this out as quickly as possible."

Marcton nodded, joined the rest of the bustling Runners. Cleve stood to the side, grim-faced and sour, more affected by Derek's death than he'd like to admit.

Carl Duncan woke up amidst the commotion, spat his wallet out of his mouth into his lap, said, "Having a little trouble?"

The entire crew – men, women, and children – was gathered around Palermo again, the building having been completely sealed up. Armed guards on every door, lookouts at all the windows. Palermo glared at Duncan hard, his breathing deep and steady.

"Just sayin' 'cause it looks like you might've lost someone out there. Maybe a few someones. Hard to tell. But someone's dead, that's for sure."

Palermo just stared and breathed for a moment. "Three down," he said. Then: "Got one of yours, too, friend."

Duncan looked around at all the hate staring back at him, wriggled in his chair. He wondered which of his friends it was. Decided he couldn't let emotion affect what he and the others were trying to do.

He tongued the hole where one of his missing teeth

used to be. Flinched at the pain. "So now you kill me, huh? Then what? What will that solve? You're busted, uncovered. Yeah, we removed three of your pawns from the board, you got one of ours, big whoop. You're cornered, motherfucker. Done." He turned his head and spat a great gob of blood onto the floor.

"Killing doesn't have to *solve* anything, Duncan. Sometimes it just has to be done. For no other reason than it brings great delight to the killer." Palermo stepped forward, drove his fist into Duncan's face once, hard. He considered the effectiveness of the action, then repeated this four more times. Duncan's nose crumpled. Palermo leaned down, got right in Duncan's face, locked eyes with him. "Still awake?" He slapped Duncan across the cheek twice, rousing him. "I want you to see the hammer that's about to cave your face in."

Duncan just grunted, nearly insensible. He mumbled something. Palermo leaned back, reached his hand out behind him, still looking at Duncan. Marcton handed him a large metal hammer. Palermo hefted its weight, brought it around to bear.

He moved it in front of Duncan's line of sight, smacked his face again till his eyes focused on the hammer. "See it? Do you see it, you little piece of shit?"

Duncan dribbled more blood onto himself and closed his eyes. "Just fucking do it. You'll be joining me soon enough. Soon enough... Just know that it was Bill Krebosche. His friends and family did this to you. For what you did to them. To us."

He could see Palermo's mind was whirling,

searching, but evidently the name meant nothing to him.

Right before Duncan lost consciousness, Palermo brought the hammer down. Duncan felt the first two blows, then nothing else ever again.

When Carl Duncan had been pulled out of his car and dragged inside Palermo's warehouse, William Krebosche dropped his binoculars, hung his head, and closed his eyes. He was lying flat on his belly in the deepening snow, four hundred feet away in a field close to the tracks upon which Palermo's caboose sat. From his vantage point a little while later, he saw two men – one of the Runners, and one of his uncles – get killed. He saw the two remaining Runners scramble back to the warehouse, watched as guards appeared at all the windows, knew the place would be securely sealed now. Duncan would no doubt be dead soon. But that was OK. Krebosche just needed to remember all this. Needed to remember it had actually happened. Then, Duncan's sacrifice would be worth it.

To ensure this, he'd been whispering the details of the events as they'd unfolded into a digital voice recorder tucked into the inside pocket of his parka. His memories had begun to fade minutes after he'd spoken, and he knew from experience that not only would he need to record the events themselves, but he would need to remind himself that the recording device held these memories. For this purpose, he had written CHECK RECORDING DEVICE: V. IMPORTANT on the backs of both of his hands, so he could not miss the message. Only parts of his past recordings made sense to him afterward, but he hoped that what he'd gotten tonight would be enough.

It was certainly more than he'd ever gotten before.

Krebosche stood up, brushed himself off, and thought of how he would break the news of his uncle's death to his aunt. Never a good way to tell someone their loved one has died. But this was necessary. They all knew it was necessary. And they all knew the risks going in.

Now it was up to Krebosche to make it all worth it.

NINE

When Faye's shift ended, she left the hospital by one of the side doors, near the loading dock. The sun was only just coming up, but the shadows were still thick, so she didn't notice the creature crouched low beside one of the dumpsters. She walked right past Henry where he slept in those shadows. Only Milo noticed her, and he wasn't sure what to do. He could try waking Henry, attempt again to make a physical connection – at least enough to wake him. He could also just let Faye walk by, go home, carry on with her life, and deal later with Henry's anger and disappointment at missing her.

Even if he did wake Henry, he reasoned, his friend would probably just get up and stumble after her like a deranged beast. She would be terrified, run from him, likely scream, and people would see him. What was the point in that? There was really no way this was going to end well. But he aimed to stand by Henry, no matter what.

So Milo concentrated as hard as he could, tried to make his fingers – or at least the *tips* of his fingers – substantial enough to brush against Henry's face.

He raised his hand, swiped it across Henry's cheek. Nothing. He did it again. And again. On the fourth try, whether Milo had actually succeeded or not in making his fingertips substantial, Henry roused a little, grunted. Metal flakes shivered in the wind and sprinkled at his feet as his neck lifted his giant skull from his chest.

Come on, Henry, she's here. She's walking away right now. Wake up. Wake up.

Henry stirred again, still partially asleep, but beginning to come around. One of his feet involuntarily kicked out, crashing against the bottom of the dumpster.

Twenty feet away, just as she was nearing the edge of the sidewalk, Faye jumped at the sound, turned around sharply, wide-eyed. She saw nothing but deep shadows, though something like dread crawled up inside her and nestled in.

She turned around slowly again, carried on walking. Reached the sidewalk.

Then she heard a voice like cracking rocks. It said her name.

She froze.

Nothing in that moment could have made her turn around again.

"Faye," the voice said again. So much pain, like it physically hurt the speaker to form the word.

Her heart thudded in her chest; her legs felt like jelly. The sidewalk upon which she stood suddenly felt like a sponge. Blood pumped in her ears – so much so that she wasn't sure she heard the next words from the voice correctly at all.

"It's me," it said.

The gloom was still thick, and the snow still falling hard enough that the few figures she spotted in the storm looked like nothing more than silhouettes from where she stood. She thought briefly of calling out to them, but something made her stop. Something connected to the dread that'd made its home in her belly. Something warmer this time, though. The voice now somehow familiar. Her mind raced to make the connection.

"It's me," the voice came again. Then: "Please, come... here."

The voice sounded inhuman, and she knew it was insanity to respond to it, to turn around and look – to even entertain the idea of heading in its direction.

But wasn't it someone she knew? Wasn't it–

"Henry," the jumble of rocks in the shadows croaked. "Henry..."

The connection made – as crazy and impossible as it was – she somehow felt a tiny bit settled. The first thought to come to her was: *I knew you weren't dead. I knew it.*

Snowflakes melting onto her flushed cheeks, she turned around slowly, then stared down at her feet, marveling as they brought her toward the source of the voice. The dumpster. The shadows. Perhaps death. Somehow it didn't matter. On some deep level, she was powerless to stop it.

Snow crunched under her feet, she slipped on some ice, righted herself. Tottered uncertainly to a stop about five feet away from the darkness near the bin. Breath coming quickly, puffing into the crisp early morning air, she whispered, "Henry?"

The darkness shifted, something caught the dim sunlight briefly and gleamed.

"I don't think," Henry growled, "you should see me … like this."

Speech was becoming a little easier for Henry, and the words came a bit more naturally from his mouth now. He was slowly learning how to use his new body.

"I went to check on you," Faye said, "but you–"

"–were dead. I know," Henry finished for her.

"You were so… hot. Burning up."

Henry said nothing. He moved slightly again, and Faye caught sight of something steel. Metallic. Fear knotted her guts. "What are you holding, Henry? What's in your hand?"

She took a step back. Two more before he answered.

"Nothing. Nothing."

Milo floated a few feet away, just watching, fascinated, curious how this would turn out. Feeling terrible for Henry. Anxious for Faye.

"Listen, I … something has happened to me, Faye. Don't know what to do. Where to go."

"What's wrong with your voice?" Faye couldn't respond to the content of the question. "It's… wrong."

"Sun will be up soon. Need to get somewhere darker. Away from people. Can you help me?"

"Tell me what happened, Henry. Let me see you, and we can try to figure out what to–"

Just then, a car drove by, its headlights illuminating the edges of the shadow in which Henry hid. She saw one of his legs, part of his torso, and the fingers of one hand.

Her jaw dropped, her eyes bugged, and a hand shot up to her mouth. But she stayed where she was, even though every fiber of her being was barking at her to run, get the fuck out of there *right now*.

The headlights whipped past the dumpster as fast as they'd lit it up. Henry pulled his leg in closer to his body, unsure of how much Faye had seen, knowing that at this point even a few inches was enough to have caused her reaction.

"I'm changing," Henry said. "Into something else."

Faye stared, slowly brought the hand down from her mouth, consciously lifted her jaw till she heard her teeth click together.

More people were moving around inside the hospital now. Outside, too. More cars, more buses.

"What do you need me to do?" Faye heard herself say, not entirely sure why she was still anywhere near this spot. She should've rocketed out of there as soon as she'd heard that voice – and *certainly* the moment she'd seen... whatever it was she'd seen. This was not Henry Kyllo. It might claim to be him, might even sound a little like him under all the growling gravel, but it couldn't be. It's impossible.

And yet.

"I just need to hide till I can figure out what's going on. I didn't know where else to turn. My only real friend was Milo, and he's dead."

Milo looked hard at his friend, then. Felt something like breath come into his lungs.

Faye glanced behind her. More people still. They were bound to start coming in and out of the loading dock doors soon.

She opened her mouth to speak – maybe even to give an answer, she didn't know – when two of her co-workers walked out of the door she'd come through a few minutes ago. They were laughing and talking shit about someone. One of them, a woman named Joan, looked up and saw Faye standing near the dumpster. "Faye?" she said. "What are you doing? Dumpster diving?" She and her friend, Marissa something-or-other, laughed some more, kept walking arm in arm.

"Ha," Faye said. "Your *face* is a dumpster." She tried to act as casual as she could so they wouldn't stop and come over. They were work friends, but not close: the occasional joke here and there, acting silly in the break room, that sort of thing.

They just made faces, flipped her the bird, and kept walking, headed for the bus stop.

Unsure exactly why she was doing this – clearly there was something incredibly wrong with Henry – she stepped closer, whispered, "Alright, then. Follow me." She felt strongly that she needed to help him, that there was truth to this. And that no one else *would* help him.

She strode past the shadows where Henry hunkered, purposely not looking, afraid to see more of whatever she'd glimpsed before in that wash of headlights. Henry said nothing as she walked past, just scrambled to gain his feet.

She opened the door to the loading dock, poked her head in, looked around.

No one coming.

She stepped inside, held the door open, but still didn't look behind her. When she felt the weight of the door removed from her hand, heard breathing close to her ear, she carried on.

Down the stairs, moving quickly. Behind her, Henry grunted, "Slow down. Can't move so fast." She ignored him. Then, two flights down, she said over her shoulder, "Keep up. I'm not waiting around," and kept going. Henry shambled along behind, occasionally forgetting his size and cracking his head off the cement stairs.

"And try to be quieter," Faye said, reaching the bottom of the staircase.

Milo grinned a little at that, whispered along in both their wakes.

"Wait here a sec," Faye said. "I'm going to check the boiler room, make sure no one's in there. Should be somewhere in there you can hide – at least for a little while."

Henry nodded, looked nervously around, expecting at any moment for someone to come out of one of the many doors along this hallway. But the hospital was still fairly sleepy at this hour of the morning. He didn't know what he'd do if someone came out and panicked at the sight of him. Would he lose his shit and just crush their tiny skull? Christ, he hoped not.

Since he'd woken up this morning, intense dread had welled up in his chest when he thought too long about what was happening. Surely his mind would also be changing as his body was, but the pre-change part of his thought processes occasionally choked on the reality of his situation. He'd feel panic burst into his brain, a mad feeling of suddenly needing to be *outside* his changing body. Then, fairly quickly, that feeling would be tamped down by another part of his brain – the part that subconsciously knew what was happening. Or that at least was becoming used to his new form. That dread filled him now, but he didn't know whether this time it was because of his own situation, or because bringing Faye into this was setting her up for whatever disastrous road must surely lie ahead.

Faye walked down to the second door on the left, opened it, went inside. Ten seconds later, she emerged, waved her arm frantically for Henry to follow. Henry, keeping his head ducked so as not to destroy the light fixtures in the hallway ceiling, closed the distance to the doorway in three strides. Once inside the boiler room, Faye closed the door behind him.

It was nearly pitch dark inside. A thin stream of weak sunlight filtered in through a small window near the back wall. Machines hummed all around Henry, easing his nervousness a little. He instantly felt more at home here. Unseen. Surrounded by steel and mechanical things.

Is that what I'm becoming? A machine? He shuddered at the thought. If he was a machine, how would he start to see Faye? What would she be to him? He brushed these thoughts aside. Shook his head quickly, physically trying to rid them from his mind.

"It's dark," he said.

"I turned out the lights," Faye said. Henry sensed her close, but not within arm's reach – not even his mammoth arms.

"Thank you," Henry said. "For hiding me here."

Faye said nothing. He sensed her move closer. Closer still.

"What happened to you, Henry?"

"I changed."

"Into what?"

"I don't know."

"Why did you come here? Why did you come to me?"

"Because Milo is dead. And I wanted to see you. I thought you could help me."

"I know. But what about other friends? In your… group. Society. Whatever it is."

Henry had never shared much about the *Inferne Cutis*. Faye knew what he was to a certain extent – knew that he was different, that he healed quickly from injuries that would kill another man. But her mind somehow separated those facts from her growing love for him. She felt no need to ask more about what he did at night when he left her apartment. Maybe simply because the less she knew, the safer she'd be. That's certainly why Henry never elaborated on his nightly Runs.

"I'm scared to go back," Henry said. "I don't know what they'll do to me."

"What do you mean? What would they do to you?"

Henry was silent for a moment. Then: "Whatever I am. Whatever this is… I don't think it's supposed to happen. It just…"

Though her eyes were starting to adjust to the darkness in the boiler room, she could still only make out Henry's general shape. But it was enough for her mouth to betray her. She said, "But I don't even know what you are."

The words were out before she knew it. She wished she could take them back. She felt Henry stiffen, felt the air around him grow somehow... colder. Even though he'd said much the same thing himself, hearing it from her was different.

"I'm sorry. I didn't mean that, Henry."

She knew her words made her sound distant, uncaring. She was trying to protect herself, but it was coming out wrong. But as close as they felt most of the time, this was uncharted territory. New boyfriends generally don't turn into *anything* more or less than human.

Behind Henry, Milo hovered, watching. He didn't know why he was here, what he hoped to achieve by hanging around his old friend, especially when he couldn't make contact. And even when he did make contact – if Milo's fingertips actually *had* brushed Henry's face – Henry didn't know what he was making contact *with*. Milo was just the cold spot in a room to Henry, perhaps a half-formed thought.

He'd stayed with him through the night, which he'd promised Henry he would. But the night was over now. Milo should get on with his afterlife. *Maybe I'll go haunt some abandoned factory somewhere,* he thought. *Or an old set of train tracks. Find a house where a bunch of people had been murdered, and whisper weird shit into the new homeowners' ears at night. Something fucking interesting, for Christ's sake.*

But he couldn't leave yet. He didn't know how he knew, but something still felt ... unfinished.

"It's... It's OK," Henry said. "You're right."

Faye stepped closer, plucked up her courage, raised her arm toward Henry, said, "Take my hand, Henry. I'll lead you somewhere safer. Someone could walk in at any time."

Henry hesitated a moment, then reached out his giant steel hand, searching. He brushed against Faye's tiny fingers, and she drew in a quick, sharp breath. "You're so cold," she said. Then her fingers found purchase on two of his fingers. She clasped them and pulled. "Come on."

She led them away from the door, away from the tiny window, away from any source of light, deeper into the boiler room. She knew her way around the boiler room because she often came down here for a sneaky smoke on particularly cold days in the dead of winter. Even so, she walked carefully, feeling ahead of her path with her right foot.

A minute later, she stopped. They were tucked into a far corner of the room, sort of an alcove, with three walls very close around them. Cleaning supplies stacked neatly near their feet. Henry clumsily kicked a broom and bucket as he stepped inside.

"Shhh, Henry, careful."

"Sorry," he said, sheepishly. "Still getting used to these big clodhoppers."

The space was small, maybe five or six square feet. They were now so close that touching was unavoidable. Milo floated just outside the alcove, watching, listening.

Tentatively, Faye reached a hand up to Henry's face. She cupped her palm, feeling the edge of his cheek. Cold as ice, hard as stone. She flinched back for a moment, and Henry flinched away, too. She recovered herself, pressed against the cheek again, this time leaving her hand there, warming the steel.

"I remember how hot you were in your apartment," Faye said. "Burning up. But dead."

"Not dead, I guess, just changing."

Her hand moved down to his neck, where sharp protrusions nestled in clumps near his collar bone.

"Careful," Henry said.

She felt around to the other side of his face, to his nose, his mouth, lips. He bent over more so she could feel his forehead, the top of his skull. He knew she needed to do this, to understand. To prepare herself for when she could no longer hide him in darkness.

She moved her hand from his head, ran it down the length of his left arm. Smooth except for thin crevices where the steel had not yet fully formed. A gentle thrumming coursed through her palm as she explored. Whatever Henry was becoming, he was still in transition, and Faye was experiencing the change in real time. Her flesh to his, connected intimately.

Faye's fingertips down Henry's arm were like a soothing balm applied to the skin of a burn victim. He felt as though he were on fire as the machinery inside him went about its work, but Faye's touch calmed him, made him feel somehow at peace with what was happening to him. Although encouraged by this, at the back of his mind, he knew that she had still not actually seen him – all of him – clearly, and that when she did, there would be no more touching, no more sympathy, nothing. She would run from him, get clear of him as fast as humanly possible.

And what would he do? Would there still be enough of who he was left to understand the rejection, to let her go? Or would he follow her, run her down, smash her to pulp?

Faye ran her hand down his right arm. This one was less formed, thicker crevices, some small holes here and there, her fingers dropping into these empty spots, then popping back out, like a tire going over potholes.

When she explored his chest, she used both hands pushed flat against him. This was different terrain. Not nearly as smooth as his head and arms. Being careful to avoid the sharper protrusions near his collar, she felt where his pectoral muscles would normally have been, and moved down from there. The metal here seemed to ripple – somehow reacting to her touch. Down, farther still, to his belly. His abdomen tensed as she neared it, then settled into a similar rippling motion as his chest. She wondered briefly what it meant, if anything. She was going to ask, but found that she couldn't form the words. She was too entranced by the motion beneath her fingers to manage speech.

After a few more moments with her hands on his stomach, she pulled them back, said, "We need to get you somewhere safe. Someone will eventually come in here for cleaning supplies."

"I know."

She waited a moment, felt her heart racing. Was she really going to say this?

"You can stay with me, but I don't know how we're going to get you to my apartment without being seen."

• • •

Milo had been floating outside the alcove, hypnotized by the scene inside. He suddenly felt something like the air pressure changing in the room. His senses prickled. He turned, drifted away from the alcove a few feet and, not more than an arm's length away, a woman stood.

Looking right at him.

Tall, long dark hair, deep red lipstick, wearing a plain red T-shirt and dark blue jeans. Her mouth moved, but no sounds came out.

Milo watched her for a few moments, then backed up, turned to look at Henry and Faye, with an *Are you two seeing this?* expression on his face. But, of course, neither of them looked in his direction. He turned back to the woman, looked down, and noticed that she, too, was floating off the ground – but where he felt insubstantial and was certain that, to others, he'd look how one expects a ghost to look, she was fully fleshed out, looked as solid as the rest of the room.

As Milo watched her, he developed a sensation of warmth that could not be traced to any particular part of his being. It was as if his entirety suddenly became warm. Heated up from the inside. He watched her lips move, tried to read the words, but couldn't make any out. But as this feeling of warmth grew, an acute sense of desperation accompanied it, and he began to feel sick. His head swam with these conflicting feelings, and he did not know what was happening to him, which only made the feeling worse. He simultaneously wanted it to stop immediately and go on forever.

Milo realized that he could literally not take his eyes

from the woman, particularly her lips. Even though he couldn't make out a single word, his attention was rapt. Were he still alive and experiencing this, Henry could've stomped over and belted him across the mouth with a frying pan-sized hand and he would still have just stood there staring.

He wanted to reach out a hand to see if he could touch her, but was unable to move. Rooted like a tree. "Whhh…" he said, his eyelids fluttering. Nothing coherent would come out, so he gave up.

Using all his willpower, he was finally able to wrench his gaze from her lips. His eyes traced her body shape once, but then snapped up to her face again. Tears formed in the corners of his eyes. His heart pounded in his chest. Palms sweaty. Mouth dry as sand.

What is this? What am I feeling? What's happening?

That's when the woman vanished.

Back in the alcove, Henry and Faye had decided that the best way for Henry to get to her apartment would be to smuggle him out in an ambulance. Or, rather, enlist the aid of an ambulance driver (Henry would never fit in a car) who could drive him to her apartment in the dead of night, then keep his mouth shut about Henry's existence.

"How can we be sure he won't tell?" Henry whispered, as best as he could, still somewhat unable to control the volume of his voice.

"He's a good friend," Faye said, realizing how unconvincing that sounded, even though the driver she had in mind, Steve Mincener, *was* a good friend, and she'd known him several years.

Henry was silent, and she knew it was because he was skeptical, but also knew there weren't a lot of options. The only choice they had was who she asked to help. If she thought Steve was their best bet, then Steve it was. Whether he told or not was out of their hands at that point.

Faye glanced at her watch. "I'll go talk to him. I'm pretty sure his shift has started. Stay here and try to hide as best you can." She allowed herself a little smirk, considering the impossibility of her statement. "Actually, better idea: follow me to the door, and we'll put something heavy in front of it so it can't be pushed open. Whoever wants in will just think it's stuck."

Faye walked out of the alcove, with Henry following behind. Even though he didn't need to, Milo stepped out of their way, still bewildered at the appearance of the beautiful woman who had vanished so suddenly. He questioned whether or not he had really seen her.

I have been under a lot of pressure lately, he thought. *But can a ghost see another ghost? And does every Runner – or Hunter, for that matter – wind up as a ghost after death? If so, where's everyone else? Have they all fucked off to Heaven or Hell, and I'm stuck here forever, doomed to float around after my best friend as he morphs into God knows what?*

Milo took one more look at the place the woman had appeared and disappeared – half expecting her to reappear again – then followed Henry and Faye to the door.

When they got there, Faye motioned Henry to *shh,* then put her ear to the door, listened for movement.

Nothing. Silence.

"Alright," she whispered, "when I'm gone, move something heavy behind the door. When I'm back, I'll knock twice, quickly, then add a third knock at the end so you'll know it's me. With any luck, I'll have Steve with me, and we can get out of here, get you safe, OK?"

Henry nodded. Faye looked at him, realizing that the light here was better than back in the alcove. And in so doing, she put reality to the images she'd drawn in her mind upon touching his face. It wasn't as terrifying as she thought it would be.

Although he was decidedly alien, his features that of a comicbook villain – all sharp angles and sinister lines – she was not frightened. This was Henry. *Her* Henry – from the hospital, from the bar, from a time before he'd become what he was now. The more she looked at him, the more comfortable she felt in his presence.

She smiled at him, touched his arm briefly, turned the doorknob, slipped out the door, and was gone.

Henry heard her footsteps echoing down the hall. With every step, he grew increasingly nervous.

What if she just leaves me here? Now that she's seen me, touched me, even in dim light, she knows what I am. What sane person would return?

Henry glanced around for something to block the door. He should do it quickly, in case someone was even now on their way for cleaning supplies.

Something heavy, something heavy…

Then it occurred to him – the quickest, easiest solution.

Henry turned his back and sat down against the door, roughly a quarter ton of steel blocking the way. As the seconds stretched into minutes, Henry's eyelids grew heavy. He fell into a deep sleep very quickly.

He dreamed he was running in a field. He felt lighter than he ever had in his life. This was pre-transformation Henry. In fact, Henry felt even lighter than that; he imagined he had no metal at all in his body. In waking life, he couldn't recall this point in his existence. He must've been lead-free at some time, but those days were lost to him. He knew only the feeling of heavy metals in his system, churning within him, eager to coalesce into what he would one day become. But this dream made him feel... what? Human? He had no idea what that felt like. Couldn't *possibly* have any idea. But this dream was wonderful. His body felt so light as he ran. As though only blood, muscle, flesh, and bone were packed inside his skin. Such a freeing feeling – one so alien to him that he didn't properly know how to process the emotions the experience stirred.

As he ran across the field, the wind whipped through his hair, around his ears, seemed to whistle right through him. He felt insubstantial, like he could run straight through solid objects.

Then: far away, perhaps coming from over the mountains that loomed on all sides, he heard thumping. The landscape rippled with each one. He continued running, but with each step, he felt heavier. Flesh and bone becoming metal again. More thumping, as if some gigantic god stomped around on the other side of the mountains, just out of sight.

Heavier, slower now. And as in most running dreams, his legs felt weighed down in cement, the horizon stretching farther and farther away. The pounding sound became thinner as Henry's feet slowed to a stop. He stood panting in the field, feeling as though this angry god would appear any second over the tip of one of the mountains, and lock him in its gaze. Rooting him to the spot forever.

When he finally swam up to reality again, he recognized the pounding of the god's fists as merely Faye's three-knock signal. He shook his head and scrambled – as much as five hundred pounds of steel can be said to scramble – to his feet. Turned, opened the door.

Faye walked in carrying a big dark blanket, followed by a short, worried-looking man. Balding. Glasses. Wearing a paramedic's uniform.

"What were you doing? Why didn't you answer?" Faye demanded as soon as the door was closed behind them.

"Nodded off. Sorry," Henry muttered.

She just stared at him. Was about to continue asking questions, realized time was of the essence. "OK, well, Steve's got the ambulance pulled up to the docking area, ready to go. I'll pop out, make sure the coast is clear – I've always wanted to say that," she said, and grinned. "Then I'll come back in, hustle you out under this big-ass blanket, and away we go. Got it?"

Henry, still half asleep, just repeated, "Got it."

"Great, let's do it." Faye then turned to Steve. "Alright, Steve, you walk out casually, get into the ambulance, then just wait for us to get in the back. Once we're underway–" And that's when she caught sight of Steve's slack-jawed expression. The blood seemed to have drained entirely from his face.

She'd told him she needed to transport something "strange" to her apartment, but didn't go into further detail. She knew if she tried to describe Henry to him, he wouldn't have believed her anyway, and would've just delayed them further by asking a million questions. But in her desire to get this done before the hospital got too busy, she'd forgotten to deal with Steve's reaction immediately upon entering the room.

She turned now to face him, put her hands on his shoulders, said, "Steve. Steve, look at me. Stop looking at Henry. Come on, Steve." She snapped her fingers in front of his face. "Come on, look at me. Focus."

Steve's jaw snapped shut with a click, his eyes slowly sliding off Henry's face like it was greased. He managed to focus on Faye's eyes. "What's… that?" he said, and backed away, out of Faye's reach, his heels smacking against the door behind him. "What is it? What is it?"

Henry dropped his gaze, looked at the floor.

Milo, too, dropped his eyes, sad to see this playing out in front of him. Embarrassed on his friend's behalf.

"I'll explain later, Steve," Faye said. "Just believe me that he's not harmful. He won't do anything to you, me, or anyone else. Something has –" she searched for the right word "– *happened* to him, Steve. It's not his fault, and I care for him, so I need you to be the friend I know you are, and just drive us to my apartment. OK?"

Steve still looked mildly horrified, but color was slowly returning to his face. "Yeah," he said. "Sure, whatever." Steve tried to tell himself the guy must just be in a suit of some kind, and maybe standing on stilts. It looked too real, though. But his mind didn't want to deal with that option, so instead ran on the automation of shock and rationalization.

He groped in the semi-dark for the door handle, grasped it, turned it. Out he went, into the hallway. The ambulance's driver-side door opened, slammed, then the engine roared to life.

A shudder ripped through Milo just then. Something unpleasant was coming. He didn't know how he knew, but felt it deep inside. A truth unbreakable, indisputable. He tried to shake it off, but it clung to him like wet gauze.

Faye turned to Henry. "Are you ready?"

Henry nodded once.

Faye flung the blanket over him as best she could. Henry helped by draping it up and over his head. When it settled, it covered about three quarters of him, which would have to do. It would be screamingly obvious to anyone if they saw thick metal legs and a blanket running around that something was suspicious, but at least they wouldn't see *all* of him, which would be much worse.

Faye cracked the door, peeked out. Nothing moved. She heard voices somewhere, though, echoing off the hallway walls, and the grounds would only get busier, so it was now or never.

She glanced back again to Henry, whispered, "Let's go," then stepped out into the hall. Henry lumbered after her, with Milo in tow. Once Henry was through the door, Faye shut it behind him, then moved ahead of him, grabbed onto one of his enormous hands and led him in the direction of the ambulance.

The voices were getting closer now, but Henry and Faye were only about twenty feet from the back of the open ambulance and safety.

"Come on, Henry, just a bit farther," Faye whispered, and tried to tug on him to speed him up. She may as well have been tugging on a car.

The sound of the ambulance's idling engine blocked out the nearby voices as they got closer, which only made her more nervous. The last ten feet of the journey were agony. With every shuffling footstep from Henry, she thought she'd hear someone yell out to them, catch them in the act. There would be no explaining this. Henry and she would be separated – probably forever. The thought created a ball of lead in her gut and brought tears to her eyes.

"Nearly there," she said. "About five more steps."

Once they were at the edge of the back doors, she lifted the blanket so Henry could see his feet and the back of the vehicle. "Step up," she said. "Quickly." She glanced around one last time. Still no one. *Is this really happening?* she thought madly. *Am I actually smuggling a metal behemoth out of a hospital furnace room?*

Henry stepped up, lost his balance, and fell forward. Luckily, due to his momentum, he toppled into the back of the ambulance rather than outside of it into the docking area. He crashed in, falling on his back and rolling to one side. Where he'd rolled, Faye saw dents in the metal underneath. The shocks of the vehicle groaned at the weight, but held.

Steve glanced back, petrified. "What the fuck!?" he hissed. "What are you doing back there? Someone's gonna hear!"

Faye hoisted herself inside, telling Henry to drag his other leg in. She stood up.

"Steve," Faye said, closing the doors. "Shut up and drive."

They drove slowly away from the hospital, snow drifting down to blanket the docking area, erasing their footprints. Milo gazed out the back window, watching the accumulation, still trying to shake the sudden feeling of menace he'd felt earlier. It wouldn't budge.

They drove in silence, Steve only occasionally craning his neck around to gawp at Henry. Blood had returned to his face, but the fear was plain in his eyes every time he swiveled in his seat to look behind him.

"Don't drive too fast," Faye said. "You'll get us pulled over."

"Least of my worries, Faye, sorry," Steve said, keeping his eyes on the road.

"Listen," Faye said, the word coming from her mouth in a sharp burst as she strode toward the front of the vehicle, leaning her head in near Steve's. "You fucking slow down right now. The last thing we need is to have an accident. I said before that my friend is not dangerous, and he's not. But I can certainly *make* him dangerous, if you'd prefer."

Steve glanced at her quickly, the fear in his eyes leveled up yet another notch. He saw that Faye meant it, said nothing – just turned his head, stared forward, and eased off the gas pedal.

Faye moved to the back of the ambulance again, leaned down near where Henry still lay prone. He shifted to sit up when she approached, wanting to at least lean his back against the side of the vehicle.

"Try not to crush too many lifesaving devices in here OK?" she said, and smiled at him.

Henry just growled low in his throat as he tried to position himself into a sitting position. He attempted a smile, but again, it came off weirdly, since he still hadn't mastered the dimensions and workings of his new face. Once he'd established himself as comfortably as possible, given the cramped interior, he mumbled, "Sorry," and cast his eyes down.

"No need to be sorry, Henry. None of this is your fault."

Now that she could see him in fairly strong light, things she originally mistook as menacing in the half-shaded areas of the hospital basement she now saw as beautiful. If you didn't know him, you'd be terrified, of course (as poor Steve clearly was), but she knew Henry. She felt she somehow knew him better than people in her life she'd known for fifteen or twenty years.

"You're at Harriston and Blumfield, right?" Steve asked.

"Yeah, the apartment building right on the corner there. Go around back. As soon as we arrive, shut the engine down. Keep us as dark as possible."

"Got it."

Faye reached out a hand, brushed it softly against

Henry's cheek. He flinched away instinctively, but only a little. He kept his eyes cast down but let her touch him. Her hand moved lower, fingers curling gently under his chin, cupping it. He flicked his eyes up at her quickly, ready to see a look of revulsion on her face, but she only smiled, her head titled on an angle.

"I'm glad you're here, Henry."

He nodded, but said nothing in return.

Milo watched nearby, touched by the scene, wishing he could reach out to Henry, as well, let his friend know he was there with him. He knew it was impossible now – and likely would be forever – but he'd never wanted to be there for Henry more than he did right this instant. He knew Henry was flagging. Everything he was going through was taxing him emotionally to the point of despair. Even through his new facial features, and the new mannerisms his body was being forced to adapt, he could still see his old friend Henry in there, struggling to keep it together. Struggling to make sense of everything. Be present. Faye was doing her best, but Milo knew if he could somehow make Henry see him, give him the knowledge that he was there, too, it might be enough to get him through.

Milo felt a sudden rush of love for his friend so strong that he didn't know where to put the emotion. It coursed through him like a rushing river. He closed his eyes, and just waited for it to pass. *I'm here, Henry*, he thought again, for the thousandth time. *Faye is here, but I'm here, too. I wish you knew. I wish I could* make *you know that.*

•••

They drove around back of Faye's apartment building, parked in a spot as close to the doors as possible. Steve cut the engine.

It was maybe thirty feet to the doors, but the sun was nearly fully up now. A few people trickled out of the building, on their way to early-start jobs, walking dogs, etc. Faye's initial plan had been to try to sit unnoticed for the day, then hustle Henry inside once darkness fell. She saw now how ridiculous that was. Steve would be missed at work, as would the ambulance.

Steve turned around in the driver's seat, said, "So what's the plan now? Use the blanket again to shuffle him inside, hope no one notices? 'Cause if so, I suggest you rethink that. No way – now that a lot of people are up and about – are you going to pull that off. No way."

Faye just sat and stared ahead, past Steve, out the front window. *What the hell am I going to do?*

Then it hit her:

"Fire alarm," she said dreamily. "That'll work, right? I'll go in, pull the fire alarm. Everyone rushes out and, in the confusion, I bring Henry in."

She looked to Steve, saw doubt in his eyes. "Risky," he said. "Super risky, but I'm not sure what other choice you have. Since I need to get back, like –" he glanced at his watch "– now."

"Fire house is pretty close," Faye mumbled. "We'd need to be quick. Get him in there before they arrive."

"Correction: *you'd* need to be quick," Steve said. "I'll be gone."

"And you're not going to say anything to *anyone*

about this, right, Steve?" Faye said, snapping out of her dreamy voice, all threat again. "*Right*?"

"Yeah, yeah, definitely, Faye. You know I'd never tell anyone. You think I want this complication in my life? I have enough of those as it is, believe me. I don't need to add this to my list. Whatever *this* is." Steve gestured to Henry. "Also, who'd believe me?"

"Alright, you ready for this? I'll go in, pull the alarm, walk out again calmly. We'll get the blanket on Henry, get him out of the ambulance, then you can leave. I'll wait till people start filing out, then we'll move past everyone. Just me and... a seven-foot tall... fucking... *giant*." Faye leaned over, put her head in her hands. "No way this is ever gonna work. Fuck!"

"Calm down, Faye. It's gonna be fine," Steve said, moving into the back part of the ambulance. He tried to put an arm around her, but she pulled away from him.

Ah, is that why you're helping me, Steve?

He moved back, cleared his throat, embarrassed, but carried on: "Let's just think for a sec. What else is out there? Near the doors, I mean. Maybe some other place he can hide till it gets dark? Whatever we do, we have to figure it out now. I already have no idea how I'm going to explain why I'm not at work and have been driving around in a fucking ambulance all morning for no apparent reason."

Faye pulled her hands away from her face, breathed deeply. Straightened out her uniform. "Alright, OK. Let's have a look." She leaned forward into the passenger seat, poked her head out just far enough so she could see outside.

Dumpster. Of course. I'm an idiot.

"The dumpster," she said, turning back to Steve. "We don't need to pull the fire alarm. We only need a diversion big enough for me to get him into the dumpster. I'll wait till people are asleep tonight, and *then* move him in. That'll give me a chance to get a bigger blanket, too – one that might actually cover all of him, head to toe. It'll still look weird if anyone sees it, but at least they won't be able to actually *see* what he is."

She glanced over at Henry, looking sheepish. She didn't mean for her words to hurt him, but she saw that they did.

"Alright, do it," Steve said, now visibly near panic at the thought of potentially losing his job. "Let's go. Come on. I gotta get back."

"Wait, what's the diversion?" Faye said.

Steve looked lost in thought for a few seconds, then said, "Just watch what I do, then move Henry when you see I've got everyone's attention. It won't be anything Hollywood-flashy, so pay attention. Just gonna spin some bullshit."

Steve moved to the back of the ambulance, took one more glance at Faye and Henry, opened the doors, then was out and walking toward the apartment building's rear entrance.

Faye turned quickly to Henry. "I'll get you out as soon as I can, Henry. I promise. It'll be well over twelve hours, but then we'll be safe, OK?"

Henry looked up at her. "Safe?" Then he dropped his eyes again. The word was hollow, meaningless in his mouth, her ears.

Milo felt that stomach-churning feeling of *wrongness* again. Knew something horrible was coming. And soon.

Faye draped the blanket over Henry as best she could. His legs would stick out the bottom, but it wouldn't be for long. Just a few feet – assuming, that was, Henry had mastered his new body enough to actually be *able* to climb into the dumpster.

"Here we go," Faye said, and smiled again. This time it felt more natural. Looked more at ease on her face.

Henry just nodded, looking grim.

She poked her head out the back, saw Steve with a small crowd of people gathered around and near him. She couldn't hear everything he was saying, but she caught wisps of sentences: "… called here by an elderly man…" "… collapsed outside the building…" "… didn't tell us the apartment number…" "… could've had a stroke, wasn't thinking clearly, maybe crawled off to try to get some help?…"

Everyone wore concerned looks on their faces, eager to be of help in finding this fictitious elderly stroke victim – or at least eager to *appear* wanting to be of help.

It wasn't perfect, but it was their best shot. "Now, Henry!" Faye whispered. "I'll guide you to the edge of the dumpster, then you hop in as quick as you can."

When Henry's weight left the ambulance, the shocks groaned again. Faye and Henry moved as silently as they could across the roughly ten feet of distance between the vehicle and the dumpster. Faye risked a quick glance at Steve and the crowd.

No one looking their way.

Henry reached the edge of the dumpster (thankfully the lid was open), reached up, felt around blindly for the lip, hoisted himself up, dropped in. He landed on a bed of snow and garbage bags. The container was nearly full of the bags, but when his full body weight hit them, he pancaked them down, and still hit the bottom – but with a muted enough sound that no one looked over.

Faye then walked as casually as possible over to Steve and his crowd of concerned citizens. Steve saw her, and promptly wrapped up his story. "Well, I really need to get back to the hospital, but if anyone sees or hears anything about this call, please let us know. Thanks, everyone, for your concern. Keep an eye out."

Steve turned and walked back to the ambulance, got in, drove away.

The crowd dispersed, muttering to each other about what a shame it was, which old man from their building it could've been, etc.

Faye looked at the dumpster as she walked through the doors of her apartment building, her heart in her throat. Hoping to hell and back that today was not a pickup day.

Across the street, Edward Palermo, hidden in shadows till now, walked slowly away.

That day turned out not to be a garbage pickup day, but Faye thought she was going to have a heart attack every time she heard a big truck go by or, worse yet, pull into the apartment building's parking lot.

The hours dragged like they were weighed down by immense anchors. Faye did everything she could think of to distract herself – watched TV, surfed the internet, played what felt like a thousand games of solitaire – but evening was slow in coming. The window of her apartment darkened by infinitesimal degrees. When night finally fell, it felt like a cool balm on her shoulders: her back and neck muscles relaxed, and she felt like she could pull in a full breath for the first time all day.

Just a few more hours, Henry. Hang in there. Just a handful of hours, then we're safe.

And there was that word again. No matter how often she said it in her mind, it never felt true. What did she think was going to happen once he was inside? He'd get a job, they'd be roommates, and everything would work out just fine? Ridiculous. This was easily the stupidest thing she'd ever done, and she had no clue why she was even doing it. Sure, they'd been dating for about a year, but there was something *more* than that at work here. She felt it like a baseline thrum under her skin. Something compellingly, inherently strange. She didn't understand her actions, but somehow they felt *right*. Was she saving him from something terrible? Probably. But what? What would actually happen to him if he was discovered?

Thinking these thoughts, puzzling over things from every angle, she drifted off into a fitful sleep.

Milo had huddled inside the dumpster with Henry, waiting for darkness.

Every once in a while, a building tenant would dump a bag of garbage or a piece of furniture on them, but other than that it was fairly silent. Just the sprinkling of snow and Henry's strange heartbeat.

Milo wasn't sure if it changed, but for whatever reason he was able to hear it quite distinctly. It wasn't the regular heartbeat he'd had (and assumed Henry had, too); this one was a triple beat: *thud-thud-thud… thud-thud-thud…* Henry nodded off a couple of times while Milo watched – each time groaning in his sleep, as if distressed by something. Milo could only imagine what weird new dreams Henry must be having. What dreams come when someone physically transforms into something else?

Once night fell, visits to the dumpster petered out entirely, and it was just the susurration of the nearby traffic that interrupted the quiet. Even the snow had let up for the most part.

Then, a few hours later, an engine that Milo recognized: an ambulance. He lifted himself out of the dumpster, hovered above the lip to see Steve pulling in.

What the hell was he *doing back?*

Steve got out of the vehicle, headed toward Faye's building.

Faye's breathing had steadied, and she was in a deep sleep when she heard faint knocking coming from somewhere. The knocking became more insistent as she surfaced through the thick webbing of her dreams. Suddenly, it was like the knocking was coming from inside her skull.

She groaned, sat forward, rubbed her head, then headed toward the door, wondering who the hell it was. She was expecting no one, and she didn't have friends who just dropped by.

She opened the door a crack to see who it was, looked out into the hallway.

"Steve? Why are you here?"

Steve stood in the hallway, trying to put a look of concern on his face. It fit about as well as ten pounds of shit in a five-pound bag.

What Faye didn't know, and what Steve wasn't about to tell her, was that he'd thought of little else but Henry all day – and that, coupled with the fact that Henry's transforming body had actually stuck in Steve's mind (where in his normal form, it wouldn't have), explained his presence here now.

"Just thought I'd see how everything went. Didja get him in yet?" He poked his head around the side of the door, trying to get a peek inside.

"No, I was –" she glanced back to the couch where she'd fallen asleep "– just watching some TV, playing some games, then I guess I nodded off."

"Oh, well, you gonna get him? Want some help?"

This from the guy who couldn't get away fast enough earlier that day, terrified – rightly so – of losing his job, or at the very least facing a harsh reprimand. Faye wanted to ask how he'd talked his way out of the situation, but found that she barely cared. Her mind hadn't fully awoken yet, was still swimming between sleep and the waking world, as yet undecided which it preferred.

"What time is it?" she asked, looking around the

room, trying to remember through the fog of sleep where on the wall the clocks in her living room were located.

"Just past eleven," Steve said, then just stood there, waiting.

"Christ!" Faye said and opened the door wider, letting Steve in. She motioned him to the couch. "Sit down. I just wanna change. Been in this uniform all day. Be back in a second."

She scurried to her bedroom down the hall. Came back a few minutes later wearing jeans and a T-shirt. She carried a big blanket. Much bigger than the one from the hospital. "Alright, let's go."

Steve's odd behavior niggled a little at the back of Faye's brain as they headed out into the hall. She had known Steve would help her when she asked this morning, but he'd never been the type to follow up in this manner once he'd lent a hand. He wasn't the overly considerate type in general. Maybe his return was tied to his apparent romantic interest in her – which she'd never suspected before he'd tried to put his arm around her.

Or maybe it was just that he was privy to an incredible secret, and was simply intensely curious now. Perhaps a combination of these factors.

Whatever the reasons for his return, she had no time to consider them right now; they had to get Henry out of the dumpster – it was already well past the time she should've gone for him, and she was terrified now that she would look inside and he would no longer be there.

•••

Downstairs in the dumpster, Milo's sense of something being incredibly wrong suddenly kicked him in the chest. And it wasn't only that Faye should have come for Henry hours ago.

Whatever it was, he felt it coming. Soon.

It began snowing heavily again.

Faye made note of how many people they passed as they walked the four flights down the stairs. Exactly one: a young guy taking his dog for a walk. That was it. But even one was too much. Too risky. She thought briefly of trying to get Henry to the elevator, then realized he probably weighed too much for that. His weight, plus hers and Steve's would easily tip the scale, and the last thing they needed was for the elevator to break down, or worse, for the line to snap entirely. No way to get out of that one.

No, it would have to be the stairs.

When they reached the rear entrance, she turned to Steve, said, "Wait here. I'll go get him. You be my eyes for this stretch of hallway. If we can get him to the stairwell, we *should* be OK."

Steve nodded, again with that weird look on his face.

Something in Faye's gut flipped over, settled strangely, and she wondered again why he'd bothered to come back.

Faye walked out the doors, looked both ways, crunched her way through the fresh snow toward the dumpster. Once beside it, she whispered, "Henry, it's Faye. I'm going to take you inside now. Don't say anything, just stand up as best you can without being seen. I'll toss a blanket on you, then you'll need to climb out. As quietly as you can."

She heard shuffling sounds inside, one semi-loud crash as Henry's elbow or knee connected with the side of the bin. She looked around quickly again. No one in sight. She craned her neck back – no one hanging out on balconies. Too cold and snowy for that. She thanked the universe this hadn't all fallen at her doorstep in the middle of summer.

She looked back to the dumpster, saw the tip of Henry's great metal cranium peek out from the top, and whispered, "Down! Lower!"

Henry's head dipped a bit. She flung the blanket up and over the lip of the bin; it settled on his head, then draped him entirely. Or at least as far down as it could go before coming to rest on garbage bags and old coffee tables.

"Climb out," Faye said. "Do it as quickly and quietly as you can, Henry."

She stepped back, kept an eye out for any movement. She glanced back toward the building, imagining for a crazy moment that Steve would be gone, having panicked. She wouldn't put it past him to have just fucked off somewhere at the very moment she needed him. But he was still there. Nervously shuffling from foot to foot, sure, but he stood right where she left him. He moved his head side to side as she watched. When he noticed her looking, he gave her a thumbs up. She returned it, feeling ludicrous.

Henry hoisted himself up surprisingly gracefully. He knocked once more against the dumpster as he pulled himself up with his massive arms, but it was even quieter than the first time. His right foot settled on the edge of the bin, then he was over, landing – once again – more gracefully than she'd ever have thought possible.

He crouched low, stayed as small as he could, and didn't move a muscle until he heard her say, "I'm going to put my hand on your head and just position you in the direction of the doors. When I say 'go,' move forward as quickly as you can, got it?"

A slight nod from beneath the blanket.

She put her hand on his head, angled it slightly, as close to the center of the doors as she could, said, "Go," then they were both moving – she, as casually as possible; he, crouched, blind, and shuffling.

The doors seemed a mile away now, and the snow crunching underfoot sounded like it was amplified through enormous speakers aimed right at her face. Her head swiveled back and forth, eyes peeled for any sign of movement. Nothing, not even the young guy walking his dog.

Faye reached the doors, opened them both as wide as she could, moved out of the way, whispered down to Henry, "Doorway." In response, he made himself smaller yet.

She moved ahead of him once he was through, got to the second set of doors, used her key on them, said again, "Doorway," and held them as wide as possible.

Both sets of doors cleared, she looked again toward Steve, who was more nervous than ever, but still stood his ground.

If Faye had been thinking clearly, she would have been even more distraught than she already was. She had forgotten about the lobby security camera.

I'll deal with that later. Can't worry about it now.

"We good?" Faye said to Steve. "Nothing, no one?"

"Not a soul, not a sound," Steve said, walked in time with Faye as they headed down the short hallway toward the stairwell.

Holy Jesus, we're almost there, Faye thought, her heart hammering, palms sweating madly.

Milo drifted in behind them, followed them into the stairwell. Henry's dead shadow.

Faye eased the door shut behind them. They were in the stairwell now. Four flights and one more hallway to safety.

Safety. Christ, don't even think the word.

"Grab a coupla corners of the blanket and lift them, Steve. Make sure he doesn't trip up the stairs."

"Got it."

Up they went. One floor, two, nearly three.

Then the door to the stairwell opened on the ground floor. Faye, Steve, and Henry all froze. Heard someone talking in pet voice.

That fucking young guy and his dog. Shit! Faye thought.

The dog barked once, twice, then they heard it and its owner climbing the stairs. They reached the first floor, were heading for the second… which is when the second-floor stairwell door crashed open with a loud bang, and a woman and her dog burst out onto the landing.

"Hey, Marcy, just came back from our late-nighter," the young guy said. "Weather's a bit shit, but not too horrific. Shouldn't be that sludgy."

"Sweet," the woman said, one of those annoying

every-word-is-a-question lilts to her nasally voice. "Don't wanna make it a long one, anyway. Just 'round the block." She bent toward her yippy little dog, said, "Isn't that right, my little boo-boo? Yes, it is!"

And she was off, tromping down the stairs in what sounded like heels.

"'Night, Marcy," the guy called after her, but she didn't reply. "Stupid bitch," Faye heard him mutter as he entered the second-floor door. It slammed shut behind him.

The ground-floor door slammed seconds afterward.

Silence. Hearts beating hard, fast. Nearly leaping out of chests.

"Go," Faye said, motioning Steve ahead of her impatiently. "Go, go, go."

Steve bounded up the last flight of stairs, opened the door to the fourth floor, poked his head out, saw no one, held it for Faye and Henry. "Clear," he said.

Less than twenty feet to her apartment now. The hallway stretched ahead of them like in a nightmare. Fifteen, ten, five –

– key frantically in lock, twisting, turning, head on a swivel, scanning the hallway –

– then... inside.

Faye closed the door as quietly as she could behind her. She lifted the blanket off Henry. He blinked against the sudden light, glanced around the apartment. Stretched himself as tall as he could under the eight-foot-ceiling, which still left him hunched, but it was better than being crouched and shuffling blindly under a blanket. He smiled a little, looked at Steve, nodded, said, "Thanks" in his hewn-from-rock voice.

Steve just looked away, then looked back, tried to hold Henry's gaze, found he couldn't. He managed a general nod, which was good enough for Henry.

Once they'd had a chance to catch their breath, Faye said, "I'm gonna go make us some coffee, settle our nerves. Henry, don't sit on any of my furniture. I don't need any kindling right now, OK?"

For a moment, Henry didn't understand, but then he got it, nodded.

"Go sit on the floor for now, till I can figure out something more comfortable for you."

Faye walked to the kitchen. Steve stood just inside the front door, staring at Henry. They locked eyes for a little too long just then, and Henry saw something in Steve's eyes he recognized very well: fear. But not *just* fear. Fear coupled with stupidity.

Milo hovered beside Henry, feeling the situation coming slowly to a head. That feeling of wrongness becoming nearly palpable, filling the air between them.

Steve glanced down the hallway, back to Henry, pulled out a cell phone, flicked on the camera app. "I won't show anyone, Henry," he said. "I just want this so I can convince myself later that it really happened. Even though you'd think this would stick hardcore, after I left, I had trouble holding on to your image in my mind. It kept slipping away." He lifted the phone and aimed it in Henry's direction. "I knew I needed to come back, to prove to myself–"

And then one of Henry's massive hands flicked up quickly from his side, shot forward, and popped Steve's head like a grape.

Blood, bone, and gristle sprayed out from between Henry's fingers, splattered the wall behind Steve. He crumpled to the ground. Bled onto the carpet and hardwood floor. Henry took three steps backward, just staring at what he'd done. A few minutes later, Faye returned from the kitchen with the coffee.

When she saw Steve's body, she stopped dead, her mouth fell open just a little, then she very deliberately moved over to the nearest flat surface, placed the coffee cups on it, and said almost too quietly for Henry to hear: "What have you done?"

TEN

Small, one-bedroom apartment. Spiral-bound notepad. The top of the first page reads: *Inferne Cutis*: Latin for "below the skin."

That's what they call themselves. Pretentious motherfuckers.

William Krebosche looked up from his notes, read the clock on his bedside table: 2:47 a.m. He'd been listening to his digital voice recorder and transcribing every word for the past three hours. Even though it was very clear, he wasn't able to salvage all of it. Some words when they entered his brain just became unintelligible, garbled by some external filter he didn't understand. Something unknown that, for whatever reason, protected the *Inferne Cutis* from scrutiny. Soon enough, the very notion of this filter would fade, just like the other memories.

As it turned three o'clock, and the recording finally ended, Krebosche leaned back in his chair, rubbed his eyes, and steeled himself for the fact that he would now have to write the entire article in one sitting, as quickly as he could, so that it made *some* kind of sense by the time it was finished. He planned to have the piece published in the local newspaper through an editor acquaintance, Paul Darby, who worked there. He hoped it would then be picked up by larger outlets, and the domino effect would take over.

He thought briefly about Edward Palermo, who should be dead right now. Once Carl Duncan had left the warehouse on Kendul's trail, and Palermo's men were back inside, Krebosche's uncle Gerald – who'd witnessed firsthand, as had William, the "accident" that set them all down this path – was supposed to kill Palermo. Just walk into his ridiculous little caboose and put him down. But in a heartbeat, that plan had gone to shit. Gerald had panicked when Palermo sent men out to search the grounds.

Krebosche would shed tears over his uncle later, but he did wish one more had been added to the list before the body count was over.

Which made him think, too, about Carl Duncan, his old high school friend –

– *his* only *friend*, his conscience didn't let him forget.

Yes, OK, only *friend, then*. Although he wasn't entirely convinced that he was capable of having what other people called friends – could count on one hand (and even that was overkill, if he was being honest) the number of people he'd ever thought of as such. And all those relationships ended horrendously, anyway, through no fault of his own. Or at least that's what he told himself. On some level, he knew there was something socially wrong with him, but he'd always been unclear what it was that drove people away. What it was *precisely*.

No word from Duncan so, yes, most certainly dead.

Or at least beyond saving. Not that Krebosche would have tried to save him, of course. As soon as their plan had been devised, Krebosche had emotionally cut ties in his mind. His heart. He was capable of this – of simply shutting that part of himself off. A clean, quick *cut*.

As for the full plan, well, Duncan following Kendul back to where the Hunters hid out would have given them more ammunition for their story, naturally, but it wasn't to be. Palermo was smart, had eyes everywhere around his warehouse. Of course he did. Krebosche expected as much, but still hoped for the best. But because he'd expected Palermo would be prepared, he'd sent Duncan in to do the up-close work – which Duncan was foolish and bullheaded enough to be more than happy to do. A loner himself, Duncan had an inflated view of his and William's friendship, which William had never downplayed. He knew he'd need people to help him carry out his plan as the time grew nearer. And family and friends (well, just "friend") worked best – there was loyalty to be mined there. And again, if he was being honest, he likely wouldn't shed much in the way of tears for his uncle, either. Gerald was just a witness, involved due to his own heartbreak. The only one in his trainwreck of a family he'd ever truly cared for was his sister. Dead now, shot in the side of the head by one of the Hunters' stray bullets...

But that road didn't bear going down right now. There was work to be done. Plans to be adjusted. Memories to be saved.

But still this memory played again in his head,

unstoppable as always:

Bright day, really bright. In memory's eye, it's blinding. He and Gerald had taken his little sister, Marla, to an afternoon movie, gone for ice cream afterward. The theatre was off the beaten path, near an industrial area, a favorite of his uncle's. Not in the greatest neighborhood, but Krebosche was OK with it since he and Gerald were both with her. Krebosche was nearly ten years older than his sister, so he'd always felt closer to a parent than a brother. Always watched out for her, never let anything bad happen.

The sun was setting and they'd had to find parking a few blocks away from the theatre. A sketchy part of town, for sure, but nothing overly alarming. Until they heard what sounded like gunshots coming from a few blocks away. Just a few at first, then a peppering. He exchanged a concerned look with his uncle, but immediately thought maybe it was a car backfiring. Maybe kids with firecrackers. Certainly nothing that–

–more shots, this time closer. Krebosche holding his sister's hand tightly, then easing up a little as they continued walking, the sense of alarm, the memories of the sounds seemingly being washed away from his mind. He looked at his uncle again, but this time there was barely a reaction on the other man's face. He just looked mildly troubled, as though thinking of something a co-worker had said to him that had bugged him that day, or replaying a mild argument he'd had with his wife. Annoyance, not alarm, not true concern. Even though the sounds were getting closer.

Looking back on it these many years later,

Krebosche thinks that what happened next might be due to the fact that children aren't as susceptible to whatever memory wipe weirdness is at play in keeping the *Inferne Cutis* hidden; children are much less likely to dismiss things with rational explanations. They're curious, fearless. Sometimes – often – to their detriment.

In Krebosche's mind, the gunshots/firecrackers/backfires dulled to a barely recognizable pulsing at the back of his skull. The three of them passed by the mouth of an alleyway as the streetlights above popped on. If they'd turned their heads at that moment, they would have seen someone getting shot by two other people. Bullets jabbing into their head, neck, and chest. As it was, in Gerald's and William's brains, there was nothing to see, no sounds to attract their attention.

And the car was just up ahead. His sister was excited, wanted to run, maybe wanted to race them to the car.

Krebosche felt his grip loosen a little bit. A little more. More yet... And then she was running ahead, nearly past the mouth of the alley now, when she suddenly lilted sideways, the side of her head burst open, a red blossom of bone and blood.

She fell, smacked the pavement hard.

Only then did the sounds filter enough into the two men's heads for them to react. Gunshots. And panic crowded into their chests. They rushed to Marla's unmoving body. Instantly knew she was dead. Looked down the alley. No sign of anyone. They didn't know it then, but the Run had simply moved on, to other alleys, other sections of the industrial park. Those involved likely had no idea about the bullet that had ricocheted off the brick of a wall, the corner of a dumpster. However it had gone astray was of little consequence. What mattered was that it had killed Krebosche's sister.

Though even now, he had to struggle to hold onto this fact. He felt something behind his forehead airbrushing, massaging the information. The wheres and hows.

But it had never been quite enough to wash it completely from his mind, his heart. The pain was more important, proved more durable than whatever this whitewashing effect was. He'd had to continually remind his uncle, nearly daily, what had happened. But for him, it stuck harder. Clung tighter.

Maybe because he was younger. Maybe because it had been his hand that'd let her go.

Shaking his head, dispelling the memory, Krebosche stood up, went to the washroom, splashed cold water on his face, then headed to the kitchen to put on a fresh pot of coffee. Time to get writing. Once the story hit – and if it did get picked up by the major newspapers – it would be all over the Internet, on people's cell phones. Everywhere. It *couldn't* be forgotten. He'd work tirelessly to spread it as far and wide as possible at every opportunity. The truth couldn't stay hidden forever – not with a massive spotlight like this shining on it. It would gain momentum. He'd get invited onto TV shows to talk about what he'd seen, what he'd heard. Whatever it was that clouded people's minds would not be able to stand up to such exposure. The story would solidify, be investigated by authorities.

And I know where they hide… the Runners, anyway, he thought. And once they were in custody, the Hunters' hideout would soon be discovered, too, he'd no doubt.

It was all just a matter of time.

Krebosche's coffeemaker beeped, signaling he had a full pot ready. He poured himself a cup, and began writing.

Five hours later, the sun having risen but still tucked away behind a thick layer of dark clouds, Krebosche had the bare bones of the piece. Some holes, some confusing bits, and a lot of questions sure to come from his editor friend. Krebosche had been tracking Palermo for nearly two years, with last night's foray planned to be the icing on the cake. But Palermo's and Kendul's deaths would have to wait. Exposing them and watching their society crumble would have to be enough for now.

Not that Krebosche knew what the *Inferne Cutis* was, exactly. For all his notes and tireless spying, he'd only come up with a partial picture of what they did. He'd only ever seen one Run – and only a very short portion of that, which had already mostly faded from his mind. Only little bits and pieces of his memory of that night still remained. Though he had also seen a woman taken into a house and never come out again. A woman he knew. Cared for.

But he blocked this path of thought, as he'd been unable to do with the memory of his sister. *Enough*, he thought. *Just… enough. No more of this tonight…*

He knew – far better than most everyone else – about the weird memory blanket that came down over everything they did. He'd never spoken to anyone who knew a single thing about this group of people. The only ones he'd been able to convince of their existence were his uncle Gerald, and his friend Carl – Gerald because he, along with Krebosche, had seen the killing that changed their lives, and Carl because he was desperate to believe he was valued, needed. He realized quickly that to convince anyone else he needed to amass evidence, gather it, organize it, footnote it, save multiple copies of it, then pore over it in hope that portions of it would stick in his mind so he wouldn't lose focus. He reread as much as possible of his notes every single day.

And now, he thought, with his finger hovering over the Send button of his email program, Paul Darby's addy in the To field of the message, *it would either be enough, or it wouldn't. Simple as that.*

He clicked the button.

"What is this crap?" Darby said on the phone fifteen minutes later. "How many times do I have to tell you to quit with this fucking paranoid bullshit?"

"It's not paranoia," Krebosche said. "I saw them kill my little sister. I think they killed another woman, too."

"You saw this with your own eyes?" Darby said.

"Yes, I did." Krebosche tried to remain calm, but irritation was creeping into his voice. He couldn't help it. He'd been dealing with Darby's attitude for at least a year, and he was reaching the end of his rope with the smug fucker.

"Uh-huh," Darby said.

Silence.

"Listen, Darby, I know this seems far-fetched, but–"

"Yeah, just a little," Darby said, cutting Krebosche off. "For instance, explain to me why no one else has heard of these mysterious gangsters. The infernal whatever-the-fucks."

"*Inferne Cutis.*"

"Yeah, them. And besides murder, what else are you accusing them of? Running around in the streets shooting at each other over near Barton and Carter – for *hours*. Like no one in the neighborhood would have heard that, maybe woken up to see what the fuck was going on. No cops would've been by to investigate the fuckton of noise that would've caused. The hospitals and the morgue just *might've* also had some record of the bodies, don't you think? Where'd they go? Vanished into the fucking ether, just like these ridiculous theories and accusations ought to?"

"I don't know how they do it, Darby," Krebosche said, knowing how weak it all sounded, "but there's some kind of… I dunno… weird *blanket* that suffuses their activity, muffles the gunshots, wipes people's memories when they do happen to see what's going on. Something makes our eyes just slide right off these people, makes our brains *cancel them out*. Hell, I tried to take pictures of the night I saw them shooting each other, and all I got back on the camera were gray and black blurs, so indistinct they could've been anything at all. The only way I know as much as I do is because of how long I've been tracking them. And the only way I've been able to do *that* is by writing myself notes, reminding myself that what I'm after is real, isn't some fucking delusion. I'm wrung out from it all, but I know I'm close to something huge here, Paul. Please, you need to work on this with me, help me figure out the missing pieces. Please."

Darby didn't say anything for about ten full seconds – so long that Krebosche thought maybe he'd hung up. But then: "Krebosche... William, listen. I know it was tough when you lost Adelina. Is that the woman you mentioned? Is that who you think they killed? 'Cause when a mind is under as much stress as yours must have been, sometimes it can't take the pressure, and it starts... inventing things that make sense. That make it easier to deal with. You know? Same goes for your sister. That was a stray bullet. Horrifying, yes, but random all the same. There's always been gang activity in that area. To be honest, and I know you don't want to hear it, but your uncle should have known better than to–"

Krebosche set his jaw. His eyes turned to hard black stones in his head as he cut Paul off. "This isn't about Adelina. Or Marla. Not like that. Not how you think. I'm not fucking delusional. I'm not."

Krebosche wanted to say more, but images of Adelina and Marla flooded his mind, making it hard to form words.

"OK, well, either way, William. We can't run this story. There's not *nearly* enough evidence or sources to–"

"I know!" Krebosche shouted, finally losing his temper. "That's why I need you to *fucking help me*, you self-important son of a bitch!"

He knew as soon as the words were out of his

mouth that the conversation was over. But it turned out that more was over than just the conversation.

"That's it, Krebosche," Darby said, his voice a hard, cold rock. "We're done. Don't call me anymore. I won't help you. Not now. Not ever."

Dial tone.

Krebosche furiously packed a duffle bag, just cramming things in – his notes, toiletries, clothes, a gun – thinking, *Fuck Darby. I'll get Palermo, and expose everything myself.* He knew it was foolhardy and would likely end horribly for him, but he wasn't sure how much he cared anymore.

He would go to a motel near the warehouse, formulate a plan there. Now that he knew he was entirely on his own, that no one (who wasn't already dead) would take him seriously, a *them or me* mentality slowly started taking shape in his head. Once it had fully taken root, his direction would be clear.

ELEVEN

I'll cut his throat while he sleeps.

The snow had let up a little, but not very much, when Krebosche pulled into the Knight's Inn motel. It was a bit of a shithole, but it was the closest motel to the warehouse. Even though he'd been in the area only hours before, he needed to consult his notes on its location, and navigate toward it as though for the first time.

When the blood starts flowing, he thought, still amped up from his conversation with Darby, *I'll tell him why I'm killing him, and those will be the last words he ever hears.*

Then another voice in his head: *Oh, yes, you're such a badass. Sending your uncle, and someone who actually liked you – as much as anyone can like you, that is – to do your dirty work. You realize those people are both dead because of you. They died horribly while you watched from afar with your ridiculous fucking binoculars plastered to your face. Did part of you hope that would happen so you could finally be rid of everyone who cared about you even a little bit? 'Cause with them gone – and ties now broken with Paul Darby at the newspaper, as well – now you can be the hero. Man of the hour.*

Krebosche tried to ignore this other voice, but it persisted.

Maybe you want to die. Maybe you're sick of dealing with this level of loss, and this is the way out. Just barrel in, guns figuratively blazing like a moron. Is that it, dummy? Is that what you really want? For all this death to be for nothing?

Krebosche closed his eyes tightly, wishing the other voice away. *No*, he thought, *that's not what I want. That's not what I want at all.*

He felt his pulse slow, his heart stop pounding, his mind clear a little.

But as calm as he became, he still felt deeply that he needed to see Palermo die. Kendul, too, if at all possible, though that was secondary. One of the two was enough, and was likely all he could hope for. He didn't give a flying fuck if the *Inferne Cutis* was exposed. Couldn't give a rat's ass if the mystery was ever solved – for him or anyone else. Palermo would die. Once that was done, he wouldn't care what happened to himself. His goal would be achieved.

He paid cash for his room, keyed the door, chucked his duffle on the bed, and immediately headed for the shower. Fifteen minutes later, he felt as though the water had swept the cobwebs from his head. A plan formed in his mind. He saw it step by step, was certain it would work. And after, while Palermo's body cooled in a puddle of his own blood, maybe Krebosche would run, maybe he wouldn't. Maybe he'd just stand there, staring at the body, hoping that wherever Adelina and Marla were – if they were anywhere at all – they could see what he'd done for them. See what they'd meant to him. What he was willing to do to make things right again. As right as they could be, anyway.

Krebosche's mind turned specifically to Adelina. The closest thing to a girlfriend he'd ever had. He had no doubt she was dead. He'd followed the men as they drove her to the outskirts of the city, shuffled her out, and led her into a rundown house. *Probably filled with crackheads and God knows who else*, he remembered thinking.

All that he was certain of now was that she went into that house under her own power – yes, being led, but upright and alive – and never came out before it was destroyed. Krebosche had been frozen in place. Had no idea how to react, what to do, who to call. He remembered crying, beating his steering wheel. But within minutes, even those strong emotions, even grief that powerful, began to wane. He felt it coming out of his pores like sweat. For some reason he was still unsure of, he had the presence of mind to write down what he could remember from the night. He scribbled it furiously, breaking the nib of his pencil halfway through, hoping to Christ he had another one with which to finish up.

Now, Krebosche got dressed, finished formulating his plan in his head, then remembered he didn't have a knife with which to cut Palermo's throat – and he assumed, as with all the other Runners, it needed to be a knife or a sword, since their bodies apparently just gobbled up bullets. It didn't have to be anything special, though; in fact, the *less* special the better.

Why waste a good knife cutting such a filthy throat?

He stuffed his gun into his waistband nonetheless – if he did decide to carry on once he'd sliced the pig's neck open, he'd want to at least put up a fight, take out a few more of Palermo's men before he died. He knew he wouldn't live long enough to take down more than two, maybe three of them, tops, but better than none.

Some distant part of him tried to argue he was also avenging Carl Duncan's and his uncle Gerald's deaths, but those internal arguments held about as much water as a sieve in his new state of mind. He was functioning on all cylinders now. No more time for bullshit.

This was for Adelina. For Marla.

And this was for him.

He put on his jacket, walked out of his motel room, spotted a Walmart across the street, headed toward it. Once inside, he made his way to the kitchen section, found the biggest knife he could. Bought it.

Then the thought struck him – with a certain amount of glee, he had to admit – that maybe hollow-point bullets would do more damage to anyone he might need to deal with after he cut Palermo's head off. Those might even kill a Runner if fired from point-blank range at the head or neck. He turned toward the ammunition section, bought some dum-dum bullets, then left the store, went back to his motel room. Undressed, went to bed.

He slept for two hours, setting his alarm for 3 a.m. It woke him in the middle of a dream in which he was covered entirely in blood. Screaming.

Pounding his fists against something. It was only upon waking, getting dressed, securing the knife down the side of his boot, the gun in his waistband, and leaving the motel room again that he realized it wasn't Palermo's blood, as he'd first assumed. It was Adelina's.

And the thing upon which he pounded his fists was enormous.

Made entirely of steel.

It felt like there would always be snow now. It had waxed and waned over the past few days, but it seemed to Krebosche that it had never actually stopped. It was only due to the temperature being fairly warm that it hadn't piled up to epic proportions. As Krebosche drove through the darkened streets, he imagined being suffocated under a mountain of snow. The thought appealed to him. He enjoyed the idea of that kind of peace, away from the noise on the streets, and in his head. It comforted him, calmed him.

He barely passed anyone on his way to the street where he planned to park, a few blocks away from the warehouse. He knew security would be tight, so getting too close would be a huge mistake.

All of this is a huge fucking mistake, he thought. But he was committed now. He felt that any choice in the matter had long since vanished. The only way through the situation was down. And down further still.

I'm about to try to cut a man's head off with something not much better than a bread knife. What a mess that's going to make. But the thought pleased him. He pictured the skin coming away in chunks as he sawed through. Blood pumping out. Drenching everything.

Tires crunching snow and gravel, he pulled his car into a dirt lot next to an abandoned building. Parked, got out. Surveyed the scene. From where he stood, he could just see the top of the warehouse. He'd need to be closer to know whether or not any lights were still on. But he supposed that was his own fault, since he, Duncan, and Gerald, were the ones who caused the breach.

As he headed toward the rear of the warehouse, where the train tracks and Palermo's caboose were located, he had to fight to keep his orientation. The streets – especially in the endlessly falling snow – all looked the same, and even when he approached a corner, the text of the street signs would appear blurred, swimming on the signposts. He had to blink and wipe his eyes, refocus, look down at his notebook, run the street names in his mind over and again. He resorted to repeating them out loud under his breath.

Around one more corner, and there was the field and the warehouse. The caboose sat like a crouching animal in the darkness.

No lights on anywhere.

Krebosche touched the knife where he'd tucked it down his boot, then the gun in his waistband. Felt his heart thudding in his chest. For all his thoughts about not caring anymore, he certainly looked like someone about to do something unwise, and was scared to death of the consequences.

Best approach is just straight up the tracks, right? Of

course, there'd be a guard at the door of the caboose, maybe two. Especially now. And probably at least a couple on the roof of the warehouse. What would make this all the more difficult was the crunching snow. There was no way to be completely stealthy.

Unless you crawl on your belly, idiot.

So he'd crawl on his belly, slither along beside the tracks, then just pop up and attack everyone? Brilliant plan. This was beginning to look more and more unlikely.

A distraction of some kind would be nice. Maybe another fool like Duncan to go die for me. The thought made even Krebosche wince – and he'd thought he was beyond pangs of conscience – at least for Duncan.

He tucked himself behind the wall of the last building before the field opened up and cover was gone. Once he left the safety of this wall, he'd be entirely exposed. Just the open field and the train tracks between him and the caboose.

He glanced up at the sky. At least the clouds were cooperating. *Can't have a fuckton of snow without clouds,* he thought. So moonlight would be at a minimum. Maybe just the occasional break in cloud cover to expose his movements.

He breathed deeply twice, three times. Decided on the belly slither. He laid himself down flat, poked his head around the side of the wall. No movement at the warehouse or the caboose. No sound. Just steadily falling snowflakes and his heart threatening to burst from his throat. Maybe the guards were hidden from view because they were afraid of getting picked off by a sniper. He didn't know. But it was now or never. He felt his resolve weakening by the second.

Just as he was about to work his way out, a voice from behind startled him.

"Looking for someone?" Palermo said.

TWELVE

"He would have told someone," Henry said. "If he hadn't already."

Faye didn't respond. She couldn't tear her eyes away from the pulped skull of her co-worker. Blood pooled around Steve's body, and the clumps that had sprayed through Henry's fingers crawled slowly down the wall like snails.

Finally: "You don't know that. You *didn't* know that."

"He wanted to take a picture, Faye."

"So he deserved to *die* for that?"

Henry was silent. At some point, tears had sprung from his eyes, grown cold now on his face. He tried to wipe them away, feeling ashamed of them. His clumsy fingers made it difficult.

He distractedly wondered what color the tears were.

Then: "Yes. He deserved to die. He would have exposed me. Exposed *us*. Or at least tried to. And I can't hide how I used to when I looked human. That was a big part of what made it easy, I imagine. Now, though... look at me. No way this will be easy to cover up, explain away. Steve said it was hard to hold on to my image in his head, sure, but he was gone for a while, yet was able to still remember me enough that he knew to come back here to look for me. That would never have happened before. Not when I looked human."

Faye left the coffees alone, forgotten. Moved to the couch. Fell into it, put her face in her hands, elbows on her knees. She didn't say anything for a long time. When she finally did, it hit Henry hard: "I want you to leave."

"Faye, listen–"

"No. Get out."

"What are you going to do with…" Henry motioned toward Steve's body.

"I'll deal with it. Just go. Get out. Now."

"Where am I supposed to go?"

She looked up at him, locked eyes. "I hardly give a fuck."

As this exchange took place, Milo felt something push upward within him. That feeling of dread had coalesced into something new. Clearly, that feeling had been warranted, and was now at least partially realized with the dead body still leaking blood on the floor. But this was something else. That cold ball of lead in his belly felt like it was heating up; he felt like *he* was heating up somehow. Becoming more… substantial?

He reached a hand out toward the table upon which Faye had placed the coffee cups. Closer to the cup handle. Closer. Then his fingers passed right through.

But just as his heart was sinking, something caught

his eye. He lifted his gaze quickly. Standing to one side of the table was the woman he'd seen in the hospital furnace room. As before, the air pressure in the room seemed to change with her appearance. But back then, she had seemed fairly calm; now she seemed agitated. And this time, Milo thought he heard sounds coming from her mouth. He watched her lips intently, realized he could make out a word here and there. She was telling him something, staring directly at him. And just as he had been feeling more substantial himself, so she seemed more substantial to him, as well.

Concentrating harder, it was like someone had turned up the volume in his brain. Words formed – all of them at once in a sudden rush that shocked him and made him stagger back: "You cannot let him leave. You cannot let him leave. You cannot let him leave."

Milo turned back to Henry. Neither Henry nor Faye had spoken in the past minute or so. Henry just stared down at Steve's body; Faye's face was slack, her initial anger giving way to fatigue. Milo wasn't sure that she was aware Henry was even still in the room.

Milo was about to turn away from them and focus his attention back on the woman when he realized he was wrong. Faye and Henry *were* still talking; he just could no longer hear them. He watched their lips move. Henry gesticulated. Faye turned away from him. The anger was back in her features, clouded her eyes. Milo thought the look on her face bordered on hatred.

He turned back to the woman, who was still repeating, "You cannot let him leave," but had now added "They'll kill him" to the repetitive refrain.

"I can hear you," Milo said.

"You cannot let him leave. They'll kill him. They'll kill…"

Milo stepped forward, nearly within arm's reach of the woman. She shimmered the air around her with her intensity. "I said I can hear you, I can hear you."

The woman stopped speaking. She looked momentarily shocked, her mouth hanging slightly open. She closed it. Opened it again, said, "You can?"

Milo nodded. "I cannot let him leave. They'll kill him."

The woman nodded.

Milo took another step forward, close enough now to touch her if he reached out a hand – and if he were able to touch anything at all.

"Who are you?" Milo said.

"Adelina."

"My name is Milo."

"I know."

They looked at each other for a moment longer, something powerful passing between them that neither really understood.

"Milo, you need to stop Henry any way you can. He doesn't know how important he is."

"To who? To what?"

"To me, to you, to everything and everyone."

"Um…"

"I know it sounds ridiculous, and you have no reason to believe me…"

"Well, I'm inclined to believe you to a *certain* extent, considering you're a ghost that's decided to appear to me – a ghost *myself* – so there's that."

"I'm not a ghost."

"Well, you look like a ghost. More substantial than me, sure, but still, uh, *floating* off the ground, you know?"

"You're not listening. Nothing can happen to Henry. He needs to be left alone. He needs to let his evolution run its course."

"Sure, and I'm not opposed to that – whatever it entails. That's kind of the point of everything we've been doing our whole lives, so I get it. But I can't touch anything, so that makes it a little difficult to stop massive metal behemoths from doing pretty much as they please, you know? Watch."

Milo swept one of his hands through the coffee cups on the table – or *would have* swept one of his hands through them, if his hand hadn't knocked them both off the table and onto the floor where they shattered into a hundred pieces.

Milo's mouth dropped open. He looked at Adelina. Then at Henry, then Faye. They both looked back at him.

Or *seemed* to look at him. After a pulse-pounding moment, he realized they were just looking in the direction of the noise, not at what caused it.

"What the hell?" Faye muttered.

"No idea," Henry said. "That was weird."

"Yes. Yes, it was," Faye said, her brow crinkling.

"At least they've stopped arguing," Milo said to no one in particular.

"You can make yourself visible to Henry if you keep concentrating. Keep trying," Adelina said.

"What? How do I do that? I didn't try to knock the coffee cups off the table, so I clearly have no clue how I did even that much."

"Once you've got a toehold, the more you assert yourself into physical space, the more it will accept you. The more it *has* to accept you. Trust me, just keep knocking things over. See if that works."

"This is insane," Milo muttered, but floated over to a bunch of knickknacks cluttering up another of Faye's tables in the living room. He swept an arm across them, shattering the entire lot.

Faye and Henry stepped back, both wearing identical shocked *O*s on their faces. "What the *fuck*?" Faye said, standing now. "Is this something you're doing, Henry? Because if it, it isn't fucking funny."

Henry said nothing, just stared at the spot where the knickknacks had gone flying. "Hang on a second, Faye. Hang on. I think I see… something."

"Where?"

"By that table."

Faye squinted. "I don't see anything. And what do you mean by 'something,' anyway?"

"I don't know. Just–"

A mirror in the hallway smashed.

Shoes on the mat by the door flew across the floor.

The glass doors of Faye's china cabinet exploded inward. Everything inside, on all three shelves, was dumped out onto the ground. Pieces of cups, plates, and china dolls flew in every direction.

Faye just stood rooted to the spot, her eyes closed, hands over her ears as the destruction took place around her.

Henry, on the other hand, stared hard at the place in the air from which everything seemed to be falling. And then it happened. Not in gradients – like a fuzzy TV picture becoming slowly clearer as it's tuned in – but like a balloon bursting. Suddenly, Milo was just *there* for Henry.

Henry stared at his friend, who held in his hands a large silver tray with a full teacup set on it, about to bring it down at his feet. His face was red with exertion.

"Milo?"

Milo looked up at the sound of Henry's voice.

"Henry? You can hear me?"

Henry nodded. "I can see you, too."

"Holy shit."

"Henry, who are you talking to?" Faye said. "What the hell is happening?"

Milo turned to Adelina, searched her face for an answer because words to ask a proper question would not come.

Adelina understood, said, "She can't see or hear you, Milo. I don't know if she'll ever be able to. But Henry can."

Milo turned his attention back to Henry. Felt a lump in his throat. Knew tears weren't far behind. "Henry," he said.

"Yeah, Milo, it's me. Put the tray down. You're freaking Faye out. Just set it down gently, OK?"

Milo looked down at the tray in his hands as though he'd no idea how it'd gotten there. "Yeah," he said, shaking his head clear. "Yeah, sorry."

Milo moved over to the coffee table, close to where

Faye sat still staring in disbelief at Henry. With shaking hands, Milo set the tray down.

"Henry, are you going to tell me what in the fuck is going on? Who just destroyed my apartment?"

"Milo did," Henry said. "He was just trying to… get my attention."

Faye said nothing, just sat down on the couch, trying to get her breathing back under control.

There would be no expressions of disbelief from Faye. No doubting what Henry told her. She'd just seen *something* whip around her apartment, smashing everything to bits – that much was certain. If Henry said it was his Milo, then great. Mystery solved. She had no gas left in the tank to fight him. What she wanted more than anything right now was to sleep. Close her eyes, fall away from the world.

To Henry, Milo looked somewhat insubstantial. Not transparent, but more like how someone appears backlit against the sun on the horizon. Definitely there, but with shadows hovering, seeking to obscure.

Henry took two steps toward Milo, easily closing the distance between them. They stood in front of one another for a moment, then Henry reached forward and down, made to hug Milo – but as gently as he could. He neither knew what Milo was made of, nor had complete control of his new muscles. His arms encircled Milo, and Milo waited with his eyes shut for them to go through him. But they didn't. They touched him. Held him as softly as metal could hold anything.

"Where were you?" Henry said, his mouth near Milo's head.

"I've been with you the whole time, old friend. The whole time."

Neither felt the need to say anything else, so they just stood like that, breathing, for a long moment.

When Henry pulled away and stood back up – as much as he could – he said, "Who else is here? I saw you looking at someone else earlier."

Milo glanced at Adelina, who was shimmering and smiling nearby.

"Adelina," Milo said. "A new friend."

Henry nodded, looked in the same direction as Milo. "I don't see her, but I believe you. After what's just happened here – not to mention what's happening to me right now – I'd believe anything."

Adelina said, "He might see me soon, Milo. I hope he does. It would be an honor."

Milo frowned at that, but his mind was having enough trouble keeping up with recent developments, so he just made a quick mental note to ask her later what she meant.

Milo looked at Faye, saw how frail and worn-out she seemed. "Tell her I'm sorry, would you, Henry? This was the only way I knew of reasserting myself in the physical world."

"Milo says he's sorry," Henry said to Faye. "If he wasn't dead, he'd offer to buy you new things."

Faye didn't respond. She was in no mood for humor. She was in no mood for anything. Her eyes were glazed, and she appeared to be breathing very shallowly. She sat completely still and just stared ahead into the middle distance. Seeing nothing. Not wanting to see anything.

Henry turned back to Milo. "She'll come around."

"Tell him what I told you now, Milo," Adelina said. "It's very important that he know."

"Henry, listen," Milo said. "Adelina says you can't leave the apartment. At least not yet. She says they'll kill you. Apparently, people know about you, that you've begun changing."

"Palermo has men keeping an eye on this place," Adelina said, clarifying. "You were careful, but not careful enough. They'll know if you move, and where you're moving to. There's no point in going anywhere right now. We need to figure out our next move, then proceed very carefully."

Milo related Adelina's words to Henry, who stood nodding, then said, "Well, that's fine. I'm not going to pretend I have any idea what's happening to me, why Palermo wants to kill me, or what's going on in a larger sense, but one thing is certain: someone is going to come looking for Steve. His ambulance is parked behind this building. And we need to do something about the body."

Everyone looked at Steve's cooling corpse. Everyone but Faye; she continued to stare at nothing, subconsciously fiddling with a loose thread in her pants.

"Why did you do that, anyway, Henry?" Milo asked. "I know he was going to take a picture, and that obviously wouldn't have been good, but this was… unnecessary."

"I know," Henry replied. "I know. I don't know why I did it. It happened very fast, and I didn't feel like I was in control of myself when my arm shot forward and just…" He shook his head. "I felt like what was inside me – what makes me who I am, what makes me *Henry* – was the wrong version of me. Disconnected. Lost. Replaced by something… else."

Slowly, like sunlight filtering down through murky water, something Henry said finally penetrated Faye's exhaustion and confusion. "Wait a minute," she mumbled, her eyes refocusing. "Palermo?"

"Edward Palermo," Henry said, moving toward Faye. He put a hand on her shoulder. Again, gently. Gently. "The head of the Runners. Why?"

"He visited me outside the hospital not long after I'd helped you home in that cab. Gave me his card, told me to call him if you got in contact with me again."

"So he's known about me that long?" Henry said.

"You're a terrible fugitive," Milo said.

Henry tried to smirk. Wasn't sure how it settled on his face, but it felt right. "So if he's known about me and where I am all this time, why hasn't he just gotten a pile of guys together to take me in?"

Adelina said to Milo, "He missed his window to contain Henry right at the beginning and, by the time he knew where he was, he was probably already too much for Palermo to safely handle. Now he knows you're powerful, but he doesn't know *how* powerful. At this point, I suspect he wants to see what you become before he makes a move."

Milo relayed her words to Henry.

Henry frowned. "How does Adelina know so much about all this, anyway, Milo? Who is she? How do you even know you can trust a word she says?"

"Palermo's my father," Adelina said quietly.

"Henry's becoming what I was supposed to be, but never fully became."

Milo stared at her. "Palermo's your father?"

Henry echoed Milo, astonished: "Palermo's her *father*?"

She nodded. "I was the first to ascend, or whatever you want to call it. No one had ever done it before me, so there's no proper term for it, but yes, full lead content. I achieved it years ago. My father... hid me away so no one would know."

Milo repeated her words to Faye and Henry, then said, "Why would he do that?"

"Look, we don't have time for me to explain everything right now. Henry's right that people will be looking for the ambulance driver. Probably have been for several hours."

Milo said to Henry, "OK, she says no time to get in to it, will explain later... So, body disposal. How do we get rid of it? We need to make it disappear, clean up the blood and... other bits, then figure out how to disappear ourselves. With people watching our every move. No sweat."

Just then, Henry had a horrible idea. But, like his arm flashing out and pulping Steve's head, this idea came from that same raw place of instinct. "I have an idea," he said, tentatively.

"Spill," Milo said.

"I could... pulp the body with my fists. Turn it to mush. Like baby food." He let that visual hang in the room for a moment, then said, "Or not."

Faye had only been privy to certain parts of the conversation as it was and, given her state of mind, a lot of it just went in one ear and out the other, but this last bit stuck. "You're going to do *what* to Steve's body?"

"Nah, nah, it's a great idea," Milo said, his eyes lighting up. "I know it's disgusting, but it'll work. And we need something that will work right now."

Henry turned to Faye, focused on her, tried to keep her eyes locked to his so that she would understand. "You should leave the room, Faye. This is going to be awful."

"You can't just fucking *pulp* my friend's body to baby food!"

"We have to."

She took a deep breath. "That's insane."

"I know, but it'll remove all identification from his corpse and will make it easy to... further dispose of."

"What does *that* mean?"

"He'll be easier to dispose of," Milo said, "as a liquid than as a solid."

Good thing Faye can't hear him, Henry thought, but said, "We don't need to go into more detail than that, Faye. You can leave it up to us; we'll take care of it, OK?"

"Jesus, can't we just hide the body, like *normal* murderers?"

"Shit idea," Milo said. "For countless reasons."

Henry agreed. "This is the only way to be sure the body's gone, Faye. Just let me do this." He wanted to reach a hand out to touch her face, but he knew she'd push him away. After what he'd done, after everything she'd been through, he imagined his touch now would just feel cold and monstrous.

Faye looked down at Steve's body, back up to Henry. "Where are you gonna go, Henry? How do you think you're gonna get out of here without being noticed?"

"No idea. One step a time, though, OK?"

Faye looked around the room – at her shattered belongings strewn about, the blood-spattered dead body of her friend and colleague splayed out on the floor, the giant metal man towering above her, and the two invisible people apparently standing somewhere nearby – and thought, *Fuck it. It's not like it can get much weirder, or much worse.*

"Go ahead," she said. "But use the fucking bathtub."

In the process of dealing with Steve's body, Milo discovered he could grasp and hold onto things fairly well now – not just sweep them from shelves and destroy them. When they were finished in the living room, they'd been so thorough that it would've passed a black-light inspection. They even replaced the smashed china with various knickknacks from other rooms in the apartment so that, if the cops did come looking, they wouldn't see anything obviously out of the ordinary. The busted hall mirror was just taken entirely off the wall, and a picture from one of Faye's closets hung in its place.

Once they were satisfied that the living room would pass a thorough inspection, Milo helped Henry pick up Steve's body and move it into the bathtub. To an outside observer, it would have seemed like Henry was somehow levitating the body, the head and shoulders supported by his giant metal arms, while the legs and feet were supported by nothing more than thin air.

The mostly headless body safely in the tub and the drain plugged, Henry – kneeling at the side of the tub – began pulping it. He started at the feet and legs and worked his way up, basically just grasping onto a given body part and crushing it through his enormous steel fingers until it squished out the sides. He repeated this motion until the body part – bone, muscle, flesh – was nothing more than mush. Skin was a little harder to render drain-ready, though, so they used a pair of heavy-duty scissors to cut up whatever might cause problems going down. Milo's job was to watch closely where any blood-spray went and immediately wipe it down.

Henry felt the urge to throw up several times before the job was done, but – somewhat disturbingly, Henry thought – Milo suffered no such affliction; he just looked fascinated by it all.

At one point, his hands, chest, and arms covered in grue, Henry turned to Milo and said, "You know there's something seriously wrong with you, right? No way you should be enjoying this like you are."

"I'm not *enjoying* it, Henry. I'm just interested in the process. Big difference. Besides, I'm not the one squeezing a body to paste through his fingers like a fucking trash compactor, so you're not exactly on firm moral ground to be judging anyone, you know?"

Henry had nothing to say to that, so he just got back to work.

Once they were satisfied that Steve was as mashed as he possibly could be, they turned on the hot water, opened the drain, and watched it all go down. Milo then tipped in the entire contents of the three bottles of Drāno Faye had found under the kitchen sink.

"Done," Milo said, leaning against the edge of the tub.

"Done," Henry echoed. "Just have to wash the rest of Steve off my chest, and we're set." Then he added, "You know we're going to Hell, right?"

"No such place, Henry. No such place."

In her bedroom, Faye attempted to make sense of everything that'd happened. She'd put on some heavy music to cover the sounds of crunching coming from the bathroom, but the album she'd chosen, Gojira's *The Way of All Flesh* (if she'd been thinking clearly, she wouldn't have picked such an on-the-nose record), had come to an end. The ensuing silence settled over her, and she felt like she could finally think straight.

When it had all been happening – when shit had been inexplicably flying all over her apartment, crashing everywhere, Henry talking to invisible people – she'd wanted nothing more than to just run out the door and never come back. But now that it was quiet, her affection (or whatever that simple emotion had now morphed into) for Henry had returned. Stronger than ever, it seemed. She felt vaguely as though her emotions were being if not outright controlled, then somehow manipulated. She couldn't put her finger on it, but she felt incredibly protective of Henry, but was uncertain why she should feel so strongly. Especially in light of everything that'd happened. But it was there, and she could not help how she felt. She'd dated other guys longer than a year – who *hadn't* turned into giant metal beasts – whom she would have just run the other way from entirely, if even a small portion of tonight's events had occurred in her presence.

Weirdly, an incredible sense of peace washed over her as she thought these things, so when Henry very tentatively knocked on her door, she said "Come in" with more tenderness and genuine caring than she would've thought possible.

Henry opened the door slowly and just stood there for a moment, silent, unsure what to say. Then he spoke, quietly: "It's done."

"OK," she said.

"For what it's worth, it was horrendously awful, and I'd never do it again, no matter the reason."

"You did what you had to do, Henry. I understand that."

Henry just looked at the ground. "I'm not sure that's true, but I did what I did, and it's done, so the only thing left to do was deal with it. And I did. Now I just want to get out of here. Figure out what's going on, why Palermo wants to kill me. And get you someplace safe. You didn't ask for any of this."

"But I did, Henry, I did." Faye got off the bed, walked toward him. "I helped you get to where you are now, so we're in this together, OK? As awful and confusing as it all is, it's you and me." She reached up and touched his face.

"And Milo."

"Yes," Faye said, smiled. "And Milo."

"And Adelina," Henry added after a moment.

"And maybe more people we can't see, who the fuck knows?"

They both laughed a little. Henry moved forward to hug Faye. She let him. He embraced her as softly as he could, then stepped back again.

When they returned to the living room, Milo said, "Alright, I figure we have till tomorrow morning before we'll need to leave here. The hospital will be wondering where in fuck Steve went, but they – and subsequently the cops – will have no reason to start looking here, so that'll give us a bit of breathing room. That said, no reason to hang around till they start piecing it together. We should vamoose ASAP."

"That's great, Milo," Henry said, "but where are we supposed to go? And how do we get *anywhere* without being noticed? Adelina said we're being watched by Palermo's men, right? And even if we weren't, I'm kind of gaining on eight feet tall and made nearly *entirely of metal*. Bit of a point of interest there, you know?"

"Let's just get a couple of hours sleep, then decide, OK?" Faye said. "I'm running on empty, and we should be thinking as clearly as possible when we decide our next step."

Milo and Henry exchanged glances. Until Faye said it, neither of them had really thought about how tired they were. Henry was physically beat, and Milo was emotionally tired, since physical concerns were no longer at the top of his list – though maybe they would start to be again, since he was feeling somewhat fleshy now.

Faye took Henry's silence as agreement. "Alright,

so corporeal people get the bedroom; incorporeal people have to sort themselves out. The living room is fine, if such things matter to ghosts."

"I'm not a–"

"I know, Milo," Henry said. "We just don't know what else to call you, OK?"

Milo frowned. "Maybe one day I'll be a *real* boy."

Henry laughed.

"No way I'm fitting on a bed anymore, even if you'd allow me in," Henry said, "so I'm good on the bedroom floor... Actually, I don't even need to take up your space, if you're not comfortable with it, Faye. I'm fine to go out on the living room floor."

"No," she said, quicker on the heels of his words than she wanted. "No, I mean – I want you to stay in here. With me. OK?"

Henry nodded. "We'll set the alarm for three hours from now."

"And I'll call in sick to the hospital when we're up again."

"See you guys in a few hours, then," Milo said, and hovered out the door.

When he got out to the living room, Adelina was gone.

"Really? Again?" he said to the empty room.

THIRTEEN

All around Adelina, energy swirled. She was aware of no sensation other than a strange kind of sight, but even that gave her no clue as to her whereabouts.

Although she had no way of knowing it, in those instances when she disappeared from the world she knew, Adelina reappeared here, in this near-colorless space. She floated here, in this place where time did not seem to exist. Occasionally, she would see what looked like a flash of lightning, but not much else. It seemed to her that her surroundings were constantly in flux. And though she did not feel it as a sensation, per se, she felt somewhere deep inside that she was more alone than she could ever have thought possible. Wherever she was, she was the only person who had ever been there, the only person that *would* ever be there. Her loneliness carved a channel through her psyche that got deeper every time she returned.

Warring with these emotions, however, was the supreme sense of calm she sometimes felt. When she'd first come here, immediately following her ascension, she'd felt this same overwhelming calm.

She did not know how long she floated here back then, but when she returned to her world it was with a purpose. She had appeared to Milo, tried to impart to him information received in this strange place. Information she had no recollection of receiving in any traditional way her mind could interpret, but there nonetheless.

And what she knew was incredibly important.

What she knew would change everything.

While she hovered in this strange place now, her mind turned again to Milo, who was apparently Henry's ghost familiar. Adelina had had a ghost familiar, too, right after she died, but she couldn't remember who it was. Was it one of her close friends, like Milo was to Henry, or was it someone she didn't know? She felt like she'd learned very important things from her familiar, but most – if not all – of it seemed drained from her mind.

She felt like her name started with an *M*. Marney? Mabel? Marissa? Maureen? Maura? ... Then it popped into her head: *Marla*. That was it. A little girl.

Adelina had no idea where she'd come from, but as soon as she'd died, this little girl, this *comfortable* companion was very near her. But she had eventually left her side. Gone somewhere else.

In this formless place, which she had come to call simply the Otherland, memories slipped through her fingers like tiny fish in a stream, but one conversation burbled briefly to the surface now, and she grasped at it, held on tightly, tried to remember...

When Adelina had first arrived here, her brain couldn't conceive of the near-nothingness in which it'd found itself, so it created a fictional construct from a memory of her childhood. Her mind plugged in walls with movie star posters on them, a carpeted floor on which she sat cross-legged, leafing through a celebrity gossip magazine. This was her teenage room, at home with her parents. She'd barely had any lead in her body at this point, had only just started participating in the Runs recently – fourteen being the age everyone had to start. It was quickly discovered that if you didn't start on the night of your fourteenth birthday, your friends and family began to disappear. The learning curve was incredibly fast for this, so not as many people vanished in the early days of the *Inferne Cutis* – about a hundred and fifty years ago – as one might imagine, and not a lot had disappeared since. (There had been one or two people who tried purposely missing Runs so they could get rid of family members they loathed, but whatever external force oversaw the vanishings saw through this tactic, so no one would disappear in those cases.)

Adelina flipped from page to page in her magazine, more details coming into existence as she glanced around the room: a night table; her alarm clock; her fan to help her sleep; the door – at which someone now knocked.

"Come in," she said, even though she didn't want to, had no idea who was going to come into the room.

It was the little girl she would later learn was named Marla.

Marla walked over to where Adelina sat, dropped to the ground, and sat crosslegged in the same position as Adelina.

"Hello," she said, and smiled. "My name's Marla. What's yours?"

"Adelina."

"That's a pretty name."

"So is yours," Adelina said.

Marla looked satisfied. "Thanks. My mom told me my dad named me."

"Where's your mom now?"

Marla's features darkened a bit. "I don't know. I think my dad and she got divorced a long time ago. I never really saw her much."

"Oh, I'm sorry to hear that."

Marla looked away, then down at her hands. "Look, um, I know a lot about where you are. I was shot in the head by your people, but they don't know it. I think they'd be sad if they knew, but I have no way to tell them. Maybe you could let them know?"

Adelina just stared at her, unable to process everything the little girl had said.

"Anyway," Marla continued, "I know a lot about where you are because I used to be here, too. The room was different – *looked* different, at least – but I know this was the same place."

Just then, the movie posters on the wall shimmered, seemed to phase in and out of substantiation. One of them vanished, popping right out of existence as Adelina watched. It was replaced by a sort of hazy blackness shot through with a pulsing glitter, like the edge of a star.

"So where am I?" Adelina asked.

"I don't know what it's called, but it's a different

universe from the one you came from, the one you lived in. The one we both lived in."

A deep sadness came over Marla, then – deeper than her age would seem to allow.

"And where are you, then? If you're not here, and you're not alive in our old world, where did you go?"

"I moved on to a different universe – different even from this one. There are so many universes, I can't keep track. In the one I'm visiting you from right now, I see all other universes laid out in front of me. Sort of –" Marla struggled to explain using her child's vocabulary "– like, stacked on top of one another, but still so that I can see them all at once... I know that's hard to imagine, to picture in your head, but if you went there, you'd know what I meant."

Adelina just nodded, waited for whatever Marla might say next. The dreamlike quality of the experience was morphing into something that felt more realistic, and it scared Adelina. It was better thinking that it was all just some strange hallucination.

"I need to leave soon. I shouldn't be here," Marla said. "They don't know I found my way back here, and when they find out, they're going to be mad. What I wanted to tell you – what you need to know, even though I don't think there's anything you can do about it – is that this universe I'm in... well, we create gods."

More things shifted, disappeared in Adelina's room. Everything was becoming more and more insubstantial. Lightning forked somewhere far off in the distance. Adelina saw it through the holes created by the vanishing walls, ceiling, floor.

"We create gods, Adelina, and we let them do whatever they like."

Marla began to cry.

FOURTEEN

Krebosche froze.

He desperately wanted to move – every muscle in his body screamed at him to do so, to get up and run like hell – but he couldn't. He just lay on his belly in the snow and shivered.

Gun's in my waistband. Knife's in my boot. No way I'll get to either before he shoots me.

Edward Palermo stood a couple of feet back from Krebosche. Gun trained on his head. "Let's assume for argument's sake," he said, "that you're looking for me. Well, here I am. What can I do for you?"

Krebosche said nothing, just stared ahead, eyes big and round in his head.

"Have we met?" Palermo asked. "I don't believe I've had the honor."

Silence still.

"You don't happen to be involved with that man who was here earlier, do you? Duncan, I think his name was. He didn't meet a very pleasant end."

Snow and breathing.

"Shall I just shoot you where you lay, then? Clearly you're retarded or someone has cut out your tongue.

In either scenario, you're of no use to me, and you're trespassing, so–"

"How did you…" Krebosche said, at last finding speech.

"How did I what?"

"How did you know–"

"That you were here? My men have binoculars and, unlike you, they aren't retarded. They located you bumbling around out here, playing – very poorly – at being some kind of sleuth."

"Can I stand up?"

"Slowly, yes. And with your hands clear of your body."

Krebosche pushed himself off the ground, got his knees under him, stood, arms away from his sides. His heart thumped slower now, his breathing becoming steadier.

Calm down, just calm down.

"I'm going to assume," Palermo said, "that you'll've come armed with something to harm me. What did you bring? Oh, and don't show me, just tell me first."

Krebosche thought about what to say. Should he tell him about the gun *and* the knife, or just one of them, leave himself a last-ditch option?

"Gun," he said.

"That's all?"

Krebosche nodded.

"Now, show me where, but don't move your arms."

Krebosche turned around slowly, feet crunching snow. The gun was visible in his waistband.

"Lovely. Stand very, very still as I remove it. OK?"

Krebosche nodded. Palermo moved forward, gun

trained on the back of Krebosche's head. He snatched the gun out of the waistband and stepped back quickly, popped it into his own waistband.

"One more chance: any more weapons? Be honest now."

Krebosche decided to stick to his deceit. The way Palermo was talking to him – the condescending snideness – could work for him. *He thinks I'm a fool, a retard. He thinks he can fuck with me. If I can just get one moment where he's unguarded…*

"Nothing," he said. "That's it."

"Grand. Now tell me what you're doing here. You were with the other man, Duncan, yes? In it together, were you? Come to expose our secret society?"

Krebosche said nothing.

"Do you think you're the first to try?"

Krebosche wanted to tell him he'd been tracking him for nearly a year, that he wasn't just some shitty reporter or something, sniffing around for a lead, that his little society was responsible for his sister's death, and also that – in a crazy twist of fate he still found hard to believe whenever his mind would turn to the fact – Krebosche had been *dating his fucking daughter*. And that he knew Palermo had killed her. But he held it in. Tipping his hand now would be stupid. He needed to take advantage of his anonymity.

"I don't know much at all," Krebosche said. "Duncan just said if I hadn't heard from him by a certain time, I was to come after him. Get him out."

Palermo squinted, cocked his head a little. Said nothing.

Sell it. Come on, sell it, Krebosche thought. Then,

eyes down, his voice dropping an octave in what he hoped sounded like shame, he added: "He said we'd be famous."

Palermo smirked. "Famous."

Krebosche raised his eyes again, met Palermo's. He knew the key to selling a line was to not overplay it. No hangdog expressions when shame has been offered up. Definitely no tears. And don't talk too much. The less you say, the more believable the lie is. Easier to keep track of what you've said that way, too.

"So what do you suppose I'm to do with you, Mr Famous? I can't just let you go, can I."

"Why not? Won't I just forget everything in a couple of hours? And who would believe me, anyway? Whatever weird mind scrub effect protects you works on me, too." He wanted to keep Palermo talking. "How does it work, anyway? Some kinda force field? Some Rasputin-esque shit? Divine intervention?" He dropped his arms a little during the last sentence to test Palermo's attention. Palermo immediately caught on, motioned to him with the gun to get his arms back up.

"No force field. No Rasputin shit. No God. As far as we know."

"Then what?"

"Nothing that would make the slightest bit of sense to you."

Nothing that makes the slightest bit of sense to me, either, Palermo thought, but would never say.

Krebosche blinked. "Try me."

"Enough of this," Palermo said, a darkness crossing his features. Krebosche knew he'd lost him – and probably his last chance of survival. "Enough of this Bond-villain explaining-all-my-motives drivel. Hands on your head. Start walking."

Palermo motioned again with his gun, this time to turn around and walk in the direction of the caboose and the warehouse.

Or wherever he's decided to shoot me in the face, Krebosche thought, but did as he was instructed. As he turned, his peripheral vision caught something on the roof of the warehouse: a quick gleam of light from a pair of binoculars. *So there you are, you fucker. One of you, anyway.*

The moon hung low in the sky. It looked like a true blue moon. A rarity. *One more shot at random distraction*, Krebosche thought. *If this doesn't work, I'll have to tell him who I am. What I* really *know. Hope it's enough to throw him off, give me a shot at the boot knife.*

"When I was a kid," he said, as he marched through the thickening snow, "I used to live for nights like this. Full moon, big and fat, just hanging up there in the sky like–"

"Shut your mouth, or I'll kill you right here, Mr Famous. Mr *Idiot*." Something was boiling up inside Palermo. Some nameless anger that he was finding hard to control. It had started creeping up his back the moment Krebosche had brought up the "mind scrub" thing. Palermo himself had no idea what caused it, nor did anyone else, as far as he knew. It was certainly something he and his kind welcomed, but his failure to understand *why* it happened was something that gnawed away at him. To him, something about it felt *off*. Like there were reasons beyond his fathoming for the *Inferne Cutis*'s existence – some purpose beyond his capability to understand. But that wasn't entirely it; he felt, too, that there was a kind of manipulation at work. Some sort of–

Krebosche sensed the crack in Palermo's attention as finely as if he'd been observing him during direct, face-on contact. He took one quick glance at the position of the man with binoculars on the roof, then made his move: he feinted left, then dipped immediately right and low, came up quickly with the boot knife. Palermo got a shot off, but it went wide. The next second, Krebosche – knowing his only hope at not getting pegged by the guy on the rooftop, and anyone else with eyes on them, was to make sure he had no clear shot – lunged forward and tackled Palermo, taking him out at the legs. They went down together in a heap, Palermo losing his grip on the gun in the struggle. They rolled a few times, then Krebosche maneuvered himself on top of Palermo – just long enough to drive the knife into Palermo's thigh. Not enough to hobble him (he knew if he had any shot at getting out of this, Palermo would need to be able to walk), but enough to hurt like a motherfucker. Blood erupted. Palermo screamed.

"Tell them to stand down!" Krebosche barked into Palermo's face, then quickly slipped underneath and to the right of Palermo, so as to make a clean shot still impossible – or at the very least incredibly risky. He wrapped a hand around Palermo's throat. "Fucking tell them, or I cut your head off right here and now!"

The thought then occurred to Krebosche that

Palermo's men could just open up on the both of them without fear of killing Palermo – the bullets would just add to whatever was already inside Palermo, but Krebosche would be riddled with them, and would die instantly. But what else could he do? This was the situation he found himself in, and if they opened up and this was the end, then that's the outcome. He had gone for the knife in his boot instead of the gun in Palermo's waistband because Palermo was lying on his back. The gun would certainly have made him feel more secure, but he'd foolishly envisioned an uneventful lead-up to his planned murder – not *this* ridiculous sideshow.

Now all Krebosche could do was hope the threat of the knife was enough.

"Hold your fire!" Palermo yelled. He repeated it twice more to make sure he was heard.

Krebosche quickly reached over and down and pulled the knife out of Palermo's leg, moved it up to press against his neck. Palermo screamed again, tried to kick out once. Krebosche pressed the knife against Palermo's throat until it drew blood. "Do that again. Go ahead, you shiteating fuck. Do it."

Krebosche's voice was thick with hate. Palermo felt spittle fleck his ears as Krebosche spat the words out. In that moment, Palermo recognized that this wasn't just some jumped-up reporter, too stupid to know better than to come sniffing around his warehouse – or anyone even close to that; there was genuine and intense loathing in Krebosche's voice. Palermo didn't know why yet, but he knew he –

specifically – was Krebosche's target.

"Who are you?" Palermo said, his voice just edging into territory that would betray fear. He tried to control it, tamp it down. "What do you think I did to you?"

"I won't tell you either of those things here, but I'll tell you soon. I want you to know. Before I kill you, I want you to know."

Palermo could think of nothing to say that would help his situation, so he said nothing at all. Just waited for whatever came next.

In the darkness, Krebosche saw shapes moving about – Palermo's men advancing on their position, no doubt.

"Not much time," Krebosche said quietly in Palermo's ear. "You're going to tell your men to keep back, then you're going to request a vehicle be driven out here and parked very close to us. The headlights are by no means to be trained on us, or anywhere near our position. If I see a weapon of any kind on the driver, I'll end you. Do it."

Palermo yelled out the instructions. Made it particularly clear that the driver was to be unarmed. A couple of minutes later, headlights slashed the darkness, and a small jeep bounced its way toward them. The storm was picking up, and the snow would make it even more difficult for Palermo's men to get a bead on Krebosche.

The jeep slowed to a stop near where they lay in the snow. The driver put it into gear, left the engine running, then very slowly got out and stood where Krebosche and Palermo could see him.

"Turn around," Krebosche said. "No sudden movements."

The man spun around once, as carefully as he could. Krebosche saw no obvious weapons.

"Now fuck off and don't look back. Turn your head around even once, I open him up."

The man nodded, immediately started walking away from the jeep, back in the direction of the warehouse.

"Now you and I are going to stand up very slowly and very delicately," Krebosche said to Palermo. "My cheek will remain pressed to the back of your head the entire fucking time. And you don't want to go for the gun in your waistband. Believe me. Do you understand?"

Palermo nodded.

"Right. Stand up at the same time as me. Take my lead."

Both men moved in unison to achieve a standing position. Krebosche waited for the back of his head to open up. It didn't, and within moments he was shuffling them toward the open driver's door of the jeep.

"Before we get in, and you get any bright ideas about elbowing me in the gut and making a run for it – or something equally ridiculous – I have a tidbit of information you'll be interested in, and I'll tell you much more about it once we're away from here."

"Oh, yes? And what's that?"

"It's about your daughter."

Palermo stiffened, then relaxed ever so slightly. "So

what? You know I have a daughter."

"I know you *had* a daughter, but now she's gone. Probably dead. And probably you killed her."

"That doesn't–"

"Her name was Adelina. Oh, and my sister, too, died because of you. I watched her die in front of me, the result of one of your Runs, or whatever the hell you call them. Stray bullet. Her name was Marla Krebosche."

And then Krebosche described Adelina's physical appearance, right down to the two moles – one big, one smaller – near the top of her right thigh: "Like a planet and its moon," he said. Which was what Palermo had said to his daughter when she'd asked about the birthmarks as a child.

Palermo said nothing, realized this had to be the Bill Krebosche that shithead Duncan had mentioned, nodded when Krebosche asked him if he was going to sit still in the jeep.

"I thought you might."

They got in. One arm still around Palermo's neck, the knife digging in painfully where it had already broken skin, Krebosche closed the door. He put his free hand on the steering wheel, gunned the gas.

Blue light from the moon overhead immediately filled the tracks left behind.

Through his binoculars on the warehouse rooftop, Marcton watched the taillights flicker as they receded, obscured by yet more falling snow. Below him at ground level, Cleve stood breathing heavily. When he'd driven the jeep over, he'd wanted very badly to smash the weedy little fuck's face with his boot, but he couldn't risk it. The guy was clearly a nut – but exactly how dangerous a nut, they didn't know. He may well have slit Palermo's throat if Cleve had made a move – not life-ending, of course, but if the guy knew that, too, maybe he'd just keep sawing, which *would* be life-ending. Palermo looked genuinely concerned for his own well-being, which was unusual. Cleve wasn't used to seeing Palermo so vulnerable, and it unnerved him.

Marcton and two others had had rifles trained on the kidnapper and Palermo, but no clear shot had presented itself.

Now the instant the taillights had fully receded and Marcton was sure the kidnapper could no longer see them in his rear view, he yelled down to Cleve, "You, me, and two others. We're going after them. We'll use the Hummer. Get it running; I'll be down in a sec!"

Cleve nodded, said, "Got it," and radioed two of his most trusted colleagues, told them to come to the Hummer ASAP.

When all four men were in the Hummer, Marcton in the driver's seat, they tore off after Palermo and his kidnapper.

"Any idea who that was?" Marcton asked.

"None," Cleve said. The other two shook their heads.

"And no idea where he'll be taking Palermo, either, right?"

Everyone nodded.

"Fucking great."

•••

A few blocks away, Krebosche pulled the jeep over to the side of the road, cut its lights. His car was where he'd left it, unchanged, but piling up with snow.

He jabbed the tip of the knife into Palermo's leg wound – not deep, but enough to wrench another scream from him. While Palermo writhed in pain on the seat, Krebosche grabbed his gun back from Palermo's waistband, put it in his own, quickly jumped out of the jeep, and trained the knife on Palermo.

"Your fuckhead buddies will be coming soon, no doubt. They're a fairly tight little unit, so I don't doubt they'll find us in short order. Problem is, we won't be here. And we won't be in that jeep anymore. Quit your fucking squirming and get in the car."

When he'd recovered enough to speak, Palermo glared at Krebosche, was about to let loose a string of curses and threats – a rarity for him – but then he thought of something. Something that might buy him some time.

"Wherever you'd planned to take me, Krebosche, I have a better place to go. Somewhere much more interesting."

"Oh, yeah, where's that?" Krebosche looked over his shoulder for any sign of lights, listened hard for engine noises.

"I know where the guy who killed Adelina is. I know exactly where he lives. I've got men watching his place as we speak. We could go there." Palermo raised his hands to show he meant no threat, maneuvered himself to the edge of the jeep's seat, let his weight carry him off the edge as gently as he could. Grimaced as his feet touched the ground. Used the open door for support. "Right now. We could go there. If I'm lying, you can do whatever you want to me."

"Motherfucker, I can do whatever I want to you right *now*."

Palermo nodded, tried to catch his breath. "So it would seem."

"Besides, I already know who killed Adelina: you did. I've known it for nearly a year."

Palermo's mind scrambled to put the pieces together. *Nearly a year? Why don't I know who this guy is?* No time for that now; he needed to convince him it was in his best interest not to take him wherever he had planned. At least if Palermo could get him to an address he knew, he'd have a shot at his guys being able to help him. Now that the knife was away from his neck he didn't particularly need his men to save him – even with his leg injured, he was fairly certain he could overpower Krebosche – but his curiosity was piqued, and he wanted to know who this guy was, what he knew about Adelina, how he'd been able to retain all this information for nearly a full year. "You *think* you know all sorts of things, clearly," Palermo said. "But I've already planted a seed of doubt, haven't I? What if I'm not lying? Don't you want the guy who actually pulled the trigger, not just the person you *think* ordered it?"

"Stall tactics, and I don't give a fuck, Palermo. Get your ass in the car. You can lie to me all you want in there. You can lie until I slice your head off. Oh, and by the way, even if you wrestle the knife from me, my gun's loaded with hollow points, so you'll want to think twice. I know your body eats normal bullets, but a well-placed hollow point might just take your head clean off."

"Why not just kill me now, then? Why are you waiting?"

"I want you to know who I am, and why you're dying," Krebosche said. "Once you know that, really understand it, I'll take your fucking head. Or shoot it off your shoulders. Whatever."

Palermo shuffled through the ankle-deep snow toward the car, Krebosche within arm's reach the whole time. As he passed by the back window, Krebosche swept snow off it.

Krebosche was stronger than Palermo had anticipated when he'd found him on the ground outside the warehouse. He probably *could* overpower him, but he was younger and quick. And very, very angry.

When Palermo reached the passenger side, Krebosche put the gun under his chin, said, "Get in slowly, dickbag. Slide over to the driver's side."

Palermo grunted and got in the passenger side, slid behind the wheel. Krebosche kept the gun trained on him as he sat down himself, shut the door. Snow fell in a heap from the window.

Krebosche put the keys in the ignition, said, "Start it. Drive."

"Where to?"

"Just drive, idiot. I'll direct you as we go."

Palermo turned the key, the engine flared to life.

"Windshield," Krebosche said.

Palermo activated the windshield wipers. Snow fell to either side of the blades.

"Keep the lights off."

Palermo put the car into gear, drifted away from the curb. "Left or right," he asked as they approached the first intersection.

"Left. *Away* from your warehouse. And don't indicate."

Palermo came to a complete halt at the stop sign, turned slowly, carefully.

"A little faster would be nice."

"Just trying to make sure we arrive alive."

"Not a real concern for you right now, OK?"

Palermo shut up.

They drove on in silence for a couple of minutes, Krebosche directing Palermo at intersections, keeping an eye on the mirrors for lights. Then Palermo said: "Can I have something to stop my leg bleeding?"

Krebosche turned to him, a look of incredulity on his face. "Why would I care if you bled to death?"

Palermo sighed, and they drove on in silence.

The weather combined with the hour made it so there was barely anyone out at all, so spotting a tail would be fairly easy. Losing one on these roads, however, would be a different story.

Krebosche was trying desperately not to let doubts niggle at him, but Palermo's words had, indeed, taken root. What if Palermo *did* know where the trigger man was? Krebosche hadn't actually *seen* him kill her – and one other man, and a woman, *were* in the house he'd followed them to. But did it matter? Palermo clearly had something to do with his daughter's death, was obviously someone – if not the *main* someone – to blame for it. Wasn't that enough? Would killing the actual murderer really make that much of a difference? As for his sister, he knew he'd never find her killer, since the person whose bullet ricocheted down that alleyway probably didn't even know what they'd done.

But did it truly matter who, specifically, was responsible for what happened to Adelina? With each street that went by, each corner turned, each streetlamp flickering by overhead, and the moon bathing him in its weird blue light through the car window, Krebosche knew with a growing certainty that yes, it *did* matter. It mattered very much.

They crossed the tracks, went deeper into the suburbs until Krebosche gave Palermo one final instruction: "Left up here, then turn into the first parking lot on your right. Home sweet home."

The tires crunched snow as Palermo turned the car into the parking lot. It wasn't really Krebosche's home, but Palermo didn't need to know that.

"Very back spot, in the shadow of that big-ass tree. Then kill the engine."

Palermo steered the car into the spot, cut the engine, turned his head to look at Krebosche, said, "I'm bleeding onto your lovely seat covers here. Just so you know."

"Duly noted."

Back at the abandoned jeep, headlights cut dual cones through the snow and darkness. Another vehicle – this one a black Hummer – crawled close to the jeep, sidling up to it. Cleve's arm was out the window, holding a handgun the size of his head, trained on the jeep.

"Any movement?" Marcton asked from the driver's side.

"Nothing. I think it's been ditched."

As they pulled parallel, Marcton saw that this was the case. "Fuck."

"Agreed. What now?" Cleve said, pulled his arm inside. "Does he have his cell on him?"

Marcton turned. "Probably. Why, you wanna text him: 'where r u?' Christ, Cleve, give it some thought."

Cleve looked down at his lap. "No tracking device in his phone?"

"No. No tracking device, dummy. And no, we can't do some clever shit with the GPS."

"Well, since he's got his phone still, if he can get away, he can at least try to call one of us, right?"

"Sure."

"So maybe we just go back to the warehouse and wait."

"No, Cleve, we do not just go back to the warehouse and wait."

"You know, I'm not just some fucking idiot you can talk down to like this."

Marcton grinned. "You kind of are, Cleve. Sort of. Maybe a little bit, you know?" He held up his thumb and index finger, moved them very close together. "Just this much."

Cleve knew Marcton was just winding him up. His smile showed it, and it helped cut the tension. "Seriously, though, why not just wait? What can we do out here? The weather's getting shittier by the second, and we'll be useless if we get stuck."

"In a Hummer," Marcton said. The guys in the back chuckled.

"Alright, fine, fuck you all. Do what you want." Cleve settled into a sulk. "Just trying to do what's best."

"What's best is to keep looking for Palermo. Let's just think about this for a minute. Now, where would he go, if he had any choice in the matter? Would he try to stall the guy? Yes. Alright, so what's a good stall tactic? What's a good way to buy time? Better yet," Marcton said, snapping his fingers as an idea occurred to him. "Where does he *know* we've got guys?"

Cleve just stared at him.

"The nurse's place," Marcton said. "That's the only other operation going on right now besides the regular Runs – speaking of which, if we're still on lockdown at the warehouses, will there even *be* one tonight? And if not… well, shit, let's not even think about that. Let's make sure we get this sorted so that there *can* be one. Anyway, Palermo would try to get him to the nurse's place. He'd be a fool not to."

"So, we let our guys there know to watch out for him, yeah?" Cleve said, finally catching on.

"Yes, we do, Cleve. Yes, we do. You take care of that; I'll drive." He turned in his seat. "You ladies in the back just keep holding hands. We got this."

"Adelina was my girlfriend."

Palermo met Krebosche's eyes and knew he wasn't lying.

"For a little over two years. I gather she didn't tell you."

Once Palermo had stopped his mind from flying off in several thousand directions at once, he said, "Not one word."

"Thought not. And I know you're her father."

A nod. Eyes cast down. Palermo applied pressure to his wound. A bit of blood burbled up between his fingers.

"She said you wouldn't want her with anyone but 'her own kind.'"

"True."

"And what *kind*, exactly, is that?"

Palermo looked confused. "You don't know about us?"

"I know you're up to some shifty shit, but right now I'm lucky I'm remembering why I'm even in this car with you. Five minutes away from you and we both know it'd start to haze over."

"Interesting. I thought you knew more than that. Well, good, then. I'm not telling you anything else. You're going to kill me, anyway. Why would I tell you anything else about us?"

"How about because I loved – still love – Adelina?"

Krebosche was playing dumb to see what information Palermo might give up. He knew if Palermo thought Krebosche knew all about them, he might not give any him further info.

A car went by slowly on the street, headlights cutting the shadows back. Palermo and Krebosche both tensed up. The yellow shafts carved deeper into the darkness. Moving on. Gone.

"So did I. And…" Palermo struggled with whether to tell him anything else, decided that if he *had* loved

Adelina, then he deserved to know at least this – some truth mixed in with a lie: "I didn't kill her. No one did. She just... ascended. Or something akin to that. We don't know what to call it, exactly. People have various words for it. It's only happened once."

Palermo had already tipped one of the cards in his hand – a damn big one, at that. He wasn't about to tip them all by telling Krebosche about Henry Kyllo.

"But I saw you and another man go into a house. I followed you there. You went in, *with* Adelina. A while later, after a woman showed up, you left that house – *without* Adelina – and a good portion of the house was destroyed by something – something that demolished it from the *inside*. And I never saw or heard from Adelina again."

"When we went into that house, it was to witness her transformation."

"Into what?"

"We didn't know."

"So what happened?"

"We still don't know. She just –" he motioned upward with his hands "– disappeared."

More lies. "How? Like in a fucking magic show? What destroyed most of the house? And what's this 'ascension' horseshit? What the hell are you talking about?" Krebosche's anger rose quickly in his chest. "You expect me to believe this?"

With Krebosche's outburst came a sudden wave of lightheadedness in Palermo. He was losing blood. Not fast, but fast enough that it needed to be stopped very soon, or he'd pass out.

"Seriously, can I get some sort of tourniquet on this?

If we're going to sit and chat, I need to be conscious."

"Fine, shit." Krebosche rooted around behind Palermo's seat for a couple of seconds, sure to keep an eye on him, then came up with a camera with a strap. "Use the strap."

A minute later, Palermo had the camera strap wrapped around his leg. The bleeding stopped.

"So this person you were going to bring me to – the guy who you said killed Adelina. Obviously a trap of some kind. What's there? What kind of ambush would I have been walking into?"

"Not a big one. Just two of my men stationed there, watching an apartment I asked them to keep an eye on."

"Well, clearly we're not going there now."

"Clearly."

Another car drove by, didn't turn in.

"You know," Palermo said, deciding on a different tack, realizing that trying to convince Krebosche to go somewhere – anywhere – of his choosing would never work. "I'm something of a weather tracker. All weather means something, I think. It's a harbinger of things to come. If you study it closely enough, I think you can tell what might be coming down the road for you."

Krebosche just looked at him.

"I keep notebooks," Palermo added.

"Good for you."

"Yes, actually, it is, because I think this storm means something. We've never had one like it – not in the entire time I've been keeping track, which is to say nearly my whole life."

"Fine, I'll bite. What do you think it means?"

"Damned if I know."

That hung in the air for a moment, then Krebosche said, "Alright, then. Good to know."

"I'm just saying, maybe our meeting wasn't a coincidence. Maybe we were supposed to meet like this. Maybe there's a reason for it."

"Yeah, the reason was for me to kill you." *But now*… Krebosche thought. He closed his eyes, inhaled and exhaled slowly, rubbed his head with the heel of the hand holding the gun. "But now I don't know. It's fucked. I had everything all planned out, but…" He shook his head as if trying to put his thoughts back in their proper order.

"But you're not a killer."

Krebosche looked up. "Really. Now, how do you know that?"

"You'd have done it by now. You'd have done it the moment we were safely away from the warehouse. You'd have had me park somewhere, told me who you were, cut my head off or shot me to death, left my body in the jeep to rot. But you didn't. And I don't think you will now. You don't have it in you. As much as you wish you did. It's just not there. I know what a killer looks like, and you're simply not it."

In truth, Palermo knew no such thing. But he felt there was enough truth in what he said that he had a shot at this panning out in his favor.

"I mean, you gave me a tourniquet for the leg *you* stabbed. Twice." Palermo allowed himself a smile, hoped his instincts were serving him well, and that his attempt at humor wouldn't backfire.

Krebosche seemed to have softened at Palermo's words. His scowl less severe, shoulders less tense. The gun, however, continued to be held tight in Krebosche's hand, so any sudden movements could still end very poorly for Palermo.

Krebosche thought things through, analyzing them from every angle. *Was* he a killer? Had all this preparation been for nothing? Could he let it all go so easily, just let Palermo get out of the car, walk away?

Palermo watched his face intently. He was sure he'd convinced him. Perhaps *tricked* Krebosche out of killing him. He wondered how far he could push it. When – or even *if* – he should ask to be released.

But then something snapped into Krebosche's features – a hardness that was not there before. As suddenly as a light being switched on. And Palermo had seen *this* look before. Was reasonably sure he'd had the very same look when he'd hammered Carl Duncan to death in the warehouse.

"No," Krebosche said, raising the gun to Palermo's head, pressing it hard against his skull. "I'm going to do this. Because you deserve it. Whether your stories are true or not. Adelina is fucking gone. Along with my sister. And now so are you. I doubt even you can survive a bullet at this range."

"Please, wait!" Palermo said in a rush, ashamed of his fear, but unable to control it. His mind scrambled for anything at all he could say to save his life. He realized he had only one card left to play. "I lied, OK, I lied! *Two* of our number have ascended. Henry Kyllo is the second person. He knows where Adelina is, and I swear I can take you *right to him*. I don't know why, but he didn't disappear like she did. And he knows. He knows where she is."

"More bullshit just to save your life. Forget it. You're done."

But again, nagging doubts in Krebosche's mind... Five seconds went by – the longest in Palermo's life. His eyes were closed tight, waiting for the gun to erupt.

Then the gun was removed from his head, but still hovered close. He opened his eyes, looked at Krebosche, sweat beads forming and rolling down his forehead.

His voice low and dangerous, Krebosche said slowly, "Why didn't you mention this Kyllo guy before?"

"I was trying to keep as much from you as possible. You'd've done the same in my position."

Krebosche thought about it. His head spun. He didn't know what to think anymore. But the thought that wouldn't leave his head was: *What if she isn't dead? What if I really can see her again?*

Palermo saw the wheels turning in Krebosche's head, thought maybe this final card was worth playing after all. *Not quite my final card, actually*, he thought. *Krebosche has no idea what Kyllo is, what he's become. Neither do I, for that matter. Not really. But whatever it is, it'll buy me time. And I'll be among friends.*

"Alright," Krebosche said. "We'll go see this Kyllo guy. But on the way, you're going to explain what exactly you mean by 'ascension.' And if this is part of that trap I was gonna be walking into – the one where you were gonna take me to Adelina's 'real' killer – you'd better rethink that. I see more than one person when we arrive–"

"I get it. I'm dead."

"Yeah, you're fucking dead."

"I'll have to get a message to my guys, tell them to go back to the warehouse. I'll say the place they're sitting on doesn't need watching anymore."

"Do it."

"I'll need my cellphone to send the text." Palermo held his hands away from his body. "Right side pocket in my coat."

Krebosche fished inside the pocket, drew out the phone. "I'll do it. Tell me who to–"

That's when Palermo went for the gun.

But, as Palermo had thought earlier, Krebosche was stronger than he looked, and even the element of surprise wasn't enough for the older man to overpower him. Krebosche's right hand chopped hard at Palermo's left arm. The momentary grip he'd had on Krebosche fell away, and the gun was immediately back against his head.

"Do *not* try that again." Krebosche fixed Palermo with a look so hard, he thought he was just going to blow his head off, anyway, warning be damned.

"Marcton," Palermo finally said once his breathing had calmed.

"What?"

"That's who you call. Marcton."

Krebosche took a moment, straightened the sleeves on his coat, then tapped at the phone's screen. "Found him. What do I say? And don't think I'm stupid. I'll know a code word if I hear it."

"Just say, 'Get off apartment. Go back to warehouse.'

That ought to do it."

Krebosche scrolled through some of Palermo's previous texts to Marcton, checking to see if the voice matched. If he wasn't normally so brief, that in itself might be a code, a previously agreed-upon sign of trouble. But brevity seemed to be Palermo's texting style. Krebosche was satisfied that it checked out. He typed the message with one hand, keeping an eye on Palermo the whole time. Clicked Send.

"I'll just hang on to this, shall I?" Krebosche said. "One less thing for you to think about. Now, start the car. Let's go."

Palermo turned the key, pulled out once again into the storm.

In the Hummer, Marcton's cell phone pinged.

"Check that for me, would ya, Cleve? Probably important."

Cleve reached for Marcton's phone where it sat on the dash. "Holy good fuck," he said.

"What? Who's it from?"

"Palermo."

"Christ. Read it."

"It says, 'Get off apartment. Go back to warehouse.'" Cleve looked up from the screen. "Why would he think we're at the apartment? He assigned two other Runners to that."

"Yeah, he did," Marcton said, slowing the Hummer down, pulling it over to the side of the road, popping it into Park. "It doesn't add up. Palermo obviously *knows* who he assigned to the apartment, but he still sent that text."

Cleve handed the phone to Marcton, who read the message himself. He texted back: *Got it*. "We gotta get those Runners off the apartment. Then we have to get there ourselves, but quietly, unseen."

"Quietly. Unseen. In a Hummer," said Cleve.

"Yeah," said Marcton, smirking. "In a Hummer."

"You got those guys' number to call 'em off?"

"Call the warehouse, they'll have it."

"Why don't you have it?"

"I don't know, 'cause I fucking don't, Cleve! Now call the warehouse!"

"Alright, Jesus," Cleve said, dialing. "Just thought you were Palermo's right-hand man and all that." He held the phone to his ear.

"I *am*, Cleve, but he doesn't always–"

Cleve held up a finger in a shushing motion, "It's ringing," he whispered, knowing he was bugging the shit out of Marcton.

But Marcton was in no mood for playing games. Cleve was obviously too stupid to realize how serious the situation was, but Marcton had been a high-ranking member for years longer than Cleve. Cleve was really only in the inner circle because of a good word Marcton had put in for him. Times like this, he regretted doing Cleve the favor.

He reached over, yanking the phone out of Cleve's hand – which Cleve had fully expected. He laughed, and Marcton saw red – visions of smashing his fist into Cleve's big dumb face over and again raced through his mind.

He asked for the apartment's address, then told warehouse dispatch to call off the two guys Palermo'd put there. "On Palermo's direct goddamn say-so," Marcton said, when the dispatcher gave him grief. "Just fucking do it, or it's your head when Palermo gets back." He pressed the End Call button on the phone, handed it back to Cleve, said, "Put the warehouse on my Blocked Call list for now. I don't want them able to call back and argue with me. With no other input – and no other *recourse* for input – they'll do what I asked."

Marcton put the Hummer back into gear, pulled out onto the road, headed again for the nurse's apartment. He glanced in the rearview mirror. "You two redshirts ready for action back there?"

The Runners in the backseat – Bill Tremblay and Melvin Rowe – exchanged confused looks.

"Not big *Star Trek* fans? Well, hopefully it doesn't come to that."

FIFTEEN

One of the Runners assigned to watching Faye's building sat in a beat-up old Omni, binoculars pressed to his face. He was going back and forth between the apartment he was supposed to be watching – second from the top – and a woman undressing on the floor directly above.

"This shit is fucking up our Run, ladygirl. We could be out there tonight with everyone else instead of sitting here with our dicks in our hands. Figuratively speaking."

The other Runner pressed her walkie's talk button from her position around back of the building, where she sat in a similarly beat-up Corolla. "You think there's a Run tonight with all the shit that's been going down? Ridiculous. We're on lockdown, remember? Would be nice if there was, though, so that no one would fucking *disappear*, but I just can't see this shit being resolved tonight. Also, what part of 'radio silence' don't you get, fuckweed? Stop talking."

The radio went dead for a moment, then crackled back to life.

"And quit calling me 'ladygirl.' Last time I tell you."

Fuckweed and ladygirl – old friends who'd grown up together, real names Jim Lamb and Lindsay Kinzett, respectively – had gladly taken the fairly shitty assignment, trying to get into Palermo's good books again after a monumental cockup a few weeks ago. They'd been sent in to clean up after a Run in the southern section of the city, and had left a ton of shell casings – and one severely injured Runner – on the street for any random passerby to find the next morning. It was one thing to rightfully expect that whoever found the guy would just call 911, then immediately begin to forget the experience; it was another entirely to be careless and start taking the effect for granted, essentially inviting enquiry where none was welcome.

They'd both been reamed out, and this was their penance. What neither of them knew was that after this assignment Palermo planned to kill them anyway, so they were the perfect pair to use, since it didn't matter if they saw Kyllo or not. Palermo figured he might as well get one more use out of them.

The most recent fuckup wasn't nearly their first – this had been a long time coming. They'd endangered the *Inferne Cutis* through their combined idiocy (they were trustworthy enough alone, but reverted to teenage behavior when in each other's company) more times than Palermo cared to mention.

The last movement Lamb had seen inside the apartment was a few hours ago when someone appeared to be throwing all kinds of things in all kinds of directions. Plates, cups, and china dolls smashing everywhere. Neither Lamb nor Kinzett knew what to make of it, so they just radioed in the occurrence and waited for instructions. No one at the warehouse knew what to make of it either, so no instructions came – and in the intervening time, Palermo had been kidnapped and taken "fuck knows where," as the Runner in charge at the warehouse had said, so they had a whole new set of problems to contend with on their end, effectively relegating Kinzett and Lamb's babysitting assignment to the bottom of the priority list.

What was on both of their minds, though, was what had happened to the ambulance driver Kinzett had seen enter Faye's apartment. Lamb's sightline into the apartment was decent enough to see what was taking place in a certain section of the living room, where the drapes had been partially opened, but the apartment's front door – and the surrounding area – was completely obscured. So Kinzett had seen him for only a moment as he came into view, but then lost sight of him, and never saw him again.

"Can an ambulance driver just fuck off with an ambulance all day, ladygirl?" Lamb had asked Kinzett.

"No, they'll come looking for him eventually," Kinzett had answered. "Might have to wait till the cops are alerted before we know what's going on in there. For now, we just sit and wait, as ordered. Don't go getting any bright ideas."

"Oh, right, I forgot: you're the smart one; I'm the idiot."

"Nah, we're both idiots, but you have that ridiculous penis, which clouds your judgement, so I get to be the leader."

"Yeah, I'm definitely the dickhead. No argument there."

They'd both laughed, then fallen into a comfortable silence – the kind of silence only old friends drew actual comfort from.

Now, the radio crackled again.

"How long we gotta do radio silence?"

Kinzett sighed. "Radio silence isn't something we 'do,' Lamb; it's something that just *is*, so long as you keep your mouth shut."

They were quiet for another five minutes or so, then Kinzett's cell phone buzzed on the passenger seat, scaring the shit out of her. "This better not be you, Lamb," she mumbled. "*Again.*"

She swiped the green symbol across the screen, held the phone up to her ear. "Kinzett."

"Kinzett, you and Lamb have been called back. Get off the apartment. We need everyone back at the warehouse, anyway. Figure this Palermo thing out."

"Roger that, headed back now."

Kinzett hung up the phone, pressed the button on the walkie. "Let's go back. We've been called off," she said, and started her car's engine.

"What? Why?"

"Dunno, but we're done here. Let's go. You should be happy. You just got through bitching about the assignment, and now you're questioning the reason we don't have to do it anymore? Pick a side, sasquatch."

"Sasquatch? Why you gotta call me that?"

"'Cause you're hairy as hell, that's why. When you sit in the bathtub, I bet it feels like you're sittin' on grass."

They traded a few more insults, then drove away, their headlights slicing through the last bit of snow that would fall that night. The rest of the evening would be clear.

The next morning, though, it would start to snow again.

And dead bodies in and around Faye's building – spines crushed and skulls splintered – would be the first to be touched by the snowflakes.

SIXTEEN

While Henry and Faye slept, Milo hovered around the living room, thinking, wondering where Henry was going to go, where all this was leading, and how it had all become so fucked up in the first place.

Was a simple, clean death really so much to ask for? Just lop my head off, and let me welcome the black.

Two hours into their three-hour nap, Milo was roused from his musings by headlights below. It was nearly 2 a.m., and nothing outside had moved for about an hour. The snow had finally stopped, and now lay in a thick blanket over everything.

He drifted over to the window, saw that a car had pulled into the parking lot. Two men got out. One he didn't recognize, but the other was Edward Palermo. At street level, it would be difficult to see, but looking directly down as Milo was, it was unmistakable: the man he didn't recognize had a gun in Palermo's back and was marching him toward the back entrance of Faye's building.

Milo's eyes widened, and he immediately went for Henry. Drifted through the door, concentrated on engaging with the physical world, putting his hands on Henry's broad shoulders, shaking, shaking. "Henry! Wake up! Palermo's here. Fucking Palermo. We gotta bail, man. Wake up!"

He shook and shook, but Henry wouldn't rouse. Milo concentrated harder, looked around for something to smash. Maybe that would wake him up.

"Fucking Palermo's here, Henry, *get UP!*" Shaking harder still... until finally, Henry cracked his thick metal eyelids. Subconsciously, Milo registered that Henry'd gotten even bigger in the past ninety minutes. *When's he gonna stop fucking growing? Christ.*

"Who's here? Whuh?" Henry mumbled.

"What part of 'fucking Palermo' don't you get, Henry? He's on his way up here right now, and some douchebag has a gun in his back."

Henry shook his head from side to side to clear the cobwebs. He reached an arm out. "Help me up," he said groggily.

Milo gave him a look. "Right 'cause I'm suddenly Superman and can lift small cars on my own."

Henry grunted something under his breath, used the closest wall to gain his feet instead.

"Henry? What's... what's happening?" Faye said blearily from the bed.

"We have to go," Henry said, moving beside her. "Now. Get up." Henry was awake now, the word "Palermo" cutting through the fog in his brain like a knife and kicking his ass into operating with pure efficiency.

"Why? Tell me what's –"

"No time, just get up, let's go." He put one of his hands as delicately as he could around her left arm, pulled gently.

"Shit, you're hurting me, Henry, stop it."

"We need to get out of this apartment *right now*. Palermo is coming up the stairs. He does not want pleasant things for us. We need to go."

"OK, alright," Faye said, rubbing her eyes. "I just need my shoes."

Henry looked around the room quickly. "There," he said and pointed.

Faye moved to the edge of the bed where her shoes were, put them on as quickly as her sleep-deprived mind would allow.

"OK, let's move," Henry said, and headed for the front door.

Marcton parked the conspicuous Hummer four blocks away from Faye's apartment, got out, told Cleve, Bill, and Melvin to keep quiet. "Not one sound except the crunch of snow under your boots – and even that needs to be next to silent."

They were all packing one powerful handgun each and, in addition, Bill and Melvin had sawed-off shotguns hidden under their coats.

"The nurse's apartment is just below the top floor, southwest corner," Marcton said. "Keep your eyes peeled for any movement as we approach."

When no one responded, he was impressed: just the crunching of their boots.

Five minutes before they'd arrived, Palermo had described to Krebosche as best he could what "ascension" meant. Although he neglected to mention that the last time he'd seen Henry Kyllo he was a massive creature being smuggled out of a dumpster and into Faye's building under a blanket. He wasn't entirely sure what he'd seen sticking out under that blanket, but it certainly looked like Henry's legs were made of metal.

Just like Adelina.

What he *did* tell Krebosche – yet more lies – was that Adelina had achieved the highest state she could in their order, and that the gathering at the house was just an ascension ceremony – merely a celebration of her achievement. But then something had gone wrong. As part of the ceremony, words were spoken – what they thought were simply rites of passage passed down in their holy book (they didn't *have* a holy book). And when the words were spoken, the very moment they were out of Palermo's mouth, he'd looked up and she was gone. Vanished.

"So you're a cult leader," Krebosche had said.

"I suppose I am, yes."

"And you brought your daughter up in this voodoo shit?"

"I suppose I did. But it's not voodoo."

"Might as well be. Also, I don't believe for a second that she just vanished. What *I* think is that this Kyllo guy you're taking me to – once he sees I'm not fucking around – is going to tell me what *really* happened."

Palermo had said nothing to that, just let it sit between them in the car. Palermo felt the shifting winds in his bones, and thought they might both be in for a bit of a surprise once they saw Henry Kyllo.

•••

Inside Faye's building, the south elevator moved upward quietly. It dinged softly as it passed each floor.

"Just so you know," Palermo said, "there *will* be two people when the door opens – if the nurse isn't at work, that is. I don't know her exact schedule."

"Understood," Krebosche said.

A few floors passed with neither speaking. Then:

"So you'll do the talking?" Palermo asked.

"Um, yeah," Krebosche said, jammed the gun a little harder into the back of Palermo's neck.

Just as Milo, Henry, and Faye were readying to leave, Adelina appeared in one corner of Faye's living room. Everyone was leaving; that was good. They still had a chance. But they'd waited too long.

Nothing she could do now, but watch the door. Wait to see what happened.

Milo spotted her, said her name, but she ignored him. Just continued staring at the door.

A feeling of intense dread enveloped her.

The elevator doors opened. Palermo and Krebosche stepped out. Krebosche looked up and down the hallway, saw no one. He poked Palermo in the neck to get moving.

"So what are you gonna say?" Palermo said, hoping to unnerve Krebosche, distract him from whatever plan he might have. Depending on what Kyllo had become, distracting him might be a good tactic for helping get the hell out of the way, should things get intense. And, if recent weather was any indicator – and Palermo truly believed it was – an incredibly intense situation was bound to come due sooner or later. His subconscious had felt *something* building for a while now, but when, precisely, the shit would hit the fan, he didn't know. This all just felt like he was on a track of some kind, and there was no way off – and, in all likelihood, no brakes.

"You'll see. Got it *all* worked out. Stay tuned, friend."

Stay tuned, friend? A shiver went up Palermo's back at the words. Krebosche's tone had changed. Something in his voice was different now. Even the choice of words was strange. Not like something Krebosche – what Palermo knew of him, anyway – would say.

Their feet made little to no noise on the gray carpet of the hallway. There was a stillness in the air that Palermo didn't like. Sounds seemed to be muffled. Palermo's desire for flight was suddenly incredibly strong. He had to resist the urge to bolt down the hallway.

They were only about ten feet away from the door now. Sweat popped out on Palermo's forehead. He said, "Maybe this wasn't such a good idea, Krebosche. I've got this very strange feeling. Don't you feel it? Something's… *off.*"

He tried to stop, turn around, but Krebosche jabbed him with the gun, spun him around, said, "Keep walking."

Palermo's gut twisted. He felt suddenly ill. Under no circumstances did he want to see what was behind this door.

"Nine-eighteen, you said, yeah?"

Palermo briefly considered lying, giving Krebosche another number. Was just about to when they arrived at nine-eighteen, and Krebosche said, "Yeah, that was it. Nine-eighteen. Here we are, Palermo. Anything else I should know before we knock?"

Palermo could only shake his head. His vision was blurring. He was having trouble breathing. Felt like he was sucking air through a cheesecloth.

"Alright, then, knock on the door. And don't speak unless spoken to."

Palermo raised his fist, had a momentary mindflash of whipping around fast enough to punch Krebosche with it, maybe wrestle the gun from him, shoot him, flee. But it was a ridiculous action-film fantasy; he knew he'd never be able to do it. Especially not with his nerves as frayed as they'd become. Besides, he'd tried once already and failed. Knew that as soon as he started to turn, in that split second that his intention became clear to Krebosche, the man would know, react, and bullets would tear his neck apart.

Instead, the knuckles of his fist connected with the fake wood of the apartment door.

Inside the apartment, the knock sounded. Milo, Henry, and Faye froze where they stood.

Milo looked at Adelina. She shook her head back and forth, eyes wide. "Don't answer it. Henry's not ready for this fight. He hasn't changed. He hasn't changed."

Milo said, "He *has* changed, Adelina. Look at him!"

The knock sounded again. Someone asked very politely if he could please speak with Henry Kyllo.

Adelina continued shaking her head. "Not *enough*. He hasn't changed *enough*. And it's not these men he needs to worry about. It's the ones following soon after."

Milo had no idea what other men she was talking about, and the voice on the other side of the door was getting more insistent. He turned his attention away from Adelina, hissed, "Henry, what do we do?"

Henry considered for a moment. "No other way out besides through that door, so I guess we're opening it." He turned to Faye, said, "Stand behind me."

Faye was about to protest that she could take care of herself, but quickly realized that, should there be gunfire, standing behind a giant metal behemoth was a fairly smart place to be, despite the possibility of ricochet.

Henry then realized that they basically had an invisible man at their disposal. With some effort, Milo could interact with the physical world now, but only Henry could see him. Why the hell hadn't he – or Milo – thought of this before?

"Milo, you're invisible!" Henry hissed at him.

"I know," Milo said back. Henry saw the gears turning, then Milo understood. "Oh!"

"I'll open the door. You get ready to rush them if anything looks fucked. Attacking right out of the gate will only wake the neighbors and bring unwanted attention, so I doubt they'll want to do that."

"Yeah, give me a signal or something."

"The signal will be that I'll be attacking them, too."

"Perfect." Milo smiled. Henry wanted to return the smile, set Milo at ease for whatever came next. But he didn't really feel it. He felt instead the same way Palermo felt on the other side of the door. As though things were coming to a head – that if it wasn't already a seriously deadly business, it was about to become so in very short order.

I mashed someone to baby food through my freakshow-gigantic fingers, he thought. *I think I can handle a couple of guys with knives and guns, or whatever other weapons they have. Unless they've got close air support, this* should *pan out in our favor.*

Henry wanted desperately to believe in this voice, but he was still so unsure of his size, the way he moved. Pulping something (or some*one*) – no matter how vile and repulsive an act – in a state of relative calm was not the same as fighting angry people in close quarters. And although a lot of Henry *was* metal, there were a lot of undeveloped parts on his body still in the process of changing, hardening. Some that weren't even hardening to metal, but some other substance. Some kind of rock, he thought. But these many spots were still not even close to impervious.

My Achilles heels. Plural.

The knocking was so insistent now that it would certainly wake the neighbors if they didn't open up soon.

Henry stepped forward, head scraping the ceiling. Unlocked the door, turned the knob, pulled it open.

Krebosche's face was level with Henry's stomach. He stepped back from Palermo, and his eyes traveled upward, met Henry's gaze.

Henry's rocks-in-a-grinder voice said, "Who are you?"

Krebosche took a moment to gather himself – or, rather, what he *thought* constituted gathering himself. He was so astonished that he wasn't entirely sure what was coming out of his mouth. "Are... are you Kyllo?" he said.

If I'm gonna make a real *break for it, now is certainly the time*, Palermo thought. But he didn't. He just stood there with a gun at his back, terrified. And ashamed of that fact. But in all truth, he had never imagined that Henry would have turned into what stood before him now. He was nearly as dumbstruck as Krebosche.

Henry didn't answer the question. Instead said, "Tell me who you are."

"William Krebosche. I... need to know what happened to... my girlfriend." His mind spun. He felt nausea threatening. He didn't know how to make sense of the figure before him. It was as though his brain was trying to plug in what it thought it *should* be seeing rather than what it actually saw. He felt control of the situation already slipping.

"Who was your girlfriend?"

"Adelina Palermo," Krebosche said, running on autopilot.

Everyone just stared. Milo turned his head toward Adelina, who was expressionless.

"She's... gone, William," Henry said. "She has moved on. She will not be returning."

"I know – I guess I've always known – it's just that I..." Krebosche stared at the floor. He was beginning to come apart. Felt his insides burning up, like someone had touched a hot flame to them. Like his guts were being stirred with a hot poker.

Henry saw the hurt in Krebosche's eyes, and understood it. He also understood that he had a knife or a gun – something – pointing at Palermo's head.

"Palermo said that… that you'd know where she was. And I thought maybe if I could just see her again, let her know that… See, I just want her to know how much…" Krebosche felt his mind unravelling like a spool. His face had gone pale. He staggered back farther.

Palermo just stood for a moment, uncertain what to do.

At precisely the same time, Henry was suddenly gripped with ferocious pain. It ripped up one side of his body and down the other. He doubled over in agony, went down to his knees, clutching his stomach with one hand, his head with the other. He let out a roar that not only woke the neighbors, but probably everyone on every floor of the building.

Palermo reeled back against the hallway wall, open-mouthed.

Krebosche pointed the gun at Henry. He knew it would be next to useless against him, but on some instinctual level he still ridiculously believed in its stopping power. When Henry had doubled over, he'd revealed Faye standing behind him. Krebosche saw her, trained his weapon on her instead, said in a sleepy voice, as though waking from a dream, "Hey, who's that?"

Henry roared again. Krebosche panicked and fired. Faye went down.

People started poking their heads out of their

apartments. Once they saw Krebosche with his gun out, however, they vanished again just as quickly. Doors slammed, deadbolts locked.

Milo rushed forward and tried to knock the gun from Krebosche's hand, but he was holding on to it too tightly. Krebosche felt something brush by him, nearly knock the gun from his hand. He frowned in the direction of the attack, didn't understand where it had come from, but understood that someone was after his weapon, and that was enough to focus him – it was the only thing standing between death and this roaring monster in front of him.

He held on to the gun even tighter, held it lower, down at his side, to protect it.

That's when Palermo finally got up the nerve to make a break for it. He took off down the hall as fast as his legs would carry him. Which, given his injury, wasn't that fast.

Krebosche watched him go for a second, then shot at him. The bullet hit him in the back of the thigh. Palermo staggered forward once, crumpled to the floor. Got back up, kept running, now with a limp. Burst through the door to the stairwell. Gone.

Krebosche then emptied the rest of his gun's clip into Kyllo, who felt not a single one of the bullets – even those that happened to hit what he'd thought might be his Achilles heels.

All he felt was fire as he found his feet once more.

The fire burned along his synapses, rippled up his spine, crawled over his scalp, tore at his insides.

The only clear thought he had before he started growing – visibly expanding – in height and width was: *WHAT THE ACTUAL FUCK IS THIS?*

And then there were no more clear thoughts for quite a while.

Like a snake shedding its skin, big chunks of metal began dropping off, clunking to the floor, tendrils of smoke rising from them as though they were meteors falling to the earth. He staggered, nearly fell, crashed against a wall, righted himself, roared again. It was just blind luck that none of his pieces crushed Faye to death where she lay unconscious. The bullet had hit her upper chest, close to the armpit, and just below the collar bone. Not immediately life-threatening, but she was losing blood.

More pieces of Henry came loose and fell off. His body beneath was smoother, sleeker than the previous incarnation. Every inch looked like brushed metal, much more uniform than before. If he were able to stand upright, he would have been close to ten feet tall, and would have measured about four feet wide across the chest. He had to go down on all fours to keep from crashing through the ceiling; hunching and ducking would no longer cut it.

In the hallway, Krebosche just stood there for a moment longer, staring. Then he dropped his empty gun and walked toward Henry. Tears glistened on his eyelids. His mouth hung open. All pretense of attack or defense was gone.

This new Henry breathed heavily and with difficulty, his esophagus pushing air along pathways still being forged. But his eyes worked well. They saw Krebosche approaching, narrowed, then Henry determined the threat – if any one man could be seen as any kind of threat to him now. He sprung forward on legs like pistons, forearms stacked on top of one another, thrust out ahead of him: two massive columns of steel that crashed through both sides of the doorframe.

Right before Henry's arms connected with Krebosche's upper half, Krebosche's eyes went even wider than before, and he said, "Adelina?" Whether he could actually see her, or whether he just said her name because it was the last thing he wanted to come out of his mouth before his death, Adelina would never know.

She put a hand over her mouth as Henry slammed into Krebosche with his doublestacked arms, against the wall where he'd stood to shoot Palermo as he ran away. Krebosche's legs were lifted and dragged under him, his legs nearly horizontal with the speed of the attack. There was a sickening crunch when his top half hit the wall. His torso crumpled under the pressure. Blood splashed upward in a gout, covering his neck and most of his face.

Part of the wall caved in, dust and plaster sprinkled down from overhead. The lights in the hallway flickered but stayed on.

Henry pulled his arms back, surveyed the corpse. Another spike of pain galvanized him and he lashed out again, ripping Krebosche's corpse in two at the waist, throwing the top half over his shoulder, back into the apartment, flinging the bottom half down the hall.

Henry stomped back into Faye's apartment, leaving craters in the floor with every step. The floor shuddered, threatened to cave in, but held.

Throughout it all, Milo just stood to the side out in the hallway and wondered what he could do to stop it.

When Henry went back into the apartment, Milo followed him, shouted, "Henry! Henry, stop!"

Henry did not stop. He reached the mangled top portion of Krebosche's body, picked it up, let loose a strangled cry, and threw it toward the living room window, where it shattered the glass, sailed over the balcony, out into the night.

It dropped into a snowbank in the parking lot below, face up.

"Henry!" Milo bellowed again. "Listen to me, Henry, listen to my voice!"

Henry grunted, snorted, turned toward the sound of Milo's voice.

"You need to stop, Henry," Milo said, hands out in a placating, calming gesture. "Faye needs our help. Faye needs *your* help." He had no idea if whatever was left of Henry inside this new machine could understand him – could even *recognize* him – but he had to try. "Please, Henry. Stop. Just... stop."

Henry stared at Milo, eyes hot coals in his face.

Inhaled. Exhaled.

And again.

Inside his chest, whatever now passed for his heart beat slower. Slower still. Steadied.

Inside Henry's mind, something resembling rational thought began to return. Outside in the hallway, sounds of panic reached his ears. People screamed. Someone yelled for someone else to call 911. Another wise soul pulled the fire alarm to get everyone out, in case the floor collapsed.

Adelina had just been standing there, motionless for the past few minutes while chaos engulfed her surroundings. Milo didn't know what, but something seemed to snap her out of it. She said, "This time I can feel it. I'm going back now." Then she turned to Milo, spoke his name, said, "I will try to make them see you." Then she vanished.

The building groaned with its new load. Milo feared the entire floor would buckle, sending them crashing through.

He turned back to Henry, said, "You need to pick Faye up, Henry. And then *we need to go. Right now.* Anywhere but here. We have to–"

Then it happened again.

But this time, instead of doubling Henry over, the pain curved his spine backward as it stretched to accommodate another growth spurt.

Henry's gigantic head and torso tore straight up through the ceiling into the living room above. He twisted in agony, arms flailing, knocking over the upstairs neighbor's TV, smashing it to bits. Bashing a couch and chair against the wall under the balcony window. The middle-aged couple who lived there, who'd been woken up moments before by the commotion, were half-clothed, insane with panic, but nearly to the front door. They'd both screamed when Henry burst up through the floor, then one of Henry's arms came back around the other way after knocking the furniture flying and cracked the woman hard in the chest. She fell to the floor, unconscious. The man fared worse: Henry's hand – now bigger than a trashcan lid, but far heavier – glanced off the back of his head, tearing a sizable portion away, exposing skull and brain.

He fell beside his wife, and bled out. Dead in a handful of seconds. Henry swept up the man's body with the same hand that had killed him and flung it against the living room window, some part of his brain rationalizing that this was what was to be done with corpses he had created: they were to be put out of sight. The body slammed through the window, shattered glass sprinkling outward, hit the balcony railing, and tumbled end over end down to the parking lot, landing not far from Krebosche's half-corpse.

Henry now stood upright. He was more than fifteen feet tall and close to six feet wide.

Milo – whose view was now just Henry's legs and part of his torso – still had only one thought: escape. But he decided that Henry was too far gone now. *He* needed to get Faye out of here. He would tell Henry where he was going with her – assuming his ability to interact with the physical world still held – but beyond that, he could do no more.

Sirens wailed in the distance, and he knew it was now or never. He skirted Henry's lower half, made his way over to where Faye still lay unconscious. He bent over to pick her up, noticed that a big piece of the ceiling had fallen onto her left leg. He moved to her leg, reached out for the chunk of drywall, concrete, and steel – and watched in horror as his hand passed right through.

"Come on, come on, come on – Jesus fucking Christ, come *on*," he muttered, tried again, still nothing. He closed his eyes, concentrated on the feeling of grabbing the materials. Thought of the texture of the concrete, the weight of the steel, the chalky feel of the drywall on his fingers.

Tried again: grabbed a tentative hold. Pushed on the chunk as hard as his strength would allow. It budged just enough that he was able to get her free. Her leg had a gruesome gash in it; blood pooled around the wound as the pressure of the piece of ceiling was removed.

Faye stirred at the fresh pain, looked around. "Who… who are you?" she said groggily. "What's–"

"You can fucking *see* me?"

I will try to make them see you. Adelina had said.

Fuck me, Milo thought. *Whatever Adelina did, it worked.*

"I'm Milo. Pleased to meet you and all that shit. Look, no time," he said, rapidfire. "We need to get you out of here. Henry's… unable to help. Cops and fire trucks will be here very soon, and we need to *not* be here when they arrive. I'm going to try to lift you, take you out of here. I know somewhere we can go. Not far from here."

"Henry…"

"I'll tell him where we're going, but I don't know if he can understand me anymore. He's entirely lost his marbles and is approaching the size of a school bus. He's…"

Faye was losing consciousness again, her eyelids drooping as Milo spoke. "Doesn't matter," he said. "Screw it, let's go."

He moved his arms under her, concentrating as hard as he could on the feel of her body – aware at the same time that it was an incredibly bad idea to move an injured person, but what choice did he have? If he left her here, she would die. When his arms touched flesh and bone, he breathed a huge sigh of relief, said, "Thank fuck," and hoisted her up.

The sirens were louder now, and the fire alarm was still going, but the sounds of panic in the hallway had receded.

No shit, Milo thought as he made his way toward the hallway, feeling the strange sensation of gravity again for the first time in a long while. *Apparently, a massive rampaging metal monster will clear a building pretty goddamn quick.*

Before leaving the apartment, he turned and yelled up to Henry, who was – for the moment – no longer roaring and twisting about in fury, destroying everything in his path. "Henry! I'm taking Faye to the tunnels! She's hurt badly, needs help! I don't know if you'll understand this, but you know the tunnels I mean! Underground! The old subway line!"

He coughed from the dust in the air, and from shouting everything as loudly as possible in hopes that up in the next apartment, his friend would hear him, and understand.

Hey, I'm coughing from shouting and from dust in the air. I am *a real boy, after all.*

He picked his way through the rubble, careful to watch his step, trying desperately to remember how legs that touched the ground worked.

•••

On the top floor of Faye's apartment building, Henry Kyllo's mind tried to reboot itself. It remembered the last ten minutes as a flashing haze of violence – only portions of the events remained in his head. Some of it had been purged, and only later would he learn exactly what he'd done.

For now, all his brain could latch onto was the sound of sirens, a fire alarm, what those things meant, and what he had to do about it.

He stood in an apartment he had no previous memory of being in, surrounded by rubble, blood, scraps of brain, bone, skin, and – directly behind him, near the front door – a half-dressed, unconscious, middle-aged woman. Something had happened to the living room window. It was smashed. Cold wind blew inside, stirring up the rest of the damage.

Damaged, he thought. *Like my mind. What have I done? Where is Milo? Where is Faye?*

He knew the names of these people, but couldn't put faces to those names in his head. He couldn't picture either of them.

And weren't there other people, too? Where had they gone?

He gazed down at himself, then, for the first time aware that his legs were somehow in the apartment below. He didn't know how to process that, so his brain ignored it for the moment. But he recognized that something substantial in his head had changed with his last insane growth spurt. Where before he felt he was losing control of his body, was having trouble operating it, he now felt like he'd "grown into it," for lack of a better term. It felt more comfortable. More... *him*.

Sirens again, now very close. Perhaps stopping somewhere nearby.

Probably come here to stop me. Clearly, I've done something awful. That feels like a distinct possibility. Just look around.

He thought again of his friend, Milo. Dead, but not dead. Invisible. And Faye. Wasn't there something about them both? Something–

Then the words replayed in his head in snippets, dredged up from whatever murky depths now constituted his memory:

Faye.

Injured.

Tunnels.

Subway.

These words meant something to him. Tough to know for sure right now, though. Dribbles of information were all that seemed to be allowed through. Everything else just sort of remained... over *there* somewhere. Too far for him to see, to grasp.

And now firemen were coming. He heard shouting nearby. Smelled smoke, wondered if a fire had started somewhere.

As his chest rose and fell with an efficiency he had never felt before – air filtering in and out of his (metal?) lungs so crisp and clean, he imagined his head as a fat steel balloon, drifting far above the clouds.

He closed his eyes, envisioned in great detail this trip above the earth, the scent of the breeze, the sun glinting off the metal of his arms, his legs...

His thoughts drifted back to the woman lying nearby.

Where shall we go, she and I? he thought. He knew his mind wasn't functioning properly. More clearly, yes, but not *properly*. Everything seemed slower. Nothing seemed to make much sense.

He imagined himself and the woman together this time, floating above the clouds. Maybe they were in a hot air balloon, he didn't know. The method of flight was not important. What was important was –

Tunnels. The word shot into his thoughts like a hard slap from a cold hand.

– the fact that they were together, and that they loved each other. Even though they'd only known each other a short time, they both felt that they'd been in love for as long as they could remember. Like they had never *not* been in love.

And today's trip was –

Subway.

– was something they'd been planning for weeks. Maybe he'd surprised her with it at first, then let her help him plan it. Had he won it? Entered some contest? He didn't feel like either of them had much money, so winning it seemed like a reasonable assumption.

He looked across at her, saw what he now felt sure was the shape of a hot air balloon above them, although he discovered he could not lift his head to see for sure. But that was OK because her eyes were sparkling in the sunlight where it dipped now, shining through her hair, nearing the horizon, and she was so beautiful. Just *so* beautiful that he wished they could drift up here forever. Drift across this –

Injured.

. . .

What?

His brain tried once again to reboot itself. He felt a literal redistribution of memory take place in his head, like a fragmented drive defragging, reworking itself into a more coherent version of what it once was. What it used to be.

Something clicked inside his skull.

Two firemen poked their heads around the shattered remnants of Faye's front door, axes in hand. Cursed. Yelled for cops. Yelled for anyone who would listen, then ran back down the hall.

Henry turned himself around one hundred and eighty degrees, stared directly at the woman on the floor.

Faye, he thought. The name came into his beleaguered mind like the snap of a crisply folded sheet.

Faye is injured.

Thinking of hot air balloons, sunlight filtering through soft hair, and the scent of the cleanest air he had ever smelled – all memories of a trip he'd never been on, nor would ever go on – he very gently moved his hand under the unconscious woman on the apartment floor, lifted her up. Wrapped his hand around her, tucked her close to his side, moved his other hand over and around her to protect her from any debris.

Then Henry Kyllo squatted as low as he could, angled himself toward the back parking lot, flexed his pistonlike legs.

And launched himself through the roof of the apartment building.

When he broke through, at the top of his arc, he saw the moon hanging low in the sky, tried to capture every detail of its beauty before gravity brought him down.

The roof caved in and glass exploded outward in a shower from the windows of the car Henry landed on.

He checked the condition of the woman tucked into his body: still unconscious, but otherwise unharmed. He stepped down from the car, the learning curve of dealing with the proportions of this new body exponentially curtailed from his last incarnation. He somehow felt he'd been *born* in this body.

He looked around. A small crowd of people had come out of neighboring apartment buildings when the sirens had stopped nearby. Some had likely heard the original commotion.

Firefighters and police had been scattered around, running back and forth from their vehicles to the building. When he'd landed, everyone stopped. Stared. Then panic ensued, and people ran in every direction – every direction that was *away* from Henry, of course.

Subway. Tunnels.

Henry began walking in the direction of the old subway tunnels. He assumed the police would soon be after him in force, but the ones who'd seen him – and who could properly process what they'd seen – had their hands full right now. Someone would call it in, though. And he wasn't sure if the force that protected the *Inferne Cutis* from discovery would be strong enough to play this down, wipe it clean. It would likely be too much. Too many witnesses, too scarring an event. Too strange in every way imaginable.

Probably.

But only a small portion of his mind was occupied with this line of thought. Most of his attention settled on the woman he carried. He felt as though she was Faye. The nurse. His girlfriend? She must be, mustn't she? Wasn't she the only woman in his life? He failed to see how it could be anyone else. Although his memories of Faye – and a lot of other memories, to be honest – were sketchy, so…

He was trudging through the dark streets, trying desperately to retrieve memories of Faye, when a strange sound caught his ear: hydraulics, or something close to hydraulics. He looked around, saw nothing, then looked down. At his own legs. The sound came from his legs, whenever he stepped. He hadn't noticed it before due to the noise around him, but now, cloaked in relative darkness down these side streets, he heard it clearly.

But not *quite* hydraulics. Something similar – organic tissue mixed with hydraulics? – but different enough to be noticeable. Henry stopped walking, looked down again. Air hissed from something mechanical, like a rig after hitting its brakes. But Henry had seen hydraulic systems before, and these weren't quite the same. These were more powerful, more efficient. Using some other kind of technology he was unfamiliar with.

The entrance to the old tunnels, he knew, was just another block away, and he still had not encountered anyone on the side streets and back alleys he'd chosen for his path. He started to think maybe he wouldn't see anyone, would actually go unseen the entire way. He hoped so because he wasn't sure what he'd do if someone saw him – more accurately, he was *afraid* of what he'd do if someone saw him. Disturbing flashes of what had happened at Faye's apartment occasionally bolted through his head, but nothing that made any kind of sense for the person he thought himself to be. These images felt fake – like a film he'd watched, or as though someone had poked around in his head, created false memories for some reason. Some larger plan he was part of but knew nothing about.

He hoped if someone saw him before he got underground, they would just forget. Maybe panic at first, run away, but then, by the time they reached anyone to tell about it, the memory would be trapped behind a curtain of haze.

But someone *did* see him.

And Henry saw *him*.

Palermo. Limping in his direction, his silhouette stretching out under a streetlamp.

Palermo glanced up as Henry lurched into view. Palermo stopped in his tracks. He said nothing, just stared up at Henry. His creation, to a certain extent.

Henry loomed over Palermo, stared down at him, breathing. One part of his mind recognized Palermo for who he was, the leader of the Runners. His people. Another part of his mind – the part that cared for Faye, for Milo, and the frustrated part that had no idea what he was becoming – wanted to end Palermo.

"This," Henry said. "*All* of this. It's your fault."

Palermo held up his hands, said, "Look, I just need to get back to HQ, Henry. We can sort this out. I know what's happening to you, and we can–"

Henry felt a shudder rip through his body. He lashed out with his free hand, swatted Palermo. Palermo flew through the air, smacked against a tree, his back broken.

Something in his mind – a new voice he was beginning to recognize as not of his making whatsoever – spoke up, said, *He is no longer needed.*

Henry stomped over to Palermo's twisted frame. This voice in his head now issued forth from his mouth, almost completely separate from his will: "You are no longer needed."

Henry brought a thick metal thumb down and ground Palermo's head into the snowy earth beneath.

Once Palermo was dead, the presence receded, backed down from Henry's consciousness. It felt like a darkness that had been hiding in his mind all his life had been awakened, and could now slither into and out of his brain whenever it pleased.

Henry continued walking toward the subway tunnels. One block, two.

Then about a block away from the entrance to the old tunnels, four more people saw him. They stopped as Henry lumbered into view, maybe thirty feet away from where they stood.

Marcton and Cleve pulled their weapons. Bill and Melvin followed suit. Marcton said, "Holy mother of fuck."

Then the shooting began.

•••

Five minutes earlier, Marcton, Cleve, Bill, and Melvin had been walking quietly toward the nurse's apartment. Single file.

Like Sand People, to hide our strength and numbers, Marcton thought, and chuckled.

Cleve was about to ask what was funny when Marcton slowed down, stopped, pointed. "Check it out," he said.

The other three fanned out to the sides, looked where Marcton was pointing.

Melvin said, "What the hell?"

Marcton said, "Dunno, but if Palermo's there, shit has already gone south, and we're late to the party."

From their vantage point, the building seemed to be buckling near the nurse's floor. Cracks streaked down the outer concrete. Something was going on inside the apartment, but they were too far away to see what.

Then sirens flared up behind them, getting louder.

"Ah, shit," Bill said. "Do we need to bail, Marcton?"

"Goddamnit," Marcton said. As good as a yes, so Marcton, Melvin, and Cleve turned around, started heading back to the car.

Bill was just about to do the same when the glass of the nurse's living room window shattered and the top half of a body flew out, drifted over the balcony, fell into the parking lot.

"*Fuck me*!" Bill said. The others turned around. "A fucking *body* – well, half a body – just flew out the window!"

"Shit," said Marcton. "Let's get off the street in case someone comes looking out the nurse's window. No idea who's up there or what's happening, so best to stay hidden."

When the others had already moved off the street, Marcton had to pull Cleve away by the collar, still staring up, slack-jawed and curious. "Damn, I missed it," Cleve said, a bizarre sense of wonderment filling his voice.

Getting off the street obscured their view a bit, but they could still mostly see the corner of the target building. They watched quietly in the darkness for another few minutes, aware of the sirens creeping closer. Bill and Melvin were tasked with keeping their eyes peeled in case the cops, ambulance, or fire trucks used the street they were on to get to the apartment building.

Just then, more glass shattered and another body flew out over a balcony, fell to the pavement – this time a full body, crashing through the window of the apartment directly above the nurse's. And this time Cleve saw it too.

"Wow," he said. "Just fucking wow. You know?" He glanced around at the others, a big dumb grin on his face as though he were a small child watching his first fireworks show.

Marcton didn't respond. His mind raced as he tried to put the pieces together. He stood thinking for a moment, then said, "We need to get out in front of this. Like, *now*."

"What do you want us to do?" Melvin asked.

"Lemme think, hang on. Just lemme…" He rocked side to side, weighing options, possibilities, a deep frown creasing his features. Finally: "Alright, look:

whoever's doing that shit is gonna need to vamoose *real* fucking soon with the heat that's coming down on that place, right?"

Everyone nodded.

"So. We position two at the front, two round back, and when the fucker or fuckers come out, we bag their asses. Got it?"

More nods, but Cleve looked skeptical.

Marcton sighed. "Speak up, Cleve, or forever hold your goddamn peace. We don't have all day to debate."

"Nah, it's just… Well, that seems pretty simple. And also something they'd be expecting. I mean, wouldn't it be better to have the element of surprise? Just rush in there and fuck their shit up before they even know what hit 'em?"

As much as Marcton hated to admit it, Cleve might have a point. "Alright, fine, two up the back stairs, two up the front."

"We're assuming the building *has* two sets of stairs," Melvin said.

Bill nodded. "Yeah, we can't just assume that. And what about the elevator?"

"Also," Cleve said, "fire escape."

"Jesus, when did you guys develop independent thought?" Marcton said. "Fine. Christ. Me and Cleve inside, rushing up the stairs – if there's only one set, *we'll both use that one*. Bill and Melvin, hang down at the bottom of the fire escape. Fuck the elevator – no one in a killing-spree rush is taking the time to wait for elevators."

Everyone looked satisfied with this plan.

"Great, now can we go?" Marcton said, turned, and started walking toward the building again.

"Actually," Cleve said, "is it really a good idea to split up? I mean, shouldn't we—"

There was an enormous crash then, like a bus slamming into a concrete wall. All four of them whipped their heads around in the direction of the sound.

For a moment they saw nothing, but then a dark shape nearly as big as a dump truck passed in front of the moon. The man-shaped thing seemed to hang there for longer than seemed possible, then it fell quickly to the pavement of the front parking lot. They heard an incredible crash, but could not see what happened because a line of trees and a row of bungalows obscured their view.

The event hung between the four men for a long moment, then Cleve broke the silence, saying, "So we're gonna run now, right? Like, toward *home*?"

But as much as they'd wanted to run – as much as Cleve had *really* pushed for that to happen – they hadn't. Marcton calmed his men down as best he could by telling them he'd seen the creature, or whatever it was, holding onto something. Maybe some*one*. He said it had certainly looked like a person to him for that brief moment it was lit by the moon.

"I saw it when the thing turned to position itself for its descent. I saw *something*, anyway. And what if it was Palermo? What if neither of those two dead bodies that got tossed were him, and then we just fucking *leave* because we're scared?"

"Well, shit, Marcton," Melvin countered, "if that thing *was* holding Palermo, what chance do you think he's got? I don't want to desert him, either, but we have to use our heads here."

Bill and Cleve stayed quiet while this conversation went on. They were both just jittery, looking over their shoulders every few seconds, on the verge of bolting at any moment. Somewhere nearby, someone locked their car, the horn beeping twice. Cleve nearly nearly shit himself.

But the discussion was brief, and Marcton was no longer in the mood for democracy. "I'm moving to intercept. You can leave if you want, but think on this: if you desert me out here – and maybe Palermo, too – expect to find a knife in your fucking guts the moment I get back to the warehouse."

That had effectively shut everyone up.

They began walking in the general direction of the apartment building. Not thirty seconds later, the ground shook, sounding like footsteps – but like no footsteps any of them had ever heard before.

"Holy mother of fuck," Marcton had said when the creature stomped into their line of sight.

And now here they stood, facing the creature down.

When they opened fire, the beast just stood there for a moment, head nearly level with the streetlight above them. When it realized it was under fire, it moved its arm inward to protect whatever was still tucked against its body.

Marcton quickly realized the thing was made mostly of metal, so their bullets were ricocheting madly in every direction, and that one of them could hit Palermo – or whomever was hidden inside the monster's hand. "Hold your fire!" he yelled. But at first he couldn't be heard over the cacophony. He yelled louder, his voice cracking on the first word: "*Fuck's* sake, STOP!"

The guns went dead.

The beast lifted its head, focused its gaze on them. There was no mistaking the machinery of the thing, but something in its eyes felt organic where they settled on Marcton's face. Examining him. Assessing the threat level, of course, but more than that. In fact, despite the metal exterior, there was something organic about the entire creature. Something in the way it breathed, the way it shifted its weight from side to side. Marcton would never know it, but at that very moment Henry was trying to access his memories of Marcton. They'd done several Runs together in the early years. Never became close, but Marcton would know Henry to see him – the original Henry.

Unable to retrieve any true memories, instead, weird fantastical elements of several events in Henry's past coalesced to form a picture in his mind; these elements would become the basis of Henry's thoughts about Marcton from this point forward. Enough of the elementary wiring in Henry's brain had changed, been reshaped, that he would never regain his real memories of the man.

But perhaps that was just as well, because Marcton would never even know that this was Henry Kyllo.

Now, standing in the street with the gaze of a monster fixed solely on him, Marcton was astonished to find his voice. Motioning toward the person the creature carried, he said, "Who is that?"

Marcton had no idea whether the thing spoke or understood English, but it was the only language he had with which to attempt communication. The creature seemed to understand. It looked down at its cargo, then slowly uncurled its fingers to reveal a woman. Unconscious. Not Palermo at all.

Marcton's heart sank. So one of the bodies flying out the windows was likely Palermo's. But he couldn't know for sure. Not without checking out the bodies himself. Or sending one of his guys to do so.

Unless he asked. Long shot, but why not?

"And Palermo?"

No recognition. The beast just growled low in its throat, covered the woman with its hand again, put her back at its side. She groaned a little, then. It wouldn't be long before she came around.

The monster took one tentative step forward, kept its eyes on Marcton's gun. Moved its head in the direction of the entrance to the old subway tunnels. Back to Marcton. Back to the entrance.

Something clicked in its throat. Gears whirred, ground. Something resembling human speech tried to belch its way out of the thing's neck.

Henry, of course, could've spoken if he'd wanted to, but felt he shouldn't. Felt he should let them think he was nothing remotely like them. Internally, too, he was battling with that other voice that would have just had him crush these people to death. It had gotten the better of him before, with Palermo, but now he knew about it, felt its presence curled up, ready to pounce at the back of his thoughts. Better to know where the wasp in the room was than be oblivious to its presence.

Cleve, Bill, and Melvin stiffened. Cleve took a step back, raised his gun again, said, "What are we doing here, Marcton? Your call. Letting it go? It doesn't look like it wants to hurt us, just wants to get past."

"Yeah, you're right, it's just that…" Marcton said, fascinated. The creature was hard to look away from. It looked like no machine he'd seen before. There were familiar elements, of course, and something about the way it moved was… sinewy. As though beneath all the steel were flesh and blood muscles.

It had stopped trying to push out whatever sounds it apparently thought would help get its point across, and had fallen silent.

"Come on, Marcton," Cleve said, keeping his voice low, placing a hand gently on his friend's shoulder, so as not to startle him out of his state. "Let's go."

Marcton turned to look at him.

"I think you feel it, too, man," Cleve continued. "It's like I'm standing on a sheet of very, *very* thin fucking ice here. I'm afraid to move, but every instinct I have is telling me that *now is the goddamn time to do so*."

Marcton nodded, turned to the creature, stepped backward. Put his gun away, told the other guys to do the same. They did, and everyone took several steps back, up onto the curb.

The beast looked toward the subway tunnels again.

"It's OK," Marcton said. "You can go."

The thing took another step forward, then another, then another. With each step, he kept his eyes glued to the four men. When he was fifty feet beyond them, he turned his head toward his destination and walked faster, the pistons in his legs – and the smaller ones in his arms, Marcton just noticed as his angle changed – puffing vapor out into the crisp winter air.

They watched him go, each lost in their own thoughts, trying to process what they'd seen.

As the creature turned the nearest corner, they saw that its destination was the entrance to the old subway tunnels. It ducked its head to get inside, then disappeared from view.

The first snowflake of yet another storm fell, touched Marcton's cheek near his jaw, melted, dripped down his neck. He looked up, saw the moon through a break in the clouds.

No one knew it then, but this storm was the main event.

This storm would never stop.

SEVENTEEN

Milo's trip to the subway entrance was less eventful than Henry's, but no less distressing.

He was still trying to get the hang of gravity after floating around for as long as he had been, found it severely limiting to have to move *muscles* and such. The sensation almost made him wish he were invisible again.

Somehow, Adelina had done this for him. Through whatever power she had, she had essentially brought Milo back to life. And now here he was using that life to try to save someone else's.

Faye's head bobbed against his chest while he ran – well, walked quickly. What he was doing as he took the back stairs down to the ground floor – successfully avoiding questions, or even being stopped by police or firemen – couldn't rightly be called running. His desperation to get Faye away, get her someplace safe, was overwhelming. It sped up certain experiences while slowing others down. But while his newly regained physical limitations were subjected to this effect, his brain had only one speed: overclocked.

Once outside the building, as he struggled to get

over curbs and snowbanks, his mind reeled with everything that had just taken place. Images and voices swirled in a maelstrom of confusion. Several times he needed to physically shake his head to make them stop because his vision was blurring.

If he had taken a different route to the old subway tunnels, he would have seen Henry and the four men who'd intercepted him, which would have changed the entire outcome of that situation. He might have seen Palermo, too. But he hadn't; the route he'd taken was the most direct one, on main streets. Two or three people passed him, but they were all rubberneckers, and each of them had asked if there was anything they could do to help. He had just shaken his head and carried on.

Milo, too, felt the new snowflakes falling down around him, just before he entered the old subway tunnels – not long at all after Henry had gone down. He relished their coldness on his burning skin.

When Milo was safely inside the darkness of the entrance, away from streetlights, sirens, and the eyes and offers of well-meaning strangers, he gently set Faye down on the concrete at his feet. Just to get a momentary breather.

And in that darkness, below him, down the stairs, he heard the hiss of escaping air. Saw two burning coals in the dark, and knew that his friend, Henry, was close.

Marcton was unable to move for a few minutes after the monster disappeared into the abandoned subway tunnels. He consciously sent instructions to his legs to work, but they would not listen. He wondered dreamily, his mind in a fog, if he was broken. Maybe nothing would work again, and he would just stand here in the street, as snow piled up all around him. He had an intense vision of suffocating under a mountain of white, and that's what finally got him moving.

Breath caught in his chest, and he hitched in oxygen. He blinked rapidly, looked around. Cleve, Bill, and Melvin had similar expressions, but they seemed steadier than him.

Cleve reached a hand out, said, "You alright, Marcton?"

Marcton's second and third breaths came easier. "Yeah, um… Yes. We should call the warehouse."

"Definitely," said Melvin. Waited a beat. "Any idea what that was, Marcton?"

"Nope."

"Thought not. Well, whatever it was, I'm glad it didn't stomp us. 'Cause that would have hurt."

"Only for a second," Bill said. Tried to smile. Failed, managing only a weird half-grimace. His hands shook. "I need to sit down." He moved to the curb, sat down unsteadily.

Melvin looked like he wanted to say something, but wasn't sure. He opened and closed his mouth a few times, then finally spat it out. "Should we call Kendul? Now that Palermo's, well… *gone.*"

"We don't know that for sure yet," Bill said.

"We need to confirm, at least," Marcton said. "And we can't wait for the news tomorrow." He thought about that for a second. "Not that they'd be able to identify the body."

"Can someone else go?" Bill said. "Not sure my legs would get me all the way there. They're still shaky as shit."

"I'll go," Cleve said, and headed in the direction of the nurse's building. "Might clear my head a bit."

"Don't be seen," Marcton said as Cleve walked past him. "Only get as close as you need to, then come back."

"Yep, got it." He walked away, turned a corner, and was gone.

"So. Kendul, yeah?" Melvin said.

Marcton sighed, walked over to where Bill sat on the curb, joined him. "I guess we should. They were old friends. He should hear the news from us."

"*If* Palermo's dead."

"Yeah, *if*."

But they both knew he was. Marcton, especially, felt it in his gut.

The three men passed the remaining time before Cleve's return in silence, just watching the snowflakes come down. Feeling the wind pick up. Turning their collars up against it – except for Marcton, who, as usual, still only wore a T-shirt and jeans.

Soon, Cleve came back around the corner. It was hard to tell from his face what the news was.

Marcton and Bill stood up. Melvin came closer. Cleve had to nearly shout now to be heard over the wind: "Two bodies. Well, one and a half. Neither are him."

It was not at all what Marcton expected to hear. "What? You're sure? Absolutely positive?"

"Positive, man. Didn't recognize either body. They

were both fairly smooshed and all, but their faces were pretty much intact, and I swear neither was Palermo."

Marcton turned around in the direction of the subway entrance, put his hand over his mouth, turned back, said, "Well, we don't know what happened inside. If the thing was tossing bodies out of windows, it might have left a few inside, right? We don't know the body count indoors."

Everyone nodded.

"So how do we find *that* out without trying to get inside?" Melvin said. "Rubbernecking from a safe distance is one thing, but no way we'll be able to get in there. At least not till the cops are gone... But hey," Melvin continued, "maybe Kendul can get inside. Would the leader of the Hunters have any pull with the city cops?"

"Dunno. Maybe," Marcton said. "I'm just not particularly looking forward to that conversation, you know?"

"Well, since we don't know – for sure – if Palermo's in there, you don't have to lead off with, 'Hey, so your old buddy's dead. Can you help us identify the body?'"

Marcton thought about it. "Yeah, maybe I just ask if he can put *me* in touch with someone who can get inside. That way, he won't have to find out through some dumbass cop."

"There ya go," Melvin said. "Thinkin' with your noodle now."

Marcton smirked. "OK, I'll make the call. You guys keep quiet in the background. Gonna be hard enough to hear over this wind as it is."

After calling the warehouse to get Kendul's cell

number (not the quickest task, since the Runners and the Hunters didn't exactly make a habit of gabbing to each other), he stepped a few feet back from them, dialed, waited. Kendul picked up on the fourth ring.

"Kendul."

Christ, now that he had him on the line, what would he say? How would he tiptoe around this?

"Yeah, hi, Kendul, it's Marcton. Listen," he said, deciding to dispense with pleasantries. "I need access to a building where some crazy shit has gone down. Cops are swarming it, though, so I can't get inside. I need to find out if one of ours is down. Do you have any connections, anyone you could put me in touch with?"

"Got one guy you can use: Anton Eckel." Kendul rattled off his number.

"OK, thanks. I'll—"

The line went dead.

Marcton pulled the phone away from his head, stared at the screen. "Well, shit. Didn't have to worry about prying questions from that guy."

One phone call to Eckel and ten minutes later he arrived, flashed his badge around, and strolled into the building. Marcton and his guys watched him go in from a safe vantage point a hundred feet away. Then they walked back to the Hummer through the ever-thickening snow, got in, headed back to the warehouse.

The sun would be coming up in a couple of hours, and Marcton was itching for word so he could proceed accordingly. If Palermo *was* dead inside, he was going to launch the biggest manhunt the Runners had ever been part of – and they'd been part of plenty over the years.

Well, machinehunt in this case, I guess. Or whatever the hell that thing was.

And he saw exactly where the thing went. He thought he would probably have to bring all the Runners together to explain the situation, though. This was not business as usual; this was beyond business as usual in every respect. They'd need to know exactly what they were up against.

Time was wasting, though – sure, the creature had lumbered into the old tunnels, but it could probably move fast if it wanted to, and could be anywhere by now. But the same way he'd felt Palermo was dead – deep in his gut – he sensed that the thing had retreated to the tunnels because they were a good hiding spot, tough to maneuver, tough to track through. You don't go into a nice dark hiding spot just to pop out again into the bright sunlight and keep running – not unless you're a complete idiot (especially not if you're as tall as a streetlamp), and Marcton knew the creature was anything but that. He sensed a great intelligence in those eyes, in those mannerisms.

He'd told Eckel to call him ASAP with whatever he discovered, but he hadn't heard a thing and they were almost back to the warehouse. *What the fuck was the holdup?* Just go in, poke around, see if any of the bodies inside matched the pictures of Palermo that Marcton had asked dispatch at the warehouse to email, then confirm or deny. *No reason it should be taking this long. No reason for–*

They were just pulling into the driveway of the warehouse when Marcton's phone rang; he picked it up before it even finished the first ring.

"Yeah."

"Bodies inside, but none of them Palermo's."

Marcton closed his eyes. Relief flooded through him. But then–

"However…"

"However? However what?"

"I did a quick sweep of the surrounding streets, too, and found Palermo's body next to a tree. Back broken, head pulped."

"If his head was pulped, how do you know–"

"We go way back, kid. Tattoos matched."

Silence on Marcton's end, then:

"Thanks," he said. Hung up.

Marcton steered the Hummer around the back of the warehouse, cut the lights, cut the engine, said one word: "Dead."

No one said anything. Just listened to the engine tick as it cooled.

There were about thirty steps leading down into the subway tunnels. Water-stained, crumbling, and slippery, every one of them.

Milo picked Faye up off the concrete at the mouth of the entrance, started down those steps, twice nearly losing his tentative grasp of how gravity worked. But each time he righted himself before tumbling down the steep steps – a trip which likely would have resulted in them both breaking their necks, or at least an arm or two.

As he got closer to the bottom, his mind wandered momentarily and he found himself wondering why such a clearly dangerous area wouldn't be cut off from the public. But when he reached the final step, he saw that, sure, you could maybe get drunk and fall down some wet stairs, but that's as far as you'd roll: a gate with thick bars ran across the actual entrance to the tunnels themselves. Or, rather, *used to* run across the entrance; nearly every bar had been bent out of shape, as though something massive and incredibly strong had passed straight through this spot – which, of course, it had.

And, he noticed now, as his eyes adjusted, that the stairs *had* been boarded up at street level, but someone had kicked – or otherwise split – the board in half and thrown it down here.

Milo imagined Henry squeezing his frame through this opening. *He must have been on his belly, crawling. No other way he'd've fit.*

Milo heard the hiss of air again, looked up toward the sound. His eyes had adjusted to a certain extent, but they seemed unable to penetrate deeper than a few feet into the dark.

"Henry?"

The telltale eyes were no longer visible. *Maybe his back is turned?* Milo thought. Once beyond the bars, the station opened up much wider and could easily have accommodated Henry turning around, even standing up. Partially, anyway. Only inside the tunnel where the subways actually used to run would he be able to properly stand – if he were on the tracks themselves.

A choking sound came from the dark.

"Henry, it's Milo, where are you? I can't see you."

Another choking sound, then something shuffled, scraped along the ground. Milo imagined Henry dragging his arm or leg into a different position along the concrete.

"I can't see shit in here, Henry. We need light. Can you say anything at all? Are you stuck or something? I hear you moving, so I'm just going to walk in that direction, OK? Don't make any sudden moves or you'll flatten me."

Milo checked on Faye again where she still lay in his arms, made sure she was OK. Her breathing was shallow, and she would need medical attention soon. Or at least some materials that she could work with herself, with Milo's help. Her leg wound had stopped bleeding for the most part, but the bullet had lodged in her body and he had no way of knowing how much damage it had done.

Milo set Faye down, said, "I'll be right back. We'll get you help soon. I promise."

He knew she couldn't hear him, but he felt, perhaps absurdly, that his voice could help her in some way.

"Coming now, Henry. Stay still."

Milo moved forward, past the bent-to-shit gate, into the darkness proper. It was instantly inky to the point of claustrophobia. This wasn't just lights-out-in-the-bedroom kind of dark; this was black-at-the-bottom-of-the-ocean dark. Abyss dark. What was that word he'd read in old Lovecraft stories?

Stygian. Or at least it seemed that way until his eyes began adjusting.

Now that he'd thought of Lovecraft, though, he had horrible tentacled things in his mind. Imagined their suckered awfulness groping blindly for him, wrapping around his body, squeezing the breath out of him. With these images in his head, when he bumped into Henry's leg he nearly squealed. He felt along the metal, the alien landscape of his friend's new body.

What would it feel like on the inside? Milo thought. *To be encased in this body with the same mind you had when you were a regular person. Well, a regular person to a certain extent, anyway. As "regular" as any of the* Inferne Cutis *could be. And did Henry even* have *his regular mind anymore?*

When he reached Henry's midsection, his hands fell on something warm, slightly damp. He squeezed it gently, trying to figure out what it was.

"Leave her," Henry said. His voice sounding hewn from stone. He coughed, made the same choking sounds Milo had heard earlier.

The woman groaned, squirmed where she lay cupped in Henry's palm. The bottom part of her legs hung outside of his hand.

"Is she hurt?"

Henry just breathed.

"Henry?"

More breathing. A slight twitch of one of his legs.

Milo glanced back in the direction of the entrance, saw faint light there, knew he had to get back to Faye. Knew he had to help her. If she died down here it would be his fault; he'd brought her here, so what happened to her now was on him.

What he *should* have done, he knew, was taken her to the hospital. Even just dropping her off out front, yelling for help, and running away would have been better. But some instinct had taken over. He thought bringing her to Henry *was* better for her. In some way that would keep her *safe*. He also knew that gunshot wounds always needed to be reported, which would involve cops, and that road led nowhere good for any of them.

He wondered, then, where Adelina was, whether she would ever come back.

Henry's breath seemed to quicken then. Milo heard it puffing out of his mouth farther away in the dark.

"You OK, Henry?"

Christ, it's not going to happen again*, is it? He'll bust up through the fucking street if he doubles in size again. And I'll be crushed to death.*

And then there was the faintest light splitting the black. At first, Milo couldn't sense where it was coming from; his eyes were unable to process its source. He could tell it was coming from close by, though – maybe underneath Henry? Maybe Henry himself? Some other insane transformation taking place?

He suddenly felt the need to back away, give Henry some space. *In case shit gets* expansive *again*, he thought, staggered back a few feet, feeling suddenly exposed, vulnerable.

The light got brighter, and Milo saw where it was shining from: it was the woman in Henry's hand. The woman *herself* was glowing. Mostly just the exposed parts of her skin. She wore bikini-style underwear and a tank top, so the light came mostly from her legs, arms, and face.

Milo watched as the light grew in intensity. Henry's breathing quickened even more, and now the light was sufficient for Milo to see the position in which Henry lay: he was flat out on his belly, nowhere near anything that could have gotten him stuck. Whatever reason he'd stopped – maybe to wait for Milo – he seemed to have done so, then simply found himself unable to move.

The light from the woman's skin flickered, her eyelids opened slowly; her mouth, too, opened, and she seemed to want to speak.

"Faye," Henry said, his voice a little clearer than before. Smoother. The battle in his head to keep the new darkness in his mind at bay was taking up nearly all his strength. He knew he was losing, but he also knew that once he gave up he would probably never be able to get himself back. Confusion regarding Faye still distracted him, and it was all he could do to try to maintain a grip on the true situation – or what he *felt* was the true situation. And even that seemed to be slipping through his fingers now. Everywhere in his mind was uncertainty, an ever-growing alien darkness, and a blinding, oversimplistic need to just try to *understand*.

"She's here, Henry," Milo said. "She's safe. But I don't understand what's happening with–"

The woman's skin lost some of its glow, then. Whatever internal source had been powering it was fading. Pulling back.

Then the woman slid from Henry's hand, used her

arms to steady herself. Stood up, moved away from Henry several feet.

Then she spoke.

In Adelina's voice.

Before Adelina appeared in the woman's body, she'd been back in her strange Otherland – the alien swirls and occasional lightning storms less a soothing balm than usual. She knew time was short, and the way she received messages in this place – the way she knew what to do and say when she returned to the world – was changing. Before, she was given no insight into the reasoning behind any of the things she was told. The thought would just appear in her mind and, moments later, she would appear near Milo to impart what she could. Why Milo had been chosen in the first place to receive her instructions was still a mystery.

There was certainly something compelling about him, but Adelina could never put her finger on what. She knew only that when she'd first laid eyes on him she felt awkward, but at the same time as though she'd known him for many, many years. Each time she appeared to him, she felt emotionally closer. Maybe it was nothing deeper than the fact that he was able to see her when so many others couldn't.

Whatever force sent Adelina to Milo in the first place had created the imprint of memories in her mind of a life she'd never had with him. The imprint was such that it didn't leave *true* memories – memories that could be accessed and replayed on the screen of her mind – but rather that the residue of the memory remained. These were memories that could never be given direct voice. No one event could be pointed to. The same had been done to Milo.

For a while, in the beginning, she had tried to communicate with whomever had been putting these thoughts into her head. But there was never any answer, no two-way communication. She eventually gave up. But now that she felt things coming to a head – though she had no way of knowing what *kind* of head was approaching – she felt she needed to try again.

She decided the best way would be to focus on something she could see, like a lightning fork in one of the many storms that raged around her. Once focused, she would close her eyes and try to communicate using the specific imagery still burned into her retinas. At first, it didn't seem to be working, but then she'd used this process after telling Milo that she would try to let people see him.

This time, when she asked, she felt no response per se, but felt a subtle shift. It was so small as to be no more than a molecular distinction, but enough that she knew *someone* had heard her, and what she'd requested had come to pass.

Feeling empowered by this discovery, when she'd returned to her Otherland, she tried the same thing again – this time asking that she be allowed to return herself. To let people see *her* now.

She didn't know how it would happen, or if it would happen at all, but then she had vanished from her Otherland and appeared in Henry's hand.

In another woman's body.

•••

The moment Adelina arrived in the woman's body, she sensed everything around her, immediately knew the situation. Was aware of every detail as intimately as if she'd witnessed it herself.

She sensed Milo's hesitation in speaking, said, "This woman – the woman whose body I'm in – her name is Margaret Shearman. She is very sad about her husband's death, but she wants to live. She wants to carry on without him."

"Well, yeah. Why wouldn't she?"

"Grief can be debilitating, Milo. Sometimes impossible to overcome. Impossible to see your way through."

"Are you going to let her go? She's not yours. I mean, you're not her. Whatever."

"She's got barely any life left, Milo. She's as good as dead already, and there's nothing I can do to save her."

Adelina felt something black and hateful tugging at her psyche, then, trying to yank her back to her Otherland. Some deep part of her understood at that moment that she was being manipulated – that whatever agency she had in this world was due to her own will. And that this other presence was fighting her every step of the way. She didn't know what it wanted, but she knew it didn't want to help Faye – didn't want to help anyone. Not toward any positive end, anyway. She felt shame well up inside her, felt this as strongly now as she'd felt any emotion in her entire life.

"Listen, Milo, I don't have much time. We've all been manipulated. I know that now. I feel something pulling at my thoughts."

Something hopeless, formless, filled with despair, inhabited her mind, ripped into her thoughts sharply, made her head spin, trying to cut her off, but she carried on. "I think I've been a big part of that manipulation, too. I just don't know why, or to what end. But I think we'll find out what it all means soon. I'm going to–"

She opened her mouth to continue, but then suddenly crumpled to the ground next to Faye.

"Adelina!" Milo said, crouched beside her. His initial alarm gave way to faint relief, as he realized that she'd just been pulled away from this body, back to wherever she went when she disappeared.

Henry, however, did not understand what was happening. In his addled state of mind he thought Milo had done something to "Faye" – the woman he'd brought with him in his hand from the apartment. For him, the two women on the ground blended into one.

Crouched low, back scraping the ceiling, he advanced on Milo, his eyes having adjusted enough to the near-pitch dark that her could just make out his shape. Milo glanced up at the sound, stood up, put his hands out in a supplicating manner, realizing that something protective in Henry's scrambled brain must've just clicked in.

"Whoa-whoa-whoa, Henry, hang on, man. I don't know what you think just happened, but Faye's OK."

Henry kept coming, looming over Milo now.

"Faye's fine, man. I think. I hope." He glanced down at her still-unconscious body at his feet. "Ah, Christ," he said, took three steps behind him, now backed up flat against the wall.

Henry brought his face down close to Milo's. Stared, breathed hard.

His breath smells like furnace ash, Milo thought, then shut his eyes, and waited to be pulped by Henry's massive hands.

But then: "Henry?" a thin, female voice spoke near their feet.

Milo cracked an eye, looked down at the sound, his own eyes now adjusting to the gloom. Faye was stirring.

But did Henry hear her?

"Henry! Henry, look down, man. Look *down*!"

Henry did not look down. His gaze just burned a hole in Milo's face – the only thing stopping him from flattening Milo likely being whatever recognition Henry still had of their friendship. But Milo knew that might not be enough if he actually thought Faye was dead.

Milo had to take a risk. He lifted his hands slowly upward. "Look, look," he said. "I'm moving my hands, man. Take it easy. Just wanna show you something."

Henry's eyes darted to either side of his head, tracking Milo's hands. Then the hands settled on the sides of Henry's massive cranium – Milo's arms were outstretched as far as they could go – and tried to angle it down to see Faye.

At first Henry resisted, his scowl darkening, but then he let Milo guide his gaze.

Faye, he thought. *There you are.*

By this time, Faye had maneuvered herself into a sitting position, and was rubbing her head. She glanced up to see Milo and Henry looking down at her.

"Everything hurts," she said.

"I bet," Milo replied, still breathing hard, but only mildly terrified for his safety now that Faye was awake. Milo smiled, looked at Henry. "See? She's OK. For now. I had hoped the bullet had gone right through, but I don't think it did. We need to patch her up, at the very least."

Henry moved his head away from Milo, stepped closer to Faye, leaned back, and sat down hard on his butt, making a crater in the concrete. He rested his elbows on his knees.

The Casual Monster, Milo absurdly thought.

Something like the sound of a cement mixer starting up crunched in Henry's chest, and one word came out: "Faye."

Faye looked at Milo, said, "Gimme a hand?"

Milo helped her up. She brushed herself off, careful to avoid the bullet wound.

"Henry," she said, walked toward him, realized there was nothing she could hug on his body except maybe an arm or a leg. She moved toward the closest leg, wrapped her arms around it as far as she could, like it was a tree trunk. Pressed her face against the cold steel there.

"Patch her, Milo," Henry said.

"Yeah, I was thinking about how to do that. Shirt, maybe?" Milo took off his shirt, bit into one of its edges, then tugged furiously at it till a strip came free that was long enough to wrap around Faye's armpit and shoulder. She winced as he applied pressure to the wound while he wrapped.

When he was finished, Milo shrugged what remained of his shirt back over his torso. "Better than nothing," he said.

"Barely," Faye said, and smiled.

Milo didn't know where they were going to go, but he knew that staying still wasn't a good plan, knew they needed to keep moving to avoid the police – and anyone else who might've been put into the service of catching the giant beast rampaging around the city.

"We need to keep going, Henry."

Henry appeared to think about this for a few seconds, then said, "I remembered you telling me to come here. To meet with Faye. But I also knew I needed to hide."

"You're kind of big for that, don't you think?" Milo said, but didn't get the desired reaction from Henry, who just looked away toward the tunnels. When he brought his eyes back toward Milo, they settled on the dead woman on the floor.

Milo saw him staring at her, said, "Margaret Shearman."

Henry looked at Milo blankly for a moment. Then: "What did I do?"

"Her husband died, Henry," Milo said. *Because of you*, he thought but didn't say. "And then she died of her... her wounds," he finished.

Inside Henry, something broke. Up till now, he'd been effectively distanced from nearly everything that had happened – the results of his rapid transformation into something he couldn't possibly understand. The strains on his mind and body were incredible, but he'd gained a sort of equilibrium during the recent respite from activity – from the growth spurts and the constant running away from everything he was becoming.

Flashes of the scenes in the apartment building blitzed through his brain, and he knew Margaret Shearman and her husband were not the only ones dead because of him.

He felt a sadness so profound settle in his chest that he didn't know if he could move at all, let alone continue running. Tears were no longer physically possible, it seemed, but grief assailed him where he sat on the floor of this abandoned subway tunnel. It gathered in his heart, immobilizing him.

Milo saw the shift in Henry's demeanor, but didn't know what he could do to make him feel better. He *had* killed people – some innocent, some not so innocent. Maybe through no direct fault of his own, but he was responsible. All Milo could do was try to let his friend deal with it the best way he knew how. And better still was to just keep running.

Always keep running.

"Come on. Let's use the tracks themselves, Henry. At least there you can fully stand up. He moved to take Faye's hand, started walking toward the tracks. "Seriously. Hanging out by the entrance is ridiculous. We need to get deeper inside."

Henry nodded once, slowly. He got to his feet, then, back bent under the ceiling. But instead of turning around to follow Milo and Faye, he moved one hand toward Margaret Shearman's body, did his best using his huge steel fingers to arrange her corpse so that she was lying flat, instead of crumpled in a heap.

The wind whistled through the tunnels as the storm aboveground raged on.

He turned, then, and followed his friends into the deepening darkness beyond.

Back at the warehouse, Marcton assembled his crew. They sat on crates and boxes, as they'd done when Palermo had killed Carl Duncan. It seemed like years ago.

Marcton stood in the middle of the group, pacing, still hopped up on adrenaline from the night's events. He brought everyone up to speed as quickly as he could, then opened the floor to suggestions about how to proceed. He had some ideas himself, but they were fairly weak, and he wanted to get input from his people in case something they said bolstered his own plan – if "plan" could even be applied to the handful of halfbaked notions bumbling about in his head.

As for the term "his people," he realized that's exactly what they were now – his. With Palermo gone, he was now officially in charge. The idea simultaneously thrilled and terrified him. Palermo had a certain *weight* to him. A gravitas that he wasn't at all sure he could muster. Not that he had much choice. He knew that to effectively lead, people had to believe in you. *Really* believe. They needed to feel that what you said and did was what was best for the group – whatever group you might be trying to lead. And this group had history. This group – and Kendul's Hunters, too – went back a long, long way.

As if thinking about Kendul at that moment had

somehow summoned him, he walked through the back door, his own crew in tow. Marcton had immediately called him again upon learning of Palermo's death. Even under more normal circumstances, Kendul would've been called due to his and Palermo's long relationship, but these were nothing even close to normal circumstances, and Marcton knew he could use all the help he could get. So not only was Kendul invited, so were all his Hunters.

For Marcton's Runners it felt bizarre and vaguely uncomfortable to be so close to the Hunters. As they filtered into the warehouse, the air itself seemed to stiffen somehow, became harder to breathe. A certain tightening in the muscles that every man and woman in this warehouse felt deep in his or her bones. There was an understanding between the crews – and they knew they'd all been brought together for a purpose that profoundly affected them all – but the predator/prey dynamic was ingrained, and came with no on/off switch.

"Marcton," Kendul said as he approached. He extended his hand. Marcton took it, then drew him in close. The men embraced briefly, slapped each other's backs, the clapping sound echoing loudly around the rafters.

"Kendul," Marcton said, returning the greeting, stepped back and began pacing again. He found it difficult to catch any of the thoughts whizzing around in his head and, as a result, his speech was even more clipped than usual, as if the act of providing additional details was just too taxing. He quickly filled Kendul and the Hunters in on what had happened.

Then: "Thoughts?" Marcton said to the room. "Anyone?"

A man sitting cross-legged on one of the stacks of skids piled up nearby cleared his throat, said, "Well. We fucking kill it."

A few chuckles, some uncomfortable shuffling. The man smirked, glanced around, apparently happy with his contribution.

Marcton said, "Insightful," and gave the man a withering glare that wiped the smirk off his face. "Anyone else wanna tell jokes? If so –" he lifted an arm, pointed "– there's the fucking door."

Silence. A few coughs. More uncomfortable shuffling.

"Actually, kid–" Kendul said.

"Don't fucking call me kid," Marcton said. "Do not."

Kendul raised both hands, palms out. "Actually, *Marcton*," he said, "can I have a private word? My crew can get weapons ready. Your crew can jerk it. Or whatever the fuck they do when they're not being run down by my Hunters."

A few people *way* at the back chuckled, but quickly stifled the sound.

Marcton cocked his head. "Over here, old man."

The two men broke away from the group, their footfalls like rifle reports in the ensuing silence. Once they were out of earshot, the larger group divided itself into Runners and Hunters, with only the occasional cluster of both – unlikely friendships formed in the heat of battle.

Marcton brought them back to the warehouse's

main office, closed the door behind them.

"Listen, Marcton," Kendul said, leaning against the doorframe. "This is gonna sound melodramatic, but... we have a secret weapon."

Marcton barked out a laugh, then another. When he realized Kendul wasn't joking, he frowned, said, "What, you're serious?"

Kendul waited a beat, then said, "Adelina."

Marcton's frown deepened. His mind scrambled.

"Palermo's daughter," Kendul continued when Marcton didn't respond.

Marcton moved behind the desk, sat down in the office chair – now, he realized distractedly, *his* office chair. "Yeah, I know the name. And?"

"She's alive," Kendul said.

"Like fuck she is."

"Well then fuck is alive and well, Marcton, 'cause I know exactly where she is, and I might know how to reanimate her body so that–"

"Whoa, whoa, whoa, back the fuck up, Kendul," Marcton said and stood. "What kinda crazy bullshit do you think–"

Kendul moved forward quickly, got right in Marcton's face, his voice now dropped an octave. "This *isn't* bullshit, and you need to shut your fucking hole and listen to what I have to say, you little dickhead. We don't have time for anything else. It sounds ridiculous. It sounds impossible. I get that. But that day in that house when Adelina... *changed*... whatever Palermo told you happened, that *ain't* what fucking happened, OK? He thinks she died, but she didn't." Kendul stepped away from Marcton now, slowly. He dropped his eyes to the floor, raised them back up to Marcton. "She didn't."

Marcton's face clearly showed his confusion. His mouth opened and closed several times, words nearly coming out, but never quite making the leap from thought to speech. Kendul wanted to keep explaining, knew that time was of the essence, but he also knew he had to let Marcton process this information, or nothing else he said would properly filter in.

Marcton sat back down in the chair, looked out the window into the warehouse. His eyes darted from person to person, never settling on any of them. Processing, processing…

"OK," he finally said. "Let's say Adelina *is* alive. She's one person. How the fuck does that help us?"

Kendul said, "She's not a person, kid. Not by a long shot. Not any more."

Marcton let the "kid" remark slide. Kendul's words hung in the air between them for a moment longer, then Marcton said, "You're going to have to just fucking say it, man. I am completely lost, and in no mood whatsoever for guessing games. Spit it the fuck out."

"She's a machine," Kendul said. "Well, not entirely, but mostly. About the same as what you describe this… beast as."

And just in that split-second hesitation before Kendul said "beast," Marcton had a flash of insight, knew Kendul hadn't originally intended to use that word. He was about to say something else.

"What were you going to say instead of 'beast,' there, Kendul? What do you know that you aren't saying? I find it very fucking hard to swallow that this is your only secret in this situation."

Marcton stood again, walked over to Kendul, looked hard at him, watched his eyes. Kendul was good – very good – at schooling his face, but not quite good enough for Marcton. The new leader of the Runners saw it in Kendul's eyes, saw it as though it were written right on his forehead:

"You *know*, don't you? You *know* what this thing is. Because it's happened before." Marcton saw the truth of it plain as day on Kendul's face. "And it was Adelina. Jesus fucking Christ!"

Kendul knew there was no point in trying to hide it any more. Besides, there was no time for games. Palermo was dead. The whole society was at risk of exposure with Kyllo now rampaging around. "Yeah. Henry Kyllo is the guy's name," Kendul said, sagged against the wall near the office window. "We tried to hide it again – just as we tried to hide it when Adelina ascended."

Marcton was genuinely shocked – but mostly at the first part of Kendul's little speech; he barely heard the second part. The color drained from his face. "Wait, what!? *This? This* fucking abomination is ascendance? *This* is what we become when we reach–"

"Yes!" Kendul shouted. Then: "Yes," he said again, quieter. He couldn't look Marcton in the eyes any more. Just stared down at his feet. "We didn't know what would happen if people found out. We thought it would be over. Everything. Our whole way of life. To be fair, though, we didn't know – *still* don't know – what the final ascension looks like because we stopped it happening in Adelina. Palermo couldn't bear to lose his daughter, even for something that was supposed to be an honor. We knew it would happen again, but we hoped it wouldn't be while we were leaders. But it did. And he's bigger than Adelina was, and certainly more exposed. We thought we could contain it, thought that by the time it happened, we could–"

Marcton launched himself across the room, tackled Kendul. Both men crashed against the window behind Kendul. It bulged, but didn't shatter, then they were on the floor, Marcton on top of Kendul, right fist pummeling his face over and again.

At the sound of the scuffle, Cleve, Bill, and Melvin came running. The door was open and they burst in. Cleve immediately grabbed Marcton by the shirt collar, yanked him off Kendul. It took both Cleve and Bill – one with each arm – to subdue Marcton. He didn't say a word, just stared at Kendul where he lay bleeding on the office floor, and struggled against Bill and Cleve's bulk, trying desperately to break free so he could pulverize Kendul's face some more.

Melvin stepped outside the office, told everyone everything was OK. A friendly disagreement. Sorted out in a matter of moments.

"What the fuck happened?" Cleve said in Marcton's ear. "Calm down, man. Come on. Calm down."

At Cleve's words, Marcton struggled a little less, sanity slowly filtering back into his brain. His breathing calmed, arm muscles relaxing enough so that Bill and Cleve felt safe releasing him. Marcton shrugged his shirt back into position, smoothed his hair back, said, "This piece of shit killed Palermo. It's his fault."

Bill and Cleve said nothing, just looked down to Kendul for his reaction. Kendul pulled himself into a sitting position on the floor, back against the front of the wooden office desk. Caught his breath. "Sure," he croaked, leaned to the side, coughed twice, spat up blood. "I killed him. He killed himself. I guess both are true."

Cleve and Bill just looked to both men, confused.

Kendul stood up slowly, arranged his clothing so it settled on him properly, wiped blood from his nose, said, "We let it happen, Marcton, and we shouldn't have. We should have told people. At least you. Probably others. But we didn't, and Palermo's dead. That's on me. That's on Palermo. But there was something… intangibly bleak about Adelina when she started changing. It washed over Palermo and me in that house. By stopping her ascension, we felt like we were simultaneously saving her and damning her… But listen, we can do something about it *now*. We can take Kyllo down. Bury him. Like we buried Adelina all those years ago."

"Why not just let him ascend?" Marcton said. "What's he to you? You're not saving a son or brother or something, so just let it run its course."

"Marcton, that's what I'm trying to say: I don't think ascension is a good thing. If you'd felt what we felt back then… You'll have to trust me on this. Kyllo needs to be stopped. Hell, the *Inferne Cutis* as a whole probably needs to be stopped. Palermo could have put this in clearer terms, but I think there's just something cosmically... *wrong* with us."

Marcton went silent.

"All that aside, I know where she is," Kendul continued. "And I think I know how to bring her back. I have no idea how – or even *if* – we can control her, but it's our best shot."

After a long moment Marcton said, "You said she's a machine. Like Kyllo."

"Pretty close, yeah. By the sounds of your description, she's a bit smaller than Kyllo, but probably not by a lot... And if we *can* bring her back, she needs to know that Kyllo killed her father. That could be our ace. Once she knows that, it might be enough for us to control her – to a certain extent, anyway. She can bring down Kyllo, then we put her back in the ground, just like we did the first time. Then we fucking well leave this place. Try to set up again in some other part of the country, far away. Or hell, another country *entirely*. We'll do what we've always done because what other choice is there?"

Time ticked by. Bill and Cleve remained silent, thoroughly in the dark about most of what was said, but smart enough not to ask questions right now. Outside the office, every pair of eyes was aimed toward the window. Marcton glanced out at them, felt the weight of his responsibility to them, then looked back at Kendul.

Finally, Marcton said, "We do this last thing together, then you step down. I think we can agree that your *views* on our society leave a lot to be desired

– especially in a leader. Agreed?"

Kendul turned his head, spat more blood, turned back, looked down at his boots, said, "Agreed."

"OK," Marcton said. "Show me."

EIGHTEEN

This is the house in which she was born. This is the house in which she died. Well, *kind* of died, anyway.

Three years ago, Adelina – the daughter of the Runners' leader – had been the first to achieve ascendance: full lead content in the body. Almost too perfect to be true. But she had never thought anything was perfect, and she was right about that – especially in this case.

She'd been in bed when the change came upon her. It had happened differently than it had for Henry Kyllo. For Adelina, it was swift and agonizing, completing in a matter of hours rather than days. She had gone to bed looking as she normally did, but when she woke up the next morning, sixty percent of her body had metallized overnight. She woke up screaming and didn't stop until her father and Kendul burst into her room. Kendul had been visiting as he occasionally did – secretively – for a shot or two of single malt scotch, maybe a cigar.

When Palermo saw her, he froze. As he watched, she began thrashing madly, the increased weight of her body causing the cheap wooden bed frame to crumple under her as she chopped at its sides with her metal hands and feet. It thumped to the floor, and that sound was what finally snapped Edward out of his paralysis.

He turned and ran for the phone, dialed as fast as his shaking hands would allow. Barked at a woman on the other end of the line over the soulcrushing sounds of his only daughter in horrendous pain: "She's changing!" he yelled. "Get over here and help me. I don't know what the fuck to do!"

Before she could answer him, he'd hung up.

Sandra Beiko, Palermo's second-in-command at the time, arrived twenty minutes later. Palermo explained what he could as she came inside. By the time they got up the stairs, the first wave of Adelina's change was complete. She was huddled in a far corner of the room, now roughly seventy-five percent metal and rock, and about twice her original size. Her breathing had regulated, and she appeared to be in – very understandable – shock.

Over the next ten hours, they watched her grow bigger and bigger. Watched her cycle through incoherent rage, pleading for it to stop, then sleep, then back to rage. Watched her body transform into something beautiful, something horrifying.

The three of them stood in awe, Beiko murmuring the closest thing she had to religious prayers, while Kendul just watched with rapt attention, perhaps the faintest glimpse of jealousy and envy in his eyes. *More than faint*, Palermo thought. *He wishes he was her. He wants to* be *her, wants to go through this*. That was the first time Palermo thought that maybe this was not a good thing, that maybe this was not something to aspire to. A certain blackness crept into his mind when he looked at Adelina. A bleak otherworldliness. Despair, desperation.

But there was something somehow worse than even that in Kendul's eyes – something bordering on the predatory.

The only one of them without either of these reactions was Palermo, of course. This was his daughter, and he just felt sick to his stomach. He was the only one to immediately see the fundamental change in her personality. She was losing control of who she was.

When Adelina was nearly the size of her small bedroom, Palermo took Kendul aside, talked out in the hallway while Beiko stayed inside the bedroom.

"Kendul, we have to stop this."

"*Stop it*, are you insane? This is what–"

"I know, and I don't care. This is my daughter. Something's… happening to her. She's changing on the inside, as well. I can feel it. Even when she can't speak, it's in her eyes. It's like there's someone else inside her now. If we don't stop it, I think she's going to disappear. Maybe not physically, but mentally. Emotionally. I can't…" Tears formed in Palermo's eyes. He hung his head.

Kendul put a hand on Palermo's shoulder. "I feel it, too. Something is… *off*. Corrupted. But we need to see this through. We need to see what she becomes. This is historic. I know you understand that."

That's when the screaming began. Not from Adelina this time.

Palermo flung the door to Adelina's bedroom wide open, looked up to see Beiko flailing around in both of Adelina's giant hands – his daughter whipping her back and forth like a rag doll.

Palermo stepped forward, yelled, "Adelina, stop! Stop it!"

Adelina turned toward the sound of her father's voice. Like a dog, she tilted her massive head ever so slightly one way, then stopped shaking Beiko.

Palermo lowered his voice, said, "Now put her down, Adelina. Please, put her down."

Adelina removed one hand from around Beiko's torso, but kept the other one tight. She moved the fist holding Beiko's limp body against the closest wall, pressed her knuckles flush to it, then slowly, slowly pushed the heel of the palm of her free hand against Beiko's head.

Her skull cracked, crumpled in on itself entirely. Adelina smeared the resulting mess of blood and bone along the wall in an arc, like a shooting star.

Adelina dropped the body and reached out for Kendul, something monstrous burning in her eyes.

Palermo backed out into the hallway as quickly as his feet would take him. Kendul drew his gun, started firing at her. The bullets ricocheted off her solid steel frame, bounced around the room, *thwipping* into drywall. One bullet nearly drove into Palermo's leg, but he moved in time to avoid it. He yelled for Kendul to stop and, after one of the bullets whizzed by Kendul's ear, he was shocked enough at his brush with death to stop firing.

Kendul assumed that Palermo had screamed at him

to stop firing because this was still, in some way, his daughter, but that was untrue; Palermo knew that his daughter – if she was still in there at all – was not the one who'd killed Sandra, was not the one trying to kill Kendul and himself now. He'd simply told him to cease fire for practical reasons – the bullets were bouncing off. They needed to try something else to stop her.

"It's not working, Kendul! You'll kill us both!" Palermo said. Kendul moved out of the room into the hallway, opened his mouth to speak, since it appeared that Adelina was backing off.

That's when she lunged again.

An enormous metal hand burst out of the room, into the hallway where both men stood, cracking through the bedroom doorframe, splinters flying. Adelina roared once, and it was like no sound either man had ever heard in his life. Entirely inhuman.

With no time to think – and Adelina's other hand moving to join the first, fingers almost the width of fence posts, her head dropped down to try to see them – both men opened fire. They backed away as far as they could and just emptied their weapons.

Nearly every shot bounced off, but on two occasions Palermo's scrambling, terrified mind subconsciously picked up that two or three of their shots seemed to drive home. But where? At what point on her body?

Then it came to him. As their guns clicked empty, Palermo muttered, "Joints." He turned his head toward Kendul. "Aim for the joints. They must not be fully formed or something."

Kendul nodded. "Ammo?"

"Downstairs, follow me."

Since Adelina was now blocking most of the upstairs landing, both men vaulted over the banister, dropped onto the staircase, ran to the basement.

"Shotguns will do more damage. Got a few down here," Palermo said. He moved quickly to the gun cabinet while Kendul kept watch on the stairs – not that Adelina could fit down the staircase, obviously, but she could come tumbling down it, he supposed, and just roll over them like the boulder from *Raiders of the Lost Ark*.

"Come on, man, come on," Kendul said.

Palermo smashed the glass with the butt of his gun, dropped the gun on the floor, reached inside, grabbed two shotguns, scrambled around for ammo, chucked a shotgun and some shells in Kendul's general direction, then started loading his own weapon.

There was a deep moan from upstairs, thumping, then an otherworldly scream that filled their ears, drove deep into their brains.

"Christ!" Palermo said, shaking his head from side to side, as if the noise were a tangible thing and he was trying to dislodge it from his head.

A loud crash, wood splintering. It sounded like she'd fallen through – or consciously *driven herself* through – the second-floor ceiling.

"Load up, man. She's coming," Kendul said. "She's fucking coming."

More thumping – metal on wood, metal on tile – as she clomped around the main floor, probably searching room to room, her body busting through the walls, shredding the house, gutting it like a demolition ball.

She stopped at the top of the stairs, moved her head down to see.

Palermo's base instinct was to hide. His primary thought being *if she can't see us, she can't hurt us*. But he knew they needed to try to stop her, couldn't let her just go rampaging around, destroying the street, the whole fucking city.

They had to *try* to be seen.

Going against every natural instinct in his body – every fiber of his being shouting at him to *get the fuck away!* – Palermo moved to the bottom of the stairs where he and Adelina locked eyes. Her head was enormous, eyes big metal balls set into a face composed of shards of what looked like jagged rock and steel.

She snorted once, pulled her head out of sight. Then, a second before her foot came down, Palermo knew what she was going to do, and he leaped backward out of the way.

Her right leg crashed through the basement ceiling, and she toppled down into the far side of the room, one leg very nearly touching the basement floor, the other caught on the opposite side of a steel support beam. Her bulk tilted to one side and she fell onto her back, cracking the concrete floor, sending up chunks of it to either side of her.

Palermo and Kendul knew that the moment she got to her feet, they'd be dead – knew that this was their one and only shot. There was nowhere left to go.

They opened fire.

At this range, most of the shot found its mark. Palermo concentrated on the right leg joint; Kendul fired on the right arm joint. Adelina wailed in pain. They fired and reloaded, fired and reloaded as fast as their shaking fingers would allow.

The first limb to come off was the right arm. It dropped to the basement floor with a thud, blood and some other fluid leaking out. Kendul moved on to the left arm.

The right leg was next to go. Then both men were firing into the joint of her left arm.

Adelina thrashed around on her back, reaching her remaining hand out, madly waving it back and forth blindly. Kendul was standing too close, and one of her fingers caught his right leg, shattered the bone there. He dropped, kept firing.

The left arm finally came free, more blood pumping out. Thick and dark.

With three limbs separated from her body, Adelina went from bellowing to moaning, then whimpering. Then silence.

Kendul was leaning on his right side on the ground, shaking shells free from another box of ammo, when Palermo put a hand on his shoulder, said, "It's done, James. No more."

Kendul blinked, closed his eyes tight against the pain in his leg. He nodded, rolled onto his back, dropped the shotgun, breathing heavily.

Palermo stood back up, looked at the remains of what used to be his daughter.

Arms and legs the width of telephone poles.

Torso the size of a small car.

Head the size of a truck engine, tilted to one side, eyes dead.

Nothing on the body moved.

Later, when they dug out the basement and buried her there, as far as he knew, only Kendul felt the ever so faint thrum of machinery in his bones.

He didn't know what to make of it at the time, but the feeling had stayed with him through the years. Subconscious at first, the feeling grew until it become unquestionable knowledge:

Adelina Palermo was still alive.

And the same part of him that had insisted Adelina not be stopped moments before she'd killed Sandra Beiko tore into the forefront of his mind, telling him to keep this quiet. Some diseased part of his soul that revered this abomination as a god.

NINETEEN

Marcton and Kendul stood on rubble in the basement where Adelina was buried. Kendul had brought a large duffle bag along, but hadn't opened it when they'd arrived, and hadn't told Marcton what was inside.

"She's here?" Marcton said. "Beneath us?"

Kendul nodded, thought: *And there's that faint thrumming in my bones again, but even stronger than I remember.* He still couldn't understand how Edward hadn't been able to feel it.

The house itself was mostly destroyed on the inside, but – quite miraculously – had stayed up the past three years. As amazing as that was, neither Marcton nor Kendul wanted to test their luck, so were fairly edgy, reacting to every creak and groan. From the outside it looked somewhat alright, but one wall had entirely come down, making it clear to any passerby that no one lived there, and likely hadn't for years.

"So," Marcton said. "We just start digging, do we? Then put her back together like fucking Humpty Dumpty?"

Kendul grimaced. "Something like that, yeah."

Kendul turned, picked up one of the shovels they'd brought, stuck it into the earth, started heaving dirt and small chunks of concrete over his shoulder. Marcton followed suit. Before long, they'd uncovered an arm and part of Adelina's torso.

"Fuck me running," Marcton said, stopped digging, leaned on his shovel handle. "She is here."

"Why would I lie, Marcton? What point would that have served?"

"I know, I know, it's just... Christ. I somehow didn't expect it to be true."

"Let's get some more hands in to get her out."

"Yeah," Marcton said, still dazed by confirmation of the discovery. "I'll make the call."

Three hours later, six sweating men – Kendul, Marcton, Cleve, Bill, and two random Runners – stood in a semi-circle around the two arms, one leg, and one torso-leg combination of what now constituted Adelina Palermo's body.

"Jesus," one of the randoms said.

"Crazy," said the other, looked over at Kendul and Marcton. "What is this again? Some kinda robot?"

It's you, Kendul thought. *This is you. All of you. What you'd become in your purest state.* He shuddered, said, "Yeah. Some kinda robot."

On some level, they know. Even if it was never spoken aloud, they know. They have to sense it somehow, don't they?

Kendul glanced at the four men they'd called in to help dig Adelina's body out of the basement. Cleve and Bill were part of Marcton's team, his inner circle, and they likely knew what they were looking at, but

maybe Marcton told them to shut up about it. The
other two, though – the looks on their faces indicated
to Kendul that they weren't necessarily firing on
all cylinders, so maybe this moment's profound
significance escaped them. Kendul thought that even
if they *did* know – if Marcton and Kendul just came
right out and told them – they still wouldn't really
grasp it. They might intellectually know, but anything
deeper would be impossible.

Better safe than sorry.

"What're your names?" Kendul asked, flung his
shovel into a corner of the basement. Something
nearby groaned, shifted, and everyone looked alarmed
for a moment till the noise settled, stopped.

"Harold."

"Jeremy."

"Well, Harold and Jeremy," Kendul continued.
"What if I told you that this is what you turn into
when you achieve ascendance?"

Harold and Jeremy exchanged disbelieving glances.

"*Geeeeeet* fucked!" Harold said, with a giant grin on
his big dumb face. "Seriously?"

Jeremy, possibly the smarter of the two, just shook
his head, said, "No way. Nuh-uh."

Kendul held their gazes seriously for a moment,
then dropped his eyes, laughed once, sharply, said,
"Nah, it's just some kinda robot. You guys're right."

Harold and Jeremy looked satisfied with the answer.
Easier to accept. Easier to swallow. Less horrifying
than knowing that the thing you've been taught to
aspire to – to treat as a lifelong ambition – ends with
transformation into a giant beast that your own kind

felt the need to blast *literally* limb from limb, and bury in the ground.

"Head back to the warehouse, fellas," Marcton said, nodding at Jeremy and Harold. "We'll catch up with you soon. And thanks for the help. Much appreciated."

They nodded, looking both relieved and somewhat confused.

"Oh, and don't mention the big robot, OK?"

They nodded, but Marcton knew they wouldn't be able to keep their mouths shut. It wouldn't matter soon enough, anyway. Either their plan would work, and Adelina would stop Kyllo – and they could then kill and bury her somewhere else (this time hopefully for good) – or their plan wouldn't work, and Kyllo would carry on into the outside world, destroying the way of life and the anonymity they'd been building for over a century.

Jeremy and Harold said their goodbyes and left the basement. When he heard car doors slam, Marcton said, "Not the brightest bulbs, I know, but they work like fucking dogs."

"By the way, any word of disappearances tonight from your camp?" Kendul asked.

"Not that I've heard, no. I kinda forgot about that, actually, with everything else blowing up. You?"

"No. Weird. Maybe whomever or whatever's responsible for punishing our transgressions has more on its mind tonight, too."

Marcton looked worried. "Maybe. It's still early, though, too."

Kendul nodded. The moment passed, then:

"So," Marcton said. "What now?"

The sky was darkening, and snow was still falling – hadn't stopped in days, and showed no signs of doing so.

"Well," Kendul said. "Since none of the king's horses or men are coming, I'd say we have to put her back together again ourselves."

"I don't like the Humpty Dumpty analogy," Cleve said. "Can we use Frankenstein instead?"

"You mean Frankenstein's monster," Kendul said.

"I mean fuck you," Cleve shot back.

"Alright," Marcton said, "Frankenstein's monster, it is. So how we do it? I know you said you *feel* that she's alive, Kendul – in your bones, or whatever – but she looks real fuckin' dead to the rest of us."

Kendul shot him a look, considered further arguments, but then just dropped his eyes. *I'm so goddamn tired. Exhausted by all this. Just wiped the fuck out...*

"So what do we do now?" Marcton said. "Just tell us. Just *tell* us."

Kendul looked back up at Marcton and in that instant – in a brief flash of insight – knew the kid would make a good leader. Probably better than Palermo ever was. He couldn't put his finger on what made him think it, but it was suddenly there in his mind, like a memory of childhood, brought back to the surface. Never gone, just buried for a while, but always true.

"Alright, look. I don't know exactly *how* we do it, but we need something to bring her back to *us*. I said earlier that our ace in the hole could be the fact that

Kyllo killed her father. I think that was wrong: it's not our ace in the hole; it's the only fucking card we've got."

"Séance," Cleve said.

"No," said Kendul. "Not a fucking séance. Dipshit."

"Fine, not a fucking séance. Then what?"

"I think we just need to tell her. That her father is dead. That we know who killed him. All of us. And she needs to know we truly *need* her."

"Do we need to, like, hold hands and shit?" Bill said.

"Yes. Yes, we do," Kendul said.

"Oh. Um. I was kind of joking, but… OK."

Kendul reached out his hand toward Marcton. Marcton took it, clasped it tightly. Nodded. Marcton grabbed Cleve's hand. Cleve took Bill's. Bill took Kendul's.

Every one of them wanted to make a joke to relieve the awkwardness, but no one did. Almost immediately, each man felt the thrumming Kendul had experienced – was experiencing stronger than ever now.

Snowflakes fell gently outside. Marcton watched it through one of the dirty basement windows, and just let whatever was happening fill him up. Some of the snow sifted down through the side of the house that bore no wall. It blew in under the basement door, drifted down the stairs.

"Adelina, we–" Marcton began.

"Shut up," Kendul cut him off. "Just don't. Doesn't feel right. Just think. Just… thoughts."

Silence wrapped the room so tightly, it felt like the

air was being sucked out into the night.

And Adelina heard them.

She heard them loud and clear.

Adelina felt Kendul's and the others' presence like a soft blanket draped slowly over her body. As she concentrated on connecting to their thoughts, her world of mostly formless swirls and forks of lightning began to solidify into something more concrete. Something tangible.

Crumbling walls, rubble, and dirt crisped into her mind. *I know this place*, she thought. *I know where this is. This is home. My home.*

As the scene continued to sharpen, four men took shape along the walls. *Kendul. Dad's friend. That one I know. The others… have I seen them before? I can't remember. But they're familiar.*

A warm feeling washed over her, then – the warmest feeling she'd had in as long as she could remember.

Their thoughts were intensely focused on something in the ground. Something in the dirt. Exposed.

And then Adelina saw what they saw.

At first, she only saw it as the horribly mutated machine it would appear to be to most people – even to her kind – but then memories flooded her brain, and she realized that this was her. This was her body. She was *inside* that thing.

Or *could* be.

That was also the moment she realized she'd been here all along. Stuck in the cold ground, dismembered, left to rot for years.

Why would they do this to me? What could I have done to deserve this?

But those memories would not return. The part of her that understood what all this meant – what she'd been manipulated into doing all along: the plan for Henry; the goal; what needed to be achieved – that part of her would not allow any of her experience to become truly distasteful.

Though she did not know why – or at least no *conscious* idea why – she was instrumental to what Henry was destined for. What he was *made* to do, to become.

Then, clear as a bell, this thought came to her, calming, serene: *Something inside me set all this in motion. That thing that protected our people for so long. Hid us from prying eyes. It is different now, but taken root in me. It has become me. Henry is our future. Henry must survive at all cost. He is –*

– a murderer, your father's killer –

The thought slipped beneath her radar, inserted itself into her narrative. Coming from the four men:

– Kyllo killed your father –

– we need your help –

– we need you –

– *No* – the voice within her broke in: *Kyllo must survive. He will redefine what you are. What we all are. He will reshape everything, bring about the end of –*

Then back to the men again:

– come back, come back –

– he's your father's murderer, Adelina –

– you need to stop him, you need to –

Something like breath moved through the torso

of the machine in the ground, and Marcton flinched back, tripped over busted concrete, chunks of dirt, fell flat on his back.

The other three men stared at the machine's chest.

"Un-fucking-real," Cleve said. He turned to Bill: "Did we do that? We fucking did that, didn't we?"

"I think we may have fucking done that, Cleve," Bill replied.

"Steady," Kendul breathed. "Steady on." He was concentrating on the torso now, directing his thoughts there specifically.

With Marcton out of the circle, still in shock, dazed, just staring, the remaining three men joined hands.

"Keep going," Kendul said. "Focus."

As true and as real as her previous thoughts had felt about Henry Kyllo needing to be protected, to be saved at all costs, these new thoughts were just as true and just as real: he killed her father. Rage boiled up inside her – a rage she was incapable of feeling until now.

When Palermo had died on the street outside that apartment building, she'd known it, felt it on some level, but the connection to Kyllo wasn't there. The knowledge of who killed her father hovered and flitted at the edges of her subconscious like a hummingbird: gentle, almost unnoticeable, not wanting to be detected. And, as she now knew, *actively* not wanting to be detected. Actively hiding from becoming part of her memories, her psychological makeup.

But now, realizing where she was, *what* she really was, Kendul's and the others' words, desires made more sense to her, *drove* her more than this other, manipulative, voice. This was not some indistinct, vague endgame to be played out on a grandiose stage.

This was revenge, pure and simple, and it spoke to her like nothing before ever had.

The thrumming in her chest increased: she willed it to do so. She saw clearly what she was – an organic mechanical beast broken to pieces in the cold, hard earth – and for the first time in as long as she could remember, she wanted something deeply. Down to her core. She needed to experience something she'd been denied for years:

Life.

In whatever form that took. She wanted it.

And she would have it.

Marcton stood up, brushed himself off. "Sorry, got freaked out there."

"It's fine," Kendul said. "Get back into the circle. Quickly."

Marcton moved ahead to join the circle when a fullblown breath inflated the machine's torso.

Inhale.

Exhale.

No one moved.

Then Cleve very quietly whispered, "Guys, should we try to reattach–"

And at that moment, Adelina's three disembodied limbs rose up out of the dirt, shot toward her torso, and stuck fast to her joints.

"Jesus fucking fuck," Marcton breathed.

"Never mind," Cleve said.

Power churned inside Adelina's chest. She felt

herself fill with it. A strength she'd never felt before, never known was possible.

Was this what happened before, and then at some point I lost control, and people dismembered me?

Metal and rock-hewn shards on her face contracted, lifted, resembled a scowl of sorts. She would need to get used to this body. Try to control it this time.

"Um," Marcton said. "What now?"

"Let's give her some room," Kendul said. "Come on." He waved his arms. "Step back, stay up against this wall." They moved against the farthest wall. Kendul reached over to the duffle bag he'd brought. He unzipped it, reached inside, produced four shotguns and a pile of ammo.

"Uhh," Cleve said.

"Just a precaution," Kendul said. "This is how me and Edward downed her the first time. Barely. Gotta aim for the joints."

Each man took a shotgun, loaded it, stood and waited.

Minutes that felt like hours ticked by as Adelina's mind got used to its host again. Still lying on her back in the dirt, she flexed her fingers, moved her enormous feet back and forth – no toes as such there, more just two slabs of steel with what looked like tread of some kind, like on a tank, except it didn't move. She lifted a knee up, brought it back down.

The snow had been drifting down and in through the holes in the roof and the one downed wall, had been steadily gathering, more and more blowing in as the wind had intensified. There had been about an inch or two when they'd arrived, already there from the previous few nights' snowfall, but enough now had accumulated that there were a few inches to either side of Adelina, and a solid dusting on top of her.

As she continued to experiment with her body, at one point it looked like she was attempting something specific. Cleve was the first to recognize it.

"Is she…" He trailed off, frowning.

Kendul smiled. "Yeah, I think she is."

Marcton voiced it: "Snow angel."

Adelina moved her arms up and down, her legs side to side. The movements made the ground shudder.

"Surreal," Marcton said, turned to Kendul. "I gather this is not how shit went down the first time?"

"Absolutely not. Much more running, screaming, and general death that first time. This is preferable by far."

That's when Adelina sat up, and all four men who'd resurrected her caught their breath. Snow drifted down from her arms and midsection, revealing both blackened and gleaming metal.

The men just stared and waited. For death. Or, hopefully, something less permanent.

Adelina clicked her tongue a few times; it sounded almost like someone forging a sword.

"Adelina," Kendul said, breaking the silence and startling his companions. He knew he had to keep it simple. Didn't want to clutter up her mind with a bunch of pointless questions. "What do you need from us?"

Adelina blinked. Immense power coursed through her; she found it difficult to stem its flow. But her mind was calming, filtering information, only allowing through the parts of herself she recognized. Trying like hell to keep the weight of decades of her ancestry at bay. That's what wanted in, she understood: *History*, she thought. *Longevity. Continuation.*

The big metal balls that were her eyes moved from side to side, taking the men in. They squirmed under her gaze.

"Kyllo," was all she said: granite dragged across concrete. It was all she needed to say.

And the voice that said it sounded like it had been waiting to say that particular word all its life.

TWENTY

With every step Henry Kyllo took down the subway tunnel, the walls shook.

"We need to find a light source, Henry."

No answer, just more plodding.

It was getting harder and harder to get through to Henry now. Milo realized it would be best if he concentrated on working with Faye on a plan for getting them out of here. Away from these tunnels. Away from this whole city.

"Faye, how are you doing?"

"I feel a lot better," she said, but winced when she moved her wounded arm and shoulder. "This damn thing still hurts, but not even close to as bad as before."

They carried on in silence for a while, then Faye looked up at Henry, said, "How's he doing?"

"Not great. No idea what's going on in his head, and he won't say anything. I don't know where he's gone, but I'm scared he won't be coming back."

And it was true. Henry's mood darkened with each step he took, as though the darkness around him was becoming part of him, seeping into his structure. He felt as though he'd fallen down a very deep well and could no longer see the top – the light there long extinguished. And whenever he tried to scramble back up the sides of the well, they became slick with moisture, any handhold treacherous, impossible. He knew, too, that something was moving in to replace who he'd been. He was losing his internal battle.

Up ahead, some pinpricks of light. Shuffling sounds.

The lights wobbled from side to side as the tunnel curved and they were able to better see what it was: a handful of city workers, probably down here fixing something. With the sound of Henry's thunderous steps, the lights became more frenzied as the workers figured out that whatever was stomping its way toward them was *really* big. And definitely not a subway train.

Scuffling, clattering sounds, and the lights scattered. Most vanished from sight instantly, but one stayed, low to the ground. As Henry, Milo, and Faye approached, they saw that one of the workers had dropped his flashlight. It sat in the dirt near the tracks.

"Light source," said Faye.

"Ask and ye shall receive," Milo replied, laughed.

"Well, while we're asking, another one woulda been nice," Faye said.

Milo picked up the flashlight, waved it around. The shaft of light caught the side of what appeared to be another tunnel – this one leading away from the old, disused section of the underground.

"Must lead to the tunnel that's actually in use," Milo said. "Maybe something in this old tunnel is still hooked up to the new line?"

"Or, jeez, I dunno," Faye said, "maybe they were

working in the new tunnel, heard *giant goddamn footsteps* this way, decided to come check it out, saw what it was – or at least heard it – and got the hell out of Dodge."

Milo nodded, grinned. "Yeah, that's more likely, you're right."

But as quickly as the grin appeared on Milo's face, he felt his heart sink as he thought about the situation. What was their plan here? *Hide* was not a helpful idea due to Henry's size, so besides another rampage – the first one not turning out well for anyone involved – running away was the only other option. They needed to somehow try to get out of the city without being noticed. Underground *was* the best option for that plan, but now there were two options within that choice: old tunnels or new tunnels? Milo had no idea they were linked so openly.

"Henry," Milo called up to his friend. "Listen, you've got to respond now. Which way do you wanna go? The old tunnels will be less populated – and no trains running in them – but they won't extend as far out of the city as the new ones, so… what do you think?"

Henry just breathed in, breathed out. Stared down this slightly smaller tunnel, which led to the working subway lines. Blinked every once in a while.

Milo was about to ask again, clearly frustrated, but then Henry's giant metal eyeballs swiveled around, found his friend, and some kind of understanding passed between them. Henry didn't speak, but Milo thought he saw a brand of despair on Henry's face that he would not have thought possible. It made his heart ache.

What is he thinking? What does he think he's done? What does he know *he's done?* As Milo thought this last, the sound of a subway rumbling down the line nearby filtered over to where they stood. Henry's eyes settled momentarily on Faye, then he turned his head, and continued stomping away down the old tunnel, away from the sound of the train.

Milo looked at Faye, who shrugged, said, "Guess that answers your question."

They moved ahead of Henry, Milo leading the way through the pitch dark with their newfound flashlight.

They walked along in silence for a few hundred feet, then Henry suddenly stopped, turned himself around more quickly than Milo or Faye would have expected, given his size and downturned mood.

"Whoa, whoa, Henry, what…" Milo began.

And then Henry was *running*.

The ground shook. Henry's head scraped the tunnel ceiling with each step. Nearing twenty feet tall now, if he was an inch. Bits of tile and concrete crumbled off the walls. Milo and Faye ran after him, the flashlight a feeble cone of useless light in the darkness as Henry faded from view.

"Henry! Christ! What are you doing!? Where are you *going*!?" Milo yelled after him.

Henry reached the entrance to the working subway line, ducked down, and thundered through.

Moments later, he emerged into a different tunnel, this one strung with occasional lights, and the sound of a subway train somewhere in the distance.

Henry ran toward it.

● ● ●

When Adelina stood to her full height – Kendul, Marcton, Bill, and Cleve helping her get her footing, then assisting her outside the crumbling walls of the house – she was nearly as tall as Henry, but nowhere near as bulky. Something about her, though, inspired more terror in the men's hearts than Henry had when they'd seen him entering the old subway tunnels. Some indefinable dread that latched onto their minds.

The snow was two feet thick in some places – snow drifts more than double that height. And it was still coming. Now faster and harder than any of them had ever seen snow fall in their lives.

Marcton glanced up into the slate-colored sky, said, "Chopper."

A few seconds later everyone else heard it, then they all saw it. It dipped down, then a searchlight scoured the houses several blocks over. Another chopper appeared a bit farther away. The sound of sirens.

The veil has definitely been pulled back now, Kendul thought, the ideas bubbling up from his guts, his intuition, his very evolution. *We will be hunted, exterminated, wiped from the face of the earth. Not only have we been exposed, but whatever used to protect us seems to now be actively looking to destroy us.*

"We should get moving," Kendul said. The others nodded slowly. They felt it, too. There was a wave coming. First the snow, then the people.

Seeking to bury them completely.

"The old subway tunnels is where we last saw Henry, Adelina," Marcton said. "The abandoned entrance."

Adelina gave no indication she heard him. But then she looked side to side, up and down the street. She still said nothing, but began walking in the direction of the subway tunnels.

"Uh, should we…" Cleve began.

"Follow? Yeah," Marcton said. "But in the Hummer. She's focused, alright. Now we just have to keep up. I'll bring it over. You guys keep an eye on her."

Marcton hustled to the vehicle, jumped in, started it, pulled it around. It nearly got stuck in snow twice, but he was able to wrench it out before the tires dug in.

Kendul took the passenger seat; Cleve and Bill hopped in the back. They pulled away from the house, found Adelina in the headlights. She stuck to the roads, walking right down the middle – the occasional pedestrian fleeing in terror, or just edging away slowly, unsure what they were seeing, finding it difficult to believe, and *then* running away. There was no toss-up between fight or flight – everyone turned tail and ran like hell.

The sirens sounded like they were getting closer; the helicopter searchlights would be zeroing in soon – only a matter of time till they saw, or got word of, the giant steel behemoth walking around the city.

The *second* one.

The men in the Hummer understood that this would be an all-out attack. The city would come to bear with full force. They silently pulled out whatever weapons they carried, loaded them, sat grimly and waited for it to begin.

A cop car streaked by a couple of blocks ahead, lost control in the snow, vanished from sight. They heard a crash moments later.

They're insane, Kendul thought. *They're being driven to the point where safety on any level is not a concern.*

Three blocks away from the entrance to the old subway line, two more cop cars emerged into view – these ones going slightly slower. Their searchlights swiveled, found Adelina. Both cars slammed on their brakes, slid about thirty feet in the ice and snow, stopped.

Adelina just kept stomping toward the cop cars, unfazed.

The cops spun their wheels, found purchase after fishtailing, headed straight toward Adelina. The cops riding shotgun leaned out their windows, began firing their guns at her. The bullets pinged off. Zero effect. The first car rammed into Adelina's left leg just after she brought it down to street level. The hood crumpled. The driver's head drove into the windshield, cracked it, creating a star-shaped burst of blood and glass. The passenger was thrown free, but was already dead as he flew through the air. He landed in a nearby snowbank, a discarded rag doll. His face a mask of blood. Eyes glazed over, seeing nothing.

The second car came in just under Adelina's right foot. She stomped its engine block into the ground. She fell forward on her right knee, off balance, crushed the driver to a pulp in an instant. The passenger fired his revolver at her until she moved her enormous left hand down and pushed hard toward the ground on that side of the car. Everything beneath her hand crumpled in on itself. Her hand came away streaked with blood.

Fucking kamikaze, Bill thought, true fear threading its way through his guts for the first time in as long as he could remember. *How do you fight this?*

Adelina regained her balance, looked down at herself, then up at the choppers moving in. She raised both arms, then, as if to say, *Come on. Here I am. What are you waiting for?*

She lowered her arms, kept walking toward the subway entrance.

Two blocks. One block. More sirens all around them, and the choppers closing in.

Marcton pulled the Hummer over to the side of the road, hopped out, motioned for the others to follow, yelled, "Let's go! Move!"

The four men ran single file through the snow, nearly on Adelina's heels now.

That's when one of the choppers' searchlights found Adelina and opened fire. The bullets just ricocheted off her, but the double-line of heavy bullets caught Cleve and Bill in mid-stride, sent them both sprawling.

They sat up in the snow as the helicopter came around for another run.

Marcton ran back, grabbed them each by one arm, hoisted them back onto their feet, barked, "Go! Get underground now!"

Kendul had already gone under, and Adelina was squeezing herself into the entrance now, too. She hacked at the edges to make it wider, concrete falling away to either side – she was a bit smaller than Henry, but also in one hell of a rush.

She crawled in, moved deeper inside until she was able to stand somewhat comfortably.

Marcton, Bill, and Cleve scrambled down the destroyed entrance, picking their way over the rubble as they went in. Bill had the most trouble negotiating the loose chunks of concrete, his foot twice getting stuck under it.

One of the helicopters opened fire, just as a cop car came careening into view. The bullets riddled the car, killing both occupants. The cop car hopped the curb, slammed into Bill where he clambered over a small hill of rubble.

Crushed him against a wall to the left of the entrance.

He was pinned between the car and wall, the hood of the vehicle mashing his waist and part of his chest, his legs twisted and caught under the engine.

He screamed. Cleve moved toward him from the subway entrance, but Marcton pulled him back, said, "He's done, Cleve. We have to go. Come on." Pulled on Cleve's collar, spun him around roughly, pushed his back.

They ran deeper into the tunnel, caught up to Kendul and Adelina, turned back to look as the whine of a descending chopper got closer and closer. Bill screamed again, then the chopper slammed full force into the cop car, obliterating Bill in a ball of fire that rose up into the night, belching black smoke.

If everyone didn't know where all the action was before, they do now, Kendul thought.

Tears glistened on Cleve's eyelids – from smoke or grief or both, Marcton didn't know. "What the *fuck*, Marcton!? What the fuck was that? What's wrong with them? They're just fucking *divebombing* us!"

Marcton didn't respond.

"Just keep running, Cleve. Keep running," Kendul said. He turned and headed into the blackness of the tunnel, Adelina leading the way like she was a bloodhound, like she knew which way and how far Henry and the others had gone – which she did. Henry's location was like a bright red dot in the black of her mind's eye. She instinctively knew him like twins know each other, like a mother knows her own child.

Aboveground, they heard more choppers, more sirens.

Marcton clapped Cleve on the back, gently nudged him forward. Cleve took one last look at the mouth of the tunnel entrance – entirely engulfed now in fire, rubble, and black smoke.

Marcton wondered what was next. *Drones? Full missile airstrikes? Christ.*

They ran hard beneath the skin of the city then, no longer looking back for anything.

TWENTY-ONE

Moments before the subway train slammed into Henry Kyllo, these were his thoughts:

I have killed, and I will kill again.

I do not want this. I do not deserve this.

More death as a result, but at least it will be over. I will be stopped. Whatever's inside me is eating its way out. Devouring me as it goes. Who I am. Who I was. Only a hint of a shadow of me remains.

This will end it. For me, for Faye, Milo, everyone.

I need to die. I need to die.

When the train hit Henry, it drove him back a hundred yards, brakes screeching the entire way. It caved in his chest, crumpled parts of his face, severed one finger from his right hand, two from his left.

Inside the train, dozens were killed instantly, thrown around, batted from side to side as most of the cars of the train derailed, slammed into the sides of the tunnel. Glass and steel punctured lungs, ripped off limbs, crushed torsos, flattened heads, shattered spines. Many more were severely injured, and bled to death not long after the train finally came to a stop. Those who somehow made it through somewhat unscathed – mostly those at the back of the train – wandered around the wreckage crying, dazed.

When Milo and Faye heard the deafening crash, they ran toward it through the service tunnel that joined the old and new lines. Panic rose in Milo's chest. Disbelief and horror quickly replaced that feeling once they saw the devastation.

Milo shone his flashlight toward the wreckage. Henry was lying on his back several hundred feet from where Milo and Faye stood. The car at the front of the train was mostly crumpled inward, had settled across one of Henry's legs. Four or five cars beyond it were visible before there was a turn in the tunnel, and these cars were all tilted at crazy angles – one of them nearly vertical. A small pile of dead bodies had accumulated at the bottom of the closest car where it had been wrenched open by the force of the impact, spilling its contents onto the track.

Faye and Milo ran toward Henry, stopped short. Tried to block out the cries for help, screams of agony coming from seemingly every direction.

"Henry!" Milo shouted above the din. Milo put a hand on the leg that was trapped under the train car. He wanted to ask why, but he thought he knew why. So did Faye.

This was his only way out. Not escaping the city. Running forever. Out of control.

But it hadn't worked.

Milo saw Henry's shattered chest rise, pull in breath. One eye opened slowly. A nearby sparking wire caught the shiny part of that eye, and Milo had a horrible feeling that something beyond any of their comprehension was at work here. This wasn't just ascension that had gotten out of hand. This had been calculated. By who or what, Milo had no idea. But there was something ageless in the spark of that eye. Something malignant. Persistent.

Less and less remained of Henry with every passing second, but Milo would stay by his side for however long he lasted. For however long he needed his friend.

Inside Henry, the blackness he'd hoped would be his world forever stirred. It churned into recognizable shape. A recognizable *feeling*.

He was alive. He cracked an eye. The first thing he saw was Milo. Then Faye. His other eye opened, and his head turned. He saw destruction. Death.

Pain everywhere, and all his doing.

He didn't know it then, but the last words he would speak came out of his misshapen mouth. He looked at Milo, concentrated, and said, "Why can't I die? I just want to die. I can't feel myself anymore, Milo. There's something awful happening... *inside*."

And then Henry Kyllo grew again.

This time, he didn't feel it at all. The tiny portion of his personality, his consciousness – whatever made him who he was – was thrown so far back from the experience that it could have been happening to someone else.

His legs and arms grew longer, his torso stronger, wider, his head bigger, sharper – and all of him a darker metal, a coarser rock, bordering on black.

Milo dragged Faye back, as far away from Henry

as he could. Henry gained his feet, any damage from the train now fully healed, covered over. His head and shoulders burst through the tunnel ceiling, crashed through into the city street above. A few cars swerved around him, but most just shot straight into him, looks of rage and hatred on people's faces before they hit.

Henry looked up, saw the choppers in the sky, saw police cars, fire engines, ambulances everywhere – and regular people on the street charging at him, throwing themselves into their attacks, heedless of any injury they might sustain themselves.

This is humanity's last ditch effort to save itself, Henry thought, unaware where the thought had come from, but knowing its truth. *We are the Other, and we cannot be understood.*

Henry grew more, his gleaming black torso now rocketing up through the pavement, chunks cracking to either side of him.

He turned his massive head, saw a tank rolling down the street toward him. The tank fired, the shell catching him high on the cheek. Besides losing his vision momentarily, there were no adverse effects whatsoever.

Ridiculous, he thought. *I am a ridiculous cartoon monster, but I will be the end of all these people.*

The fear was contagious. More virulent than any plague in history.

The Other must be eradicated.

Far away in a war room in the country's capitol, generals seized with this inexplicable, overriding fear gave the order that nuclear missiles – along with dozens of other rockets – were to be launched in Henry Kyllo's direction. But that order was moot, since the personnel who turned the keys to launch the missiles *had already done so*.

And it was the same in as many other countries as were in range.

Humanity acted as one organism under threat of extinction, throwing everything it had at the enemy. A colossal worldwide Hail Mary to try to save itself from eradication.

Adelina Palermo walked through the dark of the old subway tunnel until she heard the crash of the train ploughing into Henry. She found the tunnel joining the old subway line with the new one, and headed down it.

Behind her, with no light source to help them, Marcton, Cleve, and Kendul simply followed Adelina's footsteps, watched for any shifting movements in the darkness that might reveal her changing direction.

When the sound of the crash reached them, rumbling through the walls, they picked up their pace, hearts in their throats – even though somewhere deep down, they knew they were running toward a lost battle.

The chaos aboveground had, to their minds, dwarfed their petty little revenge drama immeasurably. It seemed shockingly minor in the face of what was happening. All three men felt that this wasn't even about the *Inferne Cutis* any more – perhaps had *never* really been about them.

But still they plodded on.

Just grist for whatever new mill was starting up aboveground, Kendul thought, and shivered.

Adelina and the men emerged from the side tunnel joining the subway lines, and saw the destruction Henry had caused. By the time they arrived, only Henry's legs were visible, his upper portion having already burst through to the street above. They heard cars crashing. Sirens. Bombs. People were falling down through the hole Henry had created. Breaking their arms and legs from the fall. Bleeding. Dying.

Though she could not cry outwardly, internally, Adelina wept for her father. She wept for whatever was happening to the world above. She wept because she knew how this would end, had seen it in her mind well before events had progressed to this point, but was powerless to stop it, or even fully *believe* it could happen.

The possibility that she had, in fact, been one of the catalysts for it was something she consciously blotted out. There was no reserve of calm left in her body. What little of herself remained was focused solely on fighting whatever was taking her over inside. It wanted her to *help* Henry by leaving him alone. She had done her job, had kept Milo in the picture, which in turn helped keep Henry in the picture, away from prying eyes so that he could *mature*. Grow into exactly what he'd become.

She fought hard against what was inside her, even though she knew her efforts would amount to absolutely nothing of note. That nothing would change, no matter what she did.

As bombs burst above, tanks rolled down the street, firing on Henry. Helicopters and planes shot at him. People attacked with nothing more than balled-up fists.

Adelina strode toward Henry as quickly as her legs would take her.

Faye and Milo flattened themselves against a nearby wall, tried to hide from her sight as best they could. Adelina stormed right past, reached up, grabbed hold of Henry's waist and tugged down as hard as she could, eventually securing a strong enough grip to pull him back down. Once his head and arms were mostly underground again, Adelina used all her strength to throw him down the tunnel. He flew headfirst about fifty feet, turned in the air, landed on his back, skidded another twenty feet, then stopped.

People and vehicles began to stream down the hole like lemmings off a cliff.

Milo and Faye ran away from the hole, toward Henry.

Henry sat up, looked at Adelina. When their eyes met, something incredible happened – something neither of them thought could happen, not any more. They genuinely *felt* something. Something of themselves – the selves they'd given up, the selves they'd relinquished. Some kind of empathy, perhaps. Recognition. A strange kinship that neither of them understood. A feeling that no others on Earth have had, nor would ever have again. Something singular.

Adelina Palermo saw the apology in Henry Kyllo's eyes, and Henry saw and understood the pain, rage, and confusion in Adelina's. Forgiveness passed between them then.

The last of Adelina was snuffed out at that precise moment.

Milo felt her go, feeling as though he'd lost something he'd never really had to begin with. It was a hollow ache, like the hole where a pulled tooth used to sit. He didn't feel sad, exactly; he just felt a sort of slow, unnamable crumbling in his heart.

Henry was fully aware now that whatever he'd be battling, it was not Adelina. It was not that girl. It was not that woman. It was no aspect of anything he understood, or could ever understand. It was simply Other now – more Other than the world had even known.

And he knew that whatever awful, horrible thing was filling him up, very close now to snuffing Henry out entirely – it was one and the same. A cancer that grew and twisted in him, filling him up to bursting with its emptiness.

The metal giant that once was Adelina Palermo moved toward Henry. It came at him tentatively. One earthshaking step, then another. Then one more. It stood in front of him now. It blinked twice, then sat down on the ground, hung its chin on its chest, and closed its eyes.

Powered down.

Of course. This is what it wanted, Henry thought, that sick churning feeling returning to his mind. *Whatever I'm about to become – this was the plan all along.*

Henry didn't know what awaited him, in what form his existence would be after this – if such a thing were even possible – but with every shred of his remaining will, he wanted Faye and Milo to be there with him. This became his sole objective.

Henry leaned toward Milo and Faye where they crouched near one of the tunnel walls. He held out one hand, nodded his head toward it.

Faye and Milo understood. They climbed onto his hand – Milo getting on first, then turning around to hoist Faye up.

Henry closed his fingers around them protectively as much as he could, worked himself into a sitting position. He knew if he stood, he'd bash through the ceiling and onto the street again, endangering his friends.

He remained in that position, while the bombs rained down overhead, punching holes in the pavement above him. More vehicles and people crashed through to the subway tunnel. Throngs of people began crawling on Henry, climbing him, their attacks vicious, but harmless.

Henry shifted Faye to his right hand, so that he had one friend in each. He raised his arms higher so the people now swarming his legs couldn't easily climb farther up him, get access to his hands.

Milo and Faye did nothing but stare up at Henry, tears in their eyes while they waited for whatever came next.

Kendul, Marcton, and Cleve stood far enough back from the scene unfolding in the tunnel that their thoughts remained calm. They felt detached from what was happening. They did not understand why Adelina stopped advancing on Henry. They had no idea why she'd simply sat down in front of him and closed her eyes.

These three men knew only that they were witnessing the end of their city, and possibly the events that would usher in the end of their kind. They said nothing to each other, too shocked and confused to properly articulate their thoughts.

Henry Kyllo sat with his back to them. Waiting.

That's when Henry entered the final stage of his transformation.

Something like creation filled him up inside.

A slow-burn big bang.

Not long after this process started, the last vestige of Henry Kyllo would vanish from existence. But for the final two minutes of his life, he would be vaguely aware only that he was getting bigger again, and that he had saved his friends. At least for a time.

When he felt this last episode of growth coming on, he instinctively got to his feet. He curled his fingers around Faye and Milo, still one in each hand, to protect them.

His head, shoulders, and torso shot up through the tunnel ceiling, destroying it. He emerged into a different section of the street above. Chaos was everywhere. Everything was burning. Everyone was dying. It no longer even seemed connected to him any more.

Seeing this filled Henry with profound sadness, and he closed his eyes against the sight.

Several missiles landed about a mile away, exploded, lit the night. More landed closer. And

Henry continued to grow.

Hands still wrapped as tightly as possible without crushing Milo and Faye, he rose up through the ground, expanded, changed, now fully smooth and entirely black. A massive robot carved from obsidian.

Taller and taller. His head shot past the fourth floor of a glass skyscraper to which he was adjacent. He turned toward it, saw his reflection for the first time – truly saw what he'd become. And that loss of self-identity – that part of everyone that anchors who we are to how we look – was the last thing to break inside of Henry Kyllo. As he grew taller than the tenth floor of the skyscraper, he felt his consciousness drain from this machine like water down a rainspout.

When he passed the twentieth floor, he was gone from this world.

Henry, Milo's and Faye's dear friend, no longer held them; they were now simply in the hands of an unfeeling, unknowable monolith.

As Henry's torso expanded, Milo and Faye stared in terror at each other through his fingers, the gap between them becoming greater and greater. By the time Henry's head cleared the seventy-story skyscraper, his chest was nearly the width of the building itself.

And still, he continued to grow.

Missiles exploded down at his feet, and as far as the eye could see. All throughout the city, out into the countryside.

Henry grew further outward, shooting up through clouds still dumping the neverending snow onto the earth. A passenger plane crashed into one of his arms, burst into a fiery ball.

Down below, Clive, Kendul, and Marcton sat huddled near each other underground, waiting to die. When the first nuke hit, they were vaporized instantly.

The mushroom cloud rose up, engulfing Henry's legs.

At about forty thousand feet, the tiny dead people in his hands forgotten, the worldchanging machine known as Henry Kyllo dropped his arms to his sides and opened his hands. Faye's and Milo's bodies tumbled down, down through the night sky. Swallowed up by the devastation below.

Henry rose up and expanded into the stratosphere still.

Fifty thousand. Eighty thousand. A hundred thousand feet.

Henry looked around him at this height, saw the curvature of the world. And it seemed very, very small to him.

Small and worthless.

Henry grew more, out into space.

Beyond the moon.

Beyond the sun.

Beyond the solar system.

He grew and grew until the universe knew nothing but Him.

ACKNOWLEDGMENTS

Erik Mohr, for drawing on it.
  Phil Jourdan, for understanding it.
  Marc Gascoigne, for buying it.
  Paul Simpson, for editing it.
  Trish Byrne and Andrew Hook, for proofreading it.
  Penny Reeve and Mike Underwood, for pimping it.
  Nick Tyler, for editorially assisting it.
  Paul Goat Allen; Tony Burgess; Mike Carey; Craig Davidson; Brian Evenson; Christopher Golden; Brian Hodge; Stephen Graham Jones; Tim Lebbon; Jim Moore; Mark Morris; Benjamin Percy; Michael Rowe; Robert Shearman; Peter Straub; Paul Tremblay; and Peter Watts for blurbing it.

Your face, for reading it.

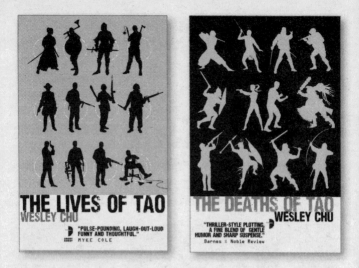

ALIENS WALK INSIDE US

"Few books begin more engagingly than *The Lives of Tao*, a science fiction romp which wears its principal strength — the wit and humour of the narrative voice — on its sleeve."
Huffington Post

"Wesley Chu is my hero... He has to be the coolest science fiction writer in the world."
Lavie Tidhar, World Fantasy Award-winning author of Osama

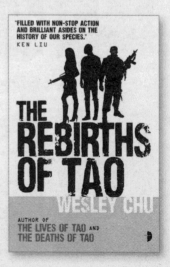

THE ROBOT RESISTANCE

angryrobotbooks.com

twitter.com/angryrobotbooks